I0566426

1

Making movies far from home is Alex's favorite thing about his job and the hardest. In the three years he and Paul have been married, they've developed a cycle: Alex goes away for a few months to film. When he returns, they cocoon together as long as they can before emerging on their very best behavior to do awards season. Then, Alex disappears for another project.

He loves the work, and he loves the adventure but being away from Paul is really fucking hard and Australia is really fucking far away. There are two months left of the six-month shoot for The Icarus Experiment. It's the longest he's ever been gone, and Alex is increasingly sure it's not something he wants to repeat. He cannot wait to get home and return to normal, or at least, what passes as normal for them.

As far as Alex can tell, Paul deals with his absence by pining and overwork. Winsome, AZ is going into its sixth and final season. While Paul has promised to take a year off when it's done, readying himself for whatever TV creation is going to be his next big adventure, there's plenty of work to keep him busy now.

Liam, meanwhile, is currently without a demanding TV shooting schedule, doing guest roles here and there and enjoying his relationships — with his wife, with Victor, and with whomever else Alex doesn't bother to keep track of. Somehow, though,

Liam has taken Alex's absence harder than anyone expected.

He hasn't stopped expressing his annoyance that while Paul visited for two weeks over Christmas, he, with Carly, a five-year-old, and his own professional obligations, couldn't make the same choice. Alex knows he's supposed to find the intensity of their friendship and emotional intimacy peculiar, but now that it's stopped bothering everyone else, he finds it difficult to care. That said, he does wish Liam could at least remember when they have a Skype date.

◆

Liam's phone vibrates in the pocket of his jeans, folded neatly along with the rest of his clothes on the floor by the side of the bed. Victor has been awake for hours but Liam is, quite reasonably, not yet ready for the world. Victor reaches for the phone to deal with the unwelcome noise.

It's a text message from Alex. Where are you? the screen reads. Waiting.

Victor silences the phone and sets it aside. Alex will try again; he always does. In the meantime, Victor pulls the white coverlet up over Liam's bare shoulders, watching the way the down settles and molds itself to the shape of Liam's body underneath. Victor made sure he was tucked in before he went to his own bed the night before, but Liam is a more restless sleeper when he's alone and managed to kick off the covers by the time Victor came back in the morning to check on him.

Victor may not desire Liam in the way Liam wishes he did, but that doesn't stop him from having a great desire to care for his body and his heart, even if he generally does both from as large a distance as he can reasonably manage. Liam's love is a terrifying gift, and Victor often wishes he were better equipped to bring him happiness. That their relationship exists at all is a testament to how hard they work for it and how well they fit in concept if not fact.

Victor kisses Liam's forehead before moving off the bed to get his laptop.

He gets an incoming Skype call from Alex almost as soon as the computer turns on and picks it up with delight as he carries the laptop out of the room.

♦

"To what do I owe the pleasure?" Victor practically purrs when he answers, settling himself at the desk in his den.

Alex lets himself laugh, because at least he knows Victor is trying to piss him off.

"Is Liam there?"

"Yes," Victor says as he twists at a ring around his little finger. It makes him look like even more of a stereotypical villain than usual.

"Is he awake?" Alex asks. He tries to ignore the fidgeting which he suspects is an intentionally targeted affectation. He imagines Victor acquiring some sort of peculiar and menacing pet in order to take the performance further.

"No."

"Ugh. He's standing me up for our Skype date." He refrains from pointing out that Victor is also not being helpful.

"He had a rough night," Victor says.

"Do I want to inquire?"

"I'm going with no," Victor says slyly.

Alex grimaces.

"That face would be easier to believe if I hadn't watched you make out with Liam on my couch."

"Jesus, Victor," Alex gapes, not quite sure where to look on the screen. He's tempted to end the call right there, but God knows what Victor would do in retaliation then. "You make it sound so sketchy."

"No, I think sketchy was when Paul — "

"Can we not talk about this?" Alex squeaks.

Victor laughs. It doesn't make him seem any less sociopathic. The last thing Alex wants to discuss is how he, Paul, Victor, Carly, and Liam got way too fucked up one night at Victor's house. There was a lot of random making out, and Paul eventually jerked Alex off not entirely in private. It's the sort of thing that would be funny and only faintly scandalous if it happened to someone else.

"You're not nearly as embarrassed by that night as you pretend," Victor says. "Even if you and Paul have a really fucked up definition of monogamy."

"You know that thing where we don't talk about that because I don't want to know about your sex life and you don't want to know about mine?" Alex says. "That was really nice. We should go back to that."

"For an actor you're remarkably unconvincing, and for a friend, remarkably inaccurate." Victor smirks.

"I'm not above hanging up on you," Alex threatens. He doesn't want to begin to examine the word friend in the context of Victor.

"You also weren't above kissing me."

"You're a bastard." Alex laughs even though he wants to die. Victor's a damn good kisser, and Alex wants to examine that fact never.

Victor decides to be merciful. "Tell me about this date with Liam," he says as if that statement is somehow less inflammatory than everything else they've just discussed.

Alex is relieved, but rolls his eyes anyway. "Appointment."

"That sounds more absurd," Victor notes.

"Then don't be an asshole."

Victor hums in thought. "Should I ask how Australia is?" It's clearly a peace offering.

"Big," Alex says after a moment. "Catalytic. Way too fucking far from everything."

2

Alex does not wear his hat. Despite having been home from Australia for a month and knowing that people will recognize him, he's hoping for a little common decency. Besides, the club is loud, crowded, and noisy, full of hundreds of men wrapped up in each other paying absolutely no attention to him and Paul edging their way toward the dance floor. It's a long way from the first time they danced together in Paul's living room, but all the important things are still right here in front of him.

Between the stress of running his very own cable TV hit and his notorious workaholic tendencies, Paul's already going gray at thirty-eight. Everyone teases him about it, but Alex loves it. Once Paul gets his arms around him, Alex wastes no time in sliding a hand up the back of Paul's neck.

"Eager?" Paul teases. He has to talk into Alex's ear to be heard over the thudding music and even then it's debatable. Alex nods and presses his forehead against Paul's. They're both already a little drunk, and he's never been able to lose himself anywhere as easily as he can in Paul's arms.

◆

Alex's eyes flutter shut when Paul slides his hands into his back pockets and pulls him closer. They're not dancing so much as grinding together, but they're hardly alone in that regard — at least they still have their shirts on, and if Alex is willing, Paul has absolutely zero desire to stop.

Paul can't hear it, but he can feel the breath of a moan on his neck when Alex gets insistent about digging his fingers into Paul's hair. He mouths at the skin above his collar. Six months apart — with only two weeks in the middle — was a very long time. The time they've had since has barely been enough to get used to sharing space with each other again, much less fall back into their relationship with all their knowledge of each other's bodies and hearts intact.

"This is possibly a bad idea," Alex murmurs at some point.

Paul isn't sure how much time has elapsed since things crossed into slightly inappropriate but totally expected territory. "I don't think you care."

"No, not really," Alex says before slipping into a whine, "but we just got here, and I don't want to go home."

"Who says we have to go home?"

"My dick."

"What? Can you not get off like this?" Paul scoffs. They might both be older than they used to be, but Alex is still a lot younger than him and the thought of making him come in his pants is both delicious and amusing.

"Paul," Alex says warningly.

His only response is to cup Alex's ass and lift him so far up onto the thigh he has between Alex's legs that his feet are barely on the ground.

"Paul!" Alex says again, and this time he's neither warning nor faking how scandalized he is.

"Come on," Paul chides. "Be impressed. You're heavier than you look."

"I'm definitely impressed," Alex says breathlessly. "But this is ridiculous."

Paul shakes his head. "The way I see it," he says, kneading at Alex's ass. "You have two options."

"Yeah?"

"You can get off right here, or you can wait until the end of tonight. Because I don't want to go home either."

Alex curls himself forward and makes a deliciously pained sound as he braces himself on Paul's shoulders. When Paul shifts one hand to the center of his back and breathes, "Yeah, that's right," in his ear, he is clearly absolutely done for. Paul groans when Alex finally smiles, sly and eager.

Paul digs his fingernails into his ass and shifts him so Alex can fuck against his thigh. He starts up a litany in Alex's ear about all the marks he'd leave on his flesh, if only Alex weren't wearing so much clothing.

"I'm not doing this alone," Alex gasps, clearly trying to hold back.

Paul laughs. "You're certainly not."

"I mean," Alex says between gasps, "that if I'm going to come on the dance floor — So. Are. You."

"What makes you think that?" Paul asks with fake disinterest.

"You don't want to go home yet," Alex pants, "And I'm not blowing you in the bathroom."

Paul laughs.

Alex responds by getting a hand between them and grabbing at Paul's very interested dick through his jeans.

"Jesus," Paul gasps. If Alex is after a challenge tonight, he seems to have found it.

"Too tacky," Alex says, clearly full of pride at being able to keep up and upping the stakes.

To Paul, it's both typical of the twenty-year-old boy Alex was when they first met and a testament to the man he's become. And if he's happy to let Paul lead and push in some things, it's only because Alex knows, absolutely, how easy it is for him to turn the tables when he wants to.

Paul has to kiss him, deep and desperate. Alex lets go of Paul's cock to grab his hips instead, rutting against him as they pant into each other's mouths.

Alex comes with a sharp gasp, his mouth frozen open. He grabs Paul around the waist so he doesn't actually fall over. Paul holds him up and runs a hand down his back until he stops shaking with it.

Before either of them catch their breath, Alex takes a step back and shoves at Paul's shoulders. Paul, eager and turned on, doesn't ask or protest as Alex steers them carefully through the crowd. He is startled though, because Alex able to function after an orgasm is not a thing Paul is used to.

At the back of the dance floor Alex shoves Paul against the wall and dives a hand down the front of his pants before Paul can register what's going on. It's hot and dark and Alex's face is dazed and intent the way it is after their best sex, when the rest of the world is gone.

"Are you out of your mind?" Paul hisses.

"You started this," Alex says, an entirely different sort of breathless now. "Prove to me you can finish it."

Paul barks out half a laugh before Alex twists his wrist just so, and then he lets his head fall back as he watches the dance floor with heavy-lidded eyes and mentally pages through every backroom fantasy he's ever had.

Alex clearly knows it, and so it only takes a smirk and a bit of encouragement from him for Paul to come all over his hand.

They clean up in the bathroom, laughing together as Alex washes his hands and then helps Paul with the mess in his underwear, neither of them giving a remote shit about the person pounding on the door because he thinks they're in there together to fuck. When they're done Alex all but drags Paul back onto the dance floor, and this time the dancing is fun. It's the perfect reminder to them both that Alex is actually home, for real, to stay. At least for a little while.

♦

It's obscenely late when they finally get back to their house and crawl into their bed drunk and sweaty and happy. Alex curls up on Paul's chest as soon as they're naked and under the covers.

Paul wraps his arms around him. "I'm glad you're home," he says, and it's different than all the other times he's said it lately. Everything feels so real, Paul can't imagine that he'll need to keep saying it after tonight.

Alex smiles into Paul's shoulder. "Me fucking too."

3

Paul moans at the sound of his ringtone. Alex curses next to him, rolls over, and says, "It'll stop."

He's not wrong, until it starts again a few moments later.

"It's still dark," Paul complains.

"Someone probably wants a ride home," Alex says. They've been drunk dialed by random combinations of Liam, Carly, Gemma, Darcy, Shawna, and Brian more than once and only sometimes by accident. Once, Paul's ex Craig called, and that was super awkward. Alex doesn't understand why all their very successful friends can't manage to call cabs like normal people.

The phone stops and starts. Again.

"That's not good."

Alex laughs, because the last time they said that about a middle-of-the-night call, he got cast in a movie.

"Where the fuck is my phone?" Paul asks, finally giving in and sitting up groggily.

"In your pants," Alex says unhelpfully.

Paul curses as he leans over the edge of the bed and gropes in the direction of the ringing. He finds it as it starts up a fourth time. Alex pulls a pillow over his head, because he's still drunk and the sound is unpleasant.

"Ellen?" Paul answers, groggy, confused, and a little concerned. At least the ringing has finally stopped.

There's a pause, and Alex hears Paul say, still groggy but a lot sharper, "What?"

"What's't?" Alex mutters, taking the pillow off his face as Paul starts pulling on his clothes while juggling the phone. Alex curses, because they're totally going to wind up giving someone a ride and that's just stupid.

It's Paul asking when and how and who else have you called, that Alex finally sits up and reaches for the light.

Paul's face is ashen as he struggles to get his arm with the phone through a sleeve. Finally, as Alex tries not to jump to all sorts of terrible conclusions, Paul runs out of steam and sits on the bed half dressed as he asks Ellen, "Are you okay?"

The answer is clearly no.

♦

"Let me call," Paul protests as Alex paces their kitchen, scrolling through his own speed-dial with unsteady hands.

"I've got this. You need to call your own people and convince them it's not a terrible April Fool's joke," Alex says shortly. The timing of the universe is always terrible, but this instance just might be the worst.

"This is six types of fucked up," Paul says under his breath.

Alex gulps some more water and finally dials Carly's number. He thinks he's relieved when she picks up on the first ring, but then she says, before Alex can get a word out, "I haven't told Liam, yet."

"Jesus Christ, Carly…."

"If you were me, how would you do that, exactly?"

"Quickly," Alex says curtly. "Before someone calls his phone."

"I have his phone."

"Carly!" Alex knows that managing Liam's relationship with the universe is sort of Carly's job, but the ethics of her choices here are making him more than a little uncomfortable.

"It can wait 'til morning. Then at least he'll get some sleep." Carly sounds angry, although with Alex or the universe at large, he's not sure.

"He's gonna be pissed at you," Alex says because he can't say anything else. Liam isn't his husband.

"Yeah, well," she snaps back, "he's gonna be a lot more pissed at Victor for being dead."

♦

Alex makes coffee while Paul starts calling people at the studio. Ellen promised to call the people at M.A.R.S., but Victor is — was — half the production company for Winsome, AZ, and that means Paul, as the other half, now has a lot of duty he can't shirk. He wishes he had any idea what the protocol is when an executive producer drops dead of a heart attack.

"Why don't we have a phone tree?" he asks as he waits for the executive at the network to pick up.

"Because no one thought Victor was a toddler in danger of having a snow day," Alex says without pause.

Paul lets it pass.

Alex pushes a cup of coffee across the table at him. Paul runs a hand through his hair and recites to a VP in network operations, whom he's always tried to avoid, everything Ellen told him about Victor's death. After the entirely necessary pause for shock — and as much grief as anyone in the business is likely to muster for someone who made a career out of being infuriating — they discuss how early they can schedule a phone meeting with the production team to figure out what the hell their plan is.

"I need to go see Liam," Alex says when Paul hangs up.

"In what world is that good choices?" Paul says wearily. "Carly's got him."

"I know, but I should be there."

"He'll call you if he needs you," Paul reasons. He does not have the bandwidth at the moment for Alex and Liam's now-platonic romance.

"I don't think you understand how bad it's going to be." Alex pauses. "I don't think I understand."

◆

There's already a thing on Variety.com that's clinical enough to not make any of this feel any more real. Alex wonders who the asshole was who called them from the ER because they overheard Ellen on the phone. No one else is reporting it yet, but that's only a matter of time. As soon as an associated actor cries in public or crashes their car, preferably at the same time, everyone will care. He gives it twenty-four hours.

When Paul hangs up from what he hopes is the last call for at least a couple of hours, Alex spins the pad Paul's been jotting notes on toward himself. As a to-do list it's wide-ranging, but hardly complete.

"When's the funeral?" Alex asks.

Paul stares at him in shock. "Shit. I don't even know if Victor has family."

"He didn't spring out of Zeus's head," Alex notes.

"Have you ever heard him mention anyone? Because I know I haven't. And I haven't from Carly. Liam?"

Alex shakes his head. "I try not to ask."

"Well, it's Jackson's problem now," Paul says, exasperated.

"Didn't he just hire that guy?"

"He's Victor's personal assistant. He'll know where the will is and how to find Victor's personal lawyer. God knows, this is not actually our problem."

Alex thinks it's the most sensible thing he's heard in hours. Unfortunately, he's unconvinced. "Pretend you're Victor and play that sentence back."

◆

By mid-afternoon, their phones are both ringing non-stop. They've yet to make a public statement — that's waiting on final decisions about what the hell is going on with Winsome and M.A.R.S. — but everyone from press to people at the studio to friends are calling. Eventually Paul silences his briefly so he can at least take a shower without interruption.

Finally there's a phone meeting with the Winsome production team, where it's decided that filming will go on tomorrow as planned. There will be a couple of days off whenever the funeral is, not that anyone knows what's going on with that anyway. Easter apparently complicates everything.

There's also another round of "Did Victor have any family?" that is immediately followed by one concerned murmur about Liam and a lot of jokes about Victor being hatched from an egg. A reptile egg, to be precise, because in times like this shitty jokes must be as sharp as fucking possible. Paul's pissed off, but he suspects Victor would be delighted.

Ellen, meanwhile, has not been in any of the M.A.R.S. meetings, but is in touch with someone who has, and keeps Paul updated with increasingly frantic emails about those talks.

The network isn't going to kill the show mid-season, but Paul knows she's not wrong to worry about how many more episodes are going to come her directorial way when it's unclear who's in charge and if it's going to continue past the current season. Anyone who was close to Victor is in either a very good or very bad position, depending on whether sentimentality wins over what a fucking consistent pain in the ass he was to anyone who was paying the bills.

Paul can't decide if he wants in on the opportunity the entire mess of a situation presents or if he's determined to stay as far away from it as possible.

♦

The calls Alex receives are less business oriented — at least, once he stops answering anything from numbers he doesn't know, because he'll be damned if he gets bullied or startled into making a statement about supporting his husband in a time of need and how he owes everything to Victor — but they're more emotional and crazy.

There's a public announcement of Victor's death in the early afternoon, which only makes the phone calls increase in frequency. Alex keeps an eye on the internet as he and Raphael text back and forth in the sort of quiet commiseration that's marked so much of their relationship since they were on Fourth together.

Paul is on the phone with Craig of all people, who has called to see if Paul is okay — Alex doesn't know what to make of that — when their doorbell rings. It's Alex's former roommate Gemma. She's followed fifteen minutes later by Darcy, Paul's starlet, who's in tears, and then Ellen, who looks like she hasn't slept at all.

Alex has no idea how their house has become mission control for dead Victor, but ultimately he's grateful to have people around. It reduces the number of phone calls getting made and gives him someone to yell in the direction of when Carly calls Alex to give him a heads up.

Apparently, Nigel is going to be in touch.

"What the fuck?" Alex asks when Carly tells him as much.

"He was Victor's best friend," Carly reminds him sharply. "And he will be useful. Don't be an asshole."

"How's Liam?"

"Thanks for your help," she says and hangs up.

Alex stares at the phone for a moment.

"Why the hell is Carly gatekeeping Liam?" he hollers to Paul who is still in the kitchen using their breakfast table as a command center.

"Leave it alone, Alex," Paul says, deep in his own distraction with his disaster of an inbox.

Nigel calls soon after and is calm and reasonable, even if his voice is heavy with the sort of shock and sorrow Alex doesn't know how to deal with. Nigel confirms that Victor doesn't have any family but doesn't really provide any further information before talking about arrangements with the sort of precision and detail that makes Alex relieved until he realizes he has, by default, been deputized into funeral planning.

"This is not my job," he protests to Gemma after Nigel finally says goodbye. Clearly he's already underestimated how fucked up this whole thing is going to get.

"You guys are Victor's family," she says. "And it's not like anybody else has time to handle this."

"Gemma, I hated him," Alex hisses like it's some sort of secret.

"No you didn't. You were just scared of whatever he saw when he looked at you, because you saw it too."

♦

That evening, despite Alex's vociferous protests, Paul sends him along with Jackson, Victor's PA, to pick out clothes for Victor for the funeral. Victor's house is as brutally clean and uncluttered as always, and Alex follows Jackson with trepidation as he leads the way upstairs.

"I'm sorry to be tagging along," Alex says, because he feels douchey about everything from being in Victor's house to involving an assistant he barely knows. Jackson's a black kid from Chicago by way of UCLA who signed up to learn from Victor's genius, not help bury him. Alex is momentarily pissed off at Paul all over again for putting him in this situation.

Jackson shrugs. "Like you're the worst thing in my day."

He heads immediately for Victor's bedroom with the air of someone who knows what he's doing, is going to do it because it needs to be done, and wants to get it over with as quickly as possible. Alex can sympathize.

Alex lingers in the hallway feeling awkward and intrusive and finally ducks into Victor's office. Maybe he can find something that might be useful for Paul in all his upcoming network meetings. There's a day planner that could be helpful, but what catches Alex's eye is the chain bracelet Victor often wore, sitting in an unused ashtray along with paperclips and loose change.

"Okay, got it," Jackson says from the doorway, carrying a garment bag. "Ready to get out of here?"

Alex nods and plucks the bracelet out of the bowl. "You should bring this too."

4

One of the very few, and very fucked up, upsides to having to get to the Cathedral for the funeral early enough to oversee various logistics, including how the flowers left over from Easter are going to be arranged by the casket, is that Alex and Paul get there before the paparazzi have the place too staked out. Alex still isn't sure exactly why he got roped into helping Nigel with this other than that he was available. Mostly, he's relieved that after today this whole ordeal — which he has definitely decided to take as Victor's parting shot toward absolutely everyone — is going to be over.

Our Lady of the Angels is exactly the sort of place that Alex thinks of when he thinks of L.A. and Victor, though he avoids this part of town like the plague. Massive and brutally modernist, the Cathedral feels as disorienting as it does inescapable. The haze of smoke blowing in from the first wildfire of the season just makes everything worse.

Alex has no doubt that Victor loved this place, even if he has no idea how much, if any, time Victor actually spent here beyond deciding he wanted to be buried in its crypt. It certainly doesn't make Alex like it any better. From the puzzlement on Nigel's face — which is admittedly warring with grief and jet lag — Alex feels confident he is not alone in his assessment. That there are Easter lilies decorating the sanctuary feels like a particularly fucked up joke. Victor may have been god of many universes, but Alex is definitely counting on him to stay dead.

Nigel's presence isn't uncomfortable exactly, but he has remained at a remove from the rest of their tangled circle over the last five years. A lot of that, Alex knows, has been simple geography and logistics: Nigel's wife and children and a career in New York that mimics, but doesn't actually involve, Hollywood magic.

Alex suspects, however, that much of it has been the wary truce between him and Liam, despite the fact that they have never been at war and were never really in competition. The only two things Alex has ever seen Liam be possessive of are Victor and cities, and it's certainly never been New York, Los Angeles, or Washington, D.C. that have been the object of Liam's rare but somewhat ugly jealousy.

♦

The descent down to the memorial chapel should be a relief after the unsettlingly pagan main sanctuary and Paul's scathing look when Alex muttered something about the "erotic baptism art" along the back wall, but it's even more uncomfortable. A staircase in three segments leads down to the crypt area below the Cathedral, and while the first set of stairs is lit normally, the second is bathed in light from a wall of windows and the Los Angeles sun. Then, a descent into the underworld as all the light is yanked away. For someone, it's surely a soothing and symbolic journey, but Alex worries that Liam will find it terrifying.

The casket stands open in front of the altar of the chapel, and it draws Alex's eyes as well as the eyes of everyone who is by now beginning to filter in. Victor looks exactly the same in death as he had when he was alive: brown, sun-weathered skin and short black hair flecked with gray, fine and unremarkable lines around his mouth and eyes.

Victor's presence was always larger than life. Now, in contrast, he looks small, almost shrunken. It's an uncomfortable feeling. As much as Alex has always resented it, Victor was a titan in his life. It feels impossible that he's dead.

Paul appears at Alex's elbow, following his gaze. "How are you doing?" he asks.

"Peculiar," Alex says, not looking at him. His eyes are finally pulled away from the casket by Paul's indrawn breath and the simultaneous click of high heels.

"He looks terrible," Paul says about Liam. Apparently, Alex isn't the only one doing peculiar.

Alex hurries to meet them, but pulls up short when he goes to hug Liam and there's no sign of Liam moving in for the same. Which is weird, because Liam hugs everyone. They stare at each other for a long moment.

"I don't know what to say to you right now," Alex manages as Paul catches up to them and hugs Carly.

Liam shrugs. "It's okay."

"Do you want a hug?" Alex asks.

Liam shakes his head. "Stoic celebrity time."

"Yeah, okay," Alex says. "That's fucked up, you know?"

Liam rolls his eyes and drifts off in the direction of the coffin. Alex watches Nigel nod to Liam from a distance and get the same in return. Whatever works, but Alex exchanges a look with Carly. When she follows Liam, Alex turns helplessly to Paul, unsure of what to do. Paul meets his eyes, which is enough to ground him and force him to let the rituals of both death and social discomfort play out.

There are a few people standing near the casket who turn to greet Liam as he passes, but he doesn't acknowledge them more than he has to. When he gets there he stands for a long moment staring down at Victor. Slowly, he lowers himself to his knees on the kneeling rail that's been placed there.

Alex makes a soft, pained sound. He's fairly certain Liam isn't religious and can only view the grace and fluidity of the gesture in the context of the little — and way too much — he knows about Liam's relationship with Victor. It's absolutely gutting and seems like something that shouldn't have an audience. He has to stifle his own impulse to turn away.

Liam reaches a hand out and gently brushes the hair back from Victor's forehead. Behind him, Carly watches with eyes already gone red. Alex waits for someone to say something terrible, but all the horror comes from Liam. He grazes his fingers across Victor's and then goes to the dead man's wrist, before deftly unfastening the bracelet Alex retrieved from the ashtray. It's completely bizarre, not just because of the circumstances, but because fine motor control has never exactly been Liam's forte.

Liam clutches the bracelet in his fist and presses it to his sternum. He bows his head slightly more for a moment, before standing. Then, as everyone in the room watches — because Liam draws eyes, always, even like this, and Alex really has no power to stop them — he leans forward and kisses Victor tenderly on the forehead.

Alex has to bite at his own hand or he's going to cry or scream, and he does not know how to deal with that impulse any more than he wants to give in to it. Eventually, Liam straightens up again. When he turns around his face is wet.

Alex goes to him, because he doesn't know how not to. If anyone had bothered to talk to him — Carly hanging up on him the day Victor died was understandable but awful, and Liam's been almost entirely radio silent since except for a couple of emails about coping through as little external stimulus as possible — he'd have a much clearer idea of what he's supposed to do.

Frankly, he's a little pissed off. Because there are rules for funerals, and no one has bothered to tell him what they are when they involve actors and people with too much money and really complicated interpersonal relationships. Funerals were so much easier back home when they were for people in his high school class Alex didn't really know or like: You said sorry, and you handed someone a casserole.

"Please don't touch me," Liam says quietly and too quickly when Alex arrives at his elbow.

It stings, more than Alex would have ever thought.

"I was with him that morning," Liam adds, as if by way of explanation.

◆

When Liam walks away and Alex instinctively leans to follow, Paul grabs Alex's elbow. Alex twists away, awkward and embarrassed, as if he's been caught out.

"Don't chase him right now," Paul tells him.

"What am I supposed to do instead?" Alex asks. He looks like he's still trying to process the implications of Victor's death.

"Nothing. I get that this is probably over for you today — "

"I'm going to be asked about Victor for the rest of my fucking life," Alex says sharply under his breath. "And I'm doing my best not to think about Liam's loss so I don't suddenly freak out over mortality."

Paul considers making a joke about being older than Alex, and Alex needing to get used to the idea, but it seems like tempting fate. He watches as Liam quietly chats with the writer/director team for his new project, and can't help but think about how fragile all of their lives are. It's not only about Victor being dead, Alex's rock climbing, or his own continued ability to draw breath. For Paul, it's about their systems and how quickly the people and things that allow them to all make magic for a living can go up in smoke.

◆

Alex drifts through the psalms and hymns of the funeral. It's all way more of the Bible than he's used to for these sorts of occasions. Paul does one of the readings, and squeezes Alex's hand tightly before he stands to walk to the lectern. Alex pays attention, because it's Paul and Alex is always proud of and interested in him, but his eyes keep drifting to Liam.

They're all in the first few pews, like the fucked up family they are. Liam stares straight ahead, not at but somewhere above where the casket is resting in front of the altar. His eyes are red, and Carly, pressed beside Alex, keeps passing him tissues. In the pew behind them, Gemma catches Alex's eye and gives him a faint and watery smile when he turns around to take in the rest of the congregation.

It's Ellen who delivers the eulogy. She'd written it too late one night last week at their house, on the notepad Paul had been using for the Winsome plans.

"I got this job because no one else wanted it," she begins. "That's probably true of most of the people in this room who have worked for Victor at some point in their careers. Let's just get it out of the way, so you all don't talk smack about me later for not saying it: Sometimes, he was an absolutely terrible human being. I'm only not putting a finer point on it 'cause we're in a church. Also, we're only in a church because he liked ritual, not because he believed in anything other than himself, and his people, which are all of you.

"A lot of you aren't prizes either. Workaholics, divas, and neurotics, as ambitious as murderous kings in many cases. And he loved every single one of you for it, although odds are, he never told you, at least not in so many words. No, Victor conveyed that information by providing opportunities, assuming loyalty, and meddling often disastrously in people's personal lives. He usually only told people they were beautiful when they were in pain, and even I couldn't always figure out when he was joking.

"But he loved people. They were his science and his religion and his avocation, and he told stories instead of becoming a therapist or an advice columnist or a teacher only because his impulse was more often curiosity than healing. But in that curiosity he honored people — you all, and the people who watched (and complained) about his shows — for what they were, instead of what they could be. And that was a vote of confidence I'd venture to say few people are lucky enough to get from anyone in life.

"Victor moved mountains in this industry, usually by pissing people off. But he believed anyone he expended even a moment of his time on could do the same thing. So if you're in this room right now, you are obligated not to let him down."

In the passenger seat Liam's hands are nearly white with how hard he's clenching them. He made it through the service and the interment of Victor's body in the cathedral mausoleum without breaking entirely, which is a relief. Carly has no idea how much longer he can do this.

She rummages in her purse for a granola bar and puts half of it in her mouth once she manages to get it unwrapped. "Oh my god, pregnancy is so gross," she says while trying to chew.

Liam, who normally finds her pregnancy-related complaints somewhat hilarious, barely reacts. It's not unexpected, but it always freaks her out when she feels this much on her own when he's right goddamn next to her.

"Granola bar?" she offers, holding the other half out to him.

He gives her a look somewhere between withering and confused. "We have to go to the food thing now."

"It's called lunch," she says softly as she starts the car.

◆

Darcy scurries up to Paul and Alex as soon as they walk into the restaurant and hugs them both tightly even though they saw her twenty minutes ago at the funeral.

"Okay, so, I didn't want to tell you this at the church, because, you know, church, but, you should probably see this." She brushes a loose strand of hair out of her face as she digs her phone out of her clutch.

Paul and Alex exchange a look.

"What's up, Darcy?" Alex asks. By now he's used to asking her gentle questions in the hope of getting somewhat tempered answers.

"Okay, so, people are totally gross," she says, which does not make Alex feel any better, as she hesitates between them and then hands Paul the phone. "And I'm really sorry."

Paul takes it cautiously. "What did you do, Darcy?" he asks warily.

"I didn't do anything!" she protests, waving a hand at the screen. "Read it."

Paul raises an eyebrow at her and then does. "Oh, fuck."

Darcy bites her lip and nods, while Alex leans in to read over Paul's shoulder. It's a stupid gossip website, and it has a rather detailed and unflattering blind that is most definitely about the two of them and the night they'd gone out dancing.

Whoever's written it has gone to great lengths to emphasize the fact that two subjects of the blind — a well-known actor, and a well-known showrunner, both connected to Victor and in a well-known relationship — were getting down and dirty in public while Victor died.

"I think I need to sit down." Alex unsteadily sinks into a chair.

Darcy runs over to Alex and crouches down in front of him, putting her hands on his knees. "Are you freaking out about being busted for public sex or the sketchy blaming you for Victor's death?"

Alex raises his head to look at her. "Darcy."

"Yes?"

"Stop talking."

◆

Aside from the appalling nature of the internet — Alex makes Darcy swear not to show anyone else the blind — the mood of the group lightens as more people filter in from the service. The M.A.R.S. team seems to be rallying with some determination to honor the dead via ridiculous stories, and Alex is happy to leave Darcy to her socializing and stay in a corner chatting with Ruth, who has remained one of Winsome's stars and whose sly sarcasm always makes large gatherings of people more bearable. Raphael and his wife Irina also serve as an island of freakishly well-adjusted calm in a sea of crazy despite having to keep an eye on their kids who are about as unprepared for funeral etiquette as Alex feels.

Paul winds up in awkwardly jovial conversation with Mark Bevers, Victor's head writer on M.A.R.S. and one of the many people in line for the dubious honor of worst week ever.

"We're back with filming on Monday," he tells Paul. "We've got a table read Tuesday, and then we're out of script that Victor was directly involved with the week after that."

Paul's eyes go wide while Alex wonders if he can politely drift away at this point. "Was he giving you that much rope or are you guys that far behind?"

Mark scowls and says, "Yes."

Ellen isn't any happier about the situation. When Alex finally extricates himself from the conversation with Paul and Mark to ask, she throws up her hands.

"No one knows if they're keeping me around, but apparently I'm still on the hook for directing a bunch of sobbing freaks. And absolutely everyone at the studio has an opinion about how Victor wanted it shot. A fitting tribute to his memory is not out-meddling him."

Alex smirks. "Tell me how you really feel."

"Like shit," she says. "Can we start drinking?"

"I think the sun's been over the yardarm since you called," Alex says.

Ellen fixes him with a look. "Yeah, it was about five hours earlier for me, thanks."

Alex pats her shoulder. One day someone is going to ask her about that; for her sake, Alex hopes it's not someone who actually deserves an answer.

◆

While Alex chats with Ellen, Paul is approached by a young South Asian woman with a streak of fuchsia in the front of her otherwise black chin-length hair.

"Hey," she says, shaking his hand. "Olivia Mallick, we've met at a couple of Victor's parties."

Paul nods, because it's clearly not a question. "Hi. Yeah, you write on M.A.R.S.?"

"Assistant," Olivia says, brushing the unfortunate technicality aside. "Look, I know this is crass, but this is Victor's funeral and it's not like he'd mind."

Paul raises his eyebrows, intrigued at a conversation that is not tending toward annoying business or banal sympathies.

"I want to write for you. You should hire me."

Paul glances across the room to where Frank Pearson — the VP he hates but keeps winding up on the phone with — and Mark are talking with their heads together. "We only have a year left, I don't know you, and you work for Mark," he says, a little blindsided by the proposition but also impressed.

"Wrong. I worked for Victor. Who promised to staff me at the end of this season. Which is not going to happen, because Mark is not going to keep Victor's promises; and he's going to run M.A.R.S. into the ground way before your year is up anyway. So. What do you need from me to make that happen?"

Paul laughs, from surprise as much as anything. He wonders if this is a little how Victor felt when Alex marched into his office and told him to kill Zach off Fourth.

"Okay," he says. "Send me what you have. I'll give it a look." It's a platitude because he doesn't necessarily expect her to be able to deliver.

But Olivia slaps a thumb drive into his hand.

"Sent," she says with a smile. "Pleasure talking with you."

"You too."

Alex appears at Paul's elbow as Olivia is walking away. "You look pleased."

Paul chuckles and tucks the thumb drive into his breast pocket. "Someone just did the equivalent of following me into the bathroom to pitch me. And I liked it."

"Well, at least someone's having fun."

♦

Liam and Carly arrive as everyone takes their seats for the meal. Liam looks a little more present than he did at the funeral, but Carly is keeping a hand or an eye on him at all times. Alex doesn't blame her. Were their situations reversed, Alex is fairly sure he wouldn't feel safe leaving Liam alone. He can't imagine what this type of loss does to a person, especially one as defined by relationships as Liam is.

"I'm so glad you finally made it," Natalie, their former co-star on The Fourth Estate, who Alex has been happy not to spend time with since the show ended years ago, says. Liam runs a finger back and forth over the hem of his napkin. "Did you get lost?"

"I drove," Carly says flatly. "And we were trying to minimize how much small talk we'd have to make with you."

Alex turns to Paul with wide eyes. He has never, ever seen Carly do anything like that, even when he's been able to tell which of Liam's lovers and ex-lovers she's less than amused by. She's always been very clear that she never wants to give anyone a reason to think Liam's other relationship choices have any bearing on the status of their marriage. Clearly, those excessively gracious — but probably wise — rules are not in effect under these circumstances.

Paul touches Alex's hand, a silent plea not to make this into more of a scene. Alex settles for glaring at Natalie, who tosses her hair but otherwise doesn't respond. He desperately wants to know what Victor ever saw in her other than her character. He wishes they were at a different table. Darcy and Jackson are definitely better company.

It's a relief when lunch is finished. Even if this hellish day isn't over yet, at least they're done with the glaringly public parts of it. Alex ends up stuck near the door of the restaurant with Paul as everyone says their goodbyes before drifting off to whatever's next.

"Thank you for all of your work," Nigel tells him as he shakes his hand. "Victor would have appreciated it."

"You mean Victor would have been disappointed we had so many of his people in one room and nothing got broken."

Nigel gives him a sad smile. "I don't think you're entirely wrong, but the ways that you are doesn't make this easier for the people who loved him more comfortably than you did."

"I didn't — "

Nigel chuckles to himself. "Give it time," he says.

♦

The post-funeral gathering, involving alcohol and no people they don't like, is at Paul and Alex's house. As far as Alex is concerned, it's one more reason to be pissed off at Victor. All he wants is to crawl into their bed and stay there with Paul. Instead, he has to be social.

Not that he tries that hard, staying mostly off to the side of the room, barefoot and in his shirtsleeves, nursing a beer while Paul, Ellen, and Raphael tell increasingly raucous stories about Victor and the incredibly impish and occasionally malevolent force he always was in their lives. Alex isn't sure if the most malignant aspects of Victor's interference in all of their lives are something none of them are actually aware of, or are just setting aside for now.

Alex knows most of the stories probably are actually funny, and as difficult as Victor made everyone's life, most of the people in this room did have a fondness for him. And while Alex has no problem making light of death or speaking ill of the dead, it feels unsettling to laugh over Victor's exploits. He's kind of afraid too much drunken grief-processing will summon him from beyond the grave.

Besides, as far as he knows, no one else in this room ever was tied to a chair by Victor for a scene, or made out with Victor while he pulled Alex's hair and lured him closer to the small submissive place that the torture scene for their TV show hadn't been able to take him. The possibility that Alex might not be the only person Victor ever treated like that is as unsettling as the possibility that he is.

At least no one else in the room is being accused of killing Victor by fucking their partner in public. The whole thing is massively fucked up.

Eventually Alex finishes his drink and sets the empty bottle down on the end table next to Darcy's glass and the whiskey bottle someone, probably Ellen, liberated from their liquor cabinet for efficiency's sake.

Paul gives Alex a concerned look when he stands up and heads out of the room, but Alex shakes his head and slips upstairs.

♦

Paul knocks on their bedroom door before he opens it.

"You okay?" he asks.

"Not really," Alex says from where he's stretched out on their bed facing the far wall. He can feel the mattress dip when Paul sits down on the edge.

"What's up?" Paul says.

"I feel like a ghoul. Liam's clearly a mess. You're going to be. Everyone's sad, and mostly I just think this is all weird."

"Well, it is weird, if that helps."

"Yeah, tell that to the blind."

Paul clearly has no idea what to say to that.

"I just got back from Australia," Alex says.

"I know."

"I don't want to go away again. It's too fucking hard."

"You don't have to do media for Icarus until November."

Alex shrugs.

"What is this about?"

"The fact that somehow I've become the bad guy in Victor's story. Which is ludicrous."

"If it's ludicrous, why are you flipping out? And God, it's the internet. Fuck that."

"I want everything to go back to the way it was."

"How's that?"

Alex doesn't say anything, because to say he misses a life without cameras on his face and where he can be a jerk with his friends on the internet, and where he and Gemma watch shitty TV while eating bad takeout in their crappy apartment, would be to say he doesn't want this life he shares with Paul. And that's not it, not really. But he wants everything to stop being so hard.

♦

When Alex doesn't answer, Paul takes a deep breath and pushes down his anxiety, because Alex being silent is Alex trying not to upset him. Paul reaches out and rubs a hand up and down Alex's arm until Alex rolls over to face him.

Paul gives him a tight smile, but the one Alex responds with is huge. Paul feels his entire being unclench at that, just in time for Alex to sit up, grab his shoulders, and kiss him hard.

Paul actually laughs into it.

"What?" Alex asks.

"Funerals. Sex."

"It's only a cliché if we're a terrible hookup."

"Everyone's still downstairs," Paul points out.

"Apparently we don't care about that," Alex informs him. "Also, they're drunk."

Paul puts a hand to his chest to push him back into the pillows.

"We shouldn't have done that," Alex blurts.

"What?"

"Last week. At the club."

"Who'd it hurt?" Paul says, brushing it away, but then Alex's eyes twist the knife. Paul sits back on his heels. "Well fuck."

"It's stupid right?"

"It's incredibly stupid. Considering the other time we did that, we did it in front of Victor and he thought it was hilarious."

"Victor was also really fucking high for that."

"Everyone was really fucking high for that," Paul says.

"You know, Victor's the first person I've kissed who's died."

♦

The sex is more awkward than it should be, and not because there is a living room full of people downstairs or because they've been rehashing some of their strange exploits. Alex wants to be obliterated, but Paul is cautious and not in the way he is when he's trying not to mark Alex up.

Alex finally mumbles, "What do you want?" He's tired and angry and a little drunk and just wants Paul to fuck him so he can fall asleep and pretend this whole day never happened.

Paul doesn't want to run the show either — he rolls over onto his back and pulls Alex on top of him. He cranes his head up for a kiss and then drops back on the pillow when he can't hold his neck up any longer.

It's not enough of an answer, but somehow Alex gets a clue and the ability to respond. He groans softly as he crawls up Paul's body, impatient and turned on and happy to shove a hand into Paul's hair before sliding it around the back of his head. Paul sucks so eagerly at Alex's cock when he starts to feed it into his mouth that Alex's breath punches out of him, and he has to close his eyes for a moment or he's going to tip right the fuck over. Paul protests, his mouth full, by pinching his ass.

Alex chuckles breathlessly and shakes his head, grabbing both of Paul's hands and drawing them up above his head. With his wrists pinned to the bed, Paul can't do anything but take it as Alex fucks his mouth. It's nothing like what they usually do, but it's dirty and hot and Alex doesn't moan out loud only because there are still people downstairs.

Paul struggles against Alex's weight on his wrists, but Alex leans more heavily on them and fucks his mouth harder. He wants to take the fragile look in Paul's eyes to its ultimate conclusion and shatter him utterly. It's not a familiar impulse, but it's completely irresistible.

Eventually, Paul does get a hand free, and jerks himself off while Alex runs a hand through Paul's hair over and over until his muscles cramp up and he comes, hard.

Paul coughs and swallows messily and comes himself while Alex blinks vision back into his eyes. He wipes his mouth with the back of his hand as Alex collapses on top of him, whining softly and burying his head in Paul's shoulder.

"What the fuck was that?" Alex asks, his voice muffled by skin.

6

The next morning Alex hauls himself out of bed when Paul gets up. He wants a few more minutes with him before he vanishes to the office again.

Given the number of guests and the volume of alcohol involved, not to mention their own activities once they went upstairs, he's not sure what he's going to find downstairs. But when they get to the kitchen, the only sign of human life is the various glasses and bottles accumulated on the counters and a note on the table.

Everyone's been sent on their way safely. Enjoy the peace and quiet. It's signed *Claire*, and there's a little smiley face next to her name. Alex can imagine Ellen's wife leaving the note before shooing the last stragglers out the door.

"They're gone," Alex breathes in relief. He drops the note back on the table and slumps against Paul. Given that all of their friends are grownups and it was a fucking wake, he'd hoped no one would actually crash, but experience has taught him not to assume maturity amongst this group. "You're sure you have to go in today?"

"It's not like my job got easier because my business partner died," Paul points out, a little sharply.

"I didn't mean it like that," Alex says.

Paul sighs. "Believe me, if I could stay home I would."

◆

Paul could accomplish everything he needs to do today from his home office, but normalcy is a powerful drug in the face of tragedy. He wants to be back at work even if the other half of his executive production team is never going to be on the *Winsome* lot again.

Of course, acting normal is one thing, but actually feeling that way is harder. Much harder. Paul looks over his shoulder half a dozen times thinking he's heard familiar footsteps or the murmur of a voice outside the door. His mother would be less skeptical of what Paul knows is just his imagination. Certainly, if Victor chose to haunt anywhere it would be his workplace, but Paul knows he only misses him.

It's only been a week since he died and it was yesterday that they put Victor in the ground — or at least, in a crypt in the mausoleum under the Cathedral. Paul wonders if any of them will ever realize he's really gone.

He's surprised when Nigel calls.

"Not to be rude," Paul says, not bothering with small talk after all of the emotion of the last week, "but I'd assumed you were looking forward to a few days of not dealing with Victor's human blast radius. What do you need?"

Nigel chuckles. Paul knows, from comments Nigel and Victor have made, that Paul is — of all their social group — consistently the most direct and least suspicious of Nigel, and that Nigel consistently appreciates it. Carly, he is fond of and can excuse. Liam and Alex are nightmares.

"I got named executor," Nigel says, which shouldn't be news to anyone. "And he named you his creative executor."

"What the hell does — "

"With Liam."

"Oh my God," Paul says. He still has no idea what that means, but it's surely nothing good.

"Yup, the bastard stuck me with all his worldly possessions and stuck you with — "

"What Alex would call the public display of the absence of his soul."

"Your husband is creepy." Nigel laughs.

"You have no idea," Paul says. "You call Liam yet?"

"What do you think? I'm relying on you to absorb the details. The less I have to navigate Victor's exhausting, possessive, and now heartbroken boyfriend, the better for everyone."

♦

Liam folds his arms across his chest, his phone dangling from one hand.

"What did he want?" Carly asks, fully prepared to call Nigel back and bitch him out if Liam is upset.

Liam shrugs.

"Words, Liam," Carly tells him.

He gives her an annoyed look.

"Well?" she asks. Sometimes he needs prodding.

"Just a minute." He's irritated and trying to collect to himself. "Victor named Paul and me creative executors of his estate."

"What the fuck does that mean?"

"I don't know. We get to figure out what to do with his creative stuff."

"Like, what? Scripts?"

"Yeah. Whatever. Stuff."

Carly sighs. More exposure to the problem is not likely to make Liam's life better. He's had a hard enough time functioning this last week, and Victor including him in this last request is going to make the challenge of facing the world that much harder.

"How do you feel about that?"

Liam shrugs. "I don't know what I'll have to do. Or if I'll have to do anything, Paul's the one who does this stuff. Maybe I won't have time."

He says it with a vague note of hope that's as wrenching to hear as anything. It's also the first time since Victor's death he's mentioned his own job. When Liam decided a couple of years ago he wanted to branch out into movies, Victor helped him pick *The Parrot Tree*. Victor knew and trusted the people involved, and Liam's enjoyed it so far even if little has gone to film and everything has been table reads and fittings.

"If the hanging out at home not talking to anybody isn't just indulging your grief while you have the time to, you're going to have to make some decisions about your movie," Carly says. It feels slightly cruel to say, but it's true. Whatever he ultimately wants or is able to do, Liam isn't best served by a lack of clarity as to the demands on his time.

"I'm not scheduled to shoot anything for a while."

"Yes, but are you going to get another week off like this? And then you're going to be on location, for six weeks, in India. How is that going to work, if you can't always *talk?*"

"I'll have a script," Liam says.

That's not strictly true, and Carly has no idea if it's supposed to be a joke about Liam's life or a comment on his ability to get lost in the work.

◆

After Paul leaves for the day, Alex calls Margaret, his manager, to check in on the general tack he wants to take regarding Victor's death. But when she asks about the blind, he wishes he hadn't.

"I absolutely do not need to know if it's true or not, and please do not tell me if it is, but for fuck's sake don't ever do that. Again or otherwise."

Alex slouches down on the couch. "Can we talk about *Icarus* promotion?"

"Sure. We should also talk about what you're planning to do next."

"I just got back from Australia a month ago," Alex says plaintively.

"That is true, but it's not relevant and you didn't answer the question."

Alex twists his wedding ring around his finger with his thumb and stares at the wall over their bookshelves, where pictures from the various trips he and Paul have taken for work and, more rarely, for vacation together are framed and hung.

"It means I don't want to think about going anywhere far away for a while. How bad an idea is it for me to guest on *Winsome?*"

The network has been nagging Paul about when he's going to get his A-list husband on the show pretty much since *Winsome* started its run. It's alternately amusing or irritating, depending on how uncomfortable he or Paul are feeling about their careers intersecting. Paul doesn't like to think that he got the show in part because he could guarantee a star like J. Alex Cook, and Alex doesn't want to be the guy who gets parts just because he's fucking — and now married to — the showrunner.

But *Winsome* needs an antagonist for its final season, and Alex is tickled to death at the idea Paul floated at him of playing a guy with whom Darcy's character forms a strange business and sexual partnership that leaves the audience guessing as to who is using who. As a bonus, Alex gets to die again, because Darcy's character is going to shoot him.

Victor asked Alex once, when they were all over at his house for dinner and then swimming, if he intended to die in every movie or show he was ever on.

"There's no suspense if I tell you yes," Alex said. Victor had cracked up.

Mostly though, Alex is glad that Paul's definitely not going to torture him to get a good performance the way Victor had for Zach's violent exit from *Fourth*.

Margaret pulls him back to the now. "Having a recurring guest role on your husband's show is adorable. Appearing in an arc for one season is adorable. Do not be a fucking regular on your husband's show."

Alex laughs darkly at all the things that are, and are not, considered acceptable in the place where their private and public lives intersect.

♦

Back in his office, Paul fishes the thumb drive from Olivia out of his computer case and plugs it in. He eats a sandwich with one hand while he scrolls through the contents of it with the other. Her writing is tight and vivid, and she studiously avoids directing from the page. Paul decides to do her a favor, just because he can. He sets the sandwich down and opens his email.

Olivia —

Monday. Be here.

Three minutes later, his phone rings.

Olivia doesn't bother to say hello. "Okay, I know that felt all *How to Get Away with Murder* sexy and stuff, but you can't 'be here' me. Make me an offer and we can fucking negotiate."

Paul laughs. "Writers' room. Monday. Six episode contract."

"I want more."

"We only have seven left."

"I want in on all seven."

"No you don't," Paul says gently. "The weekly pay is better on six weeks than eight, and I know you know it."

"I don't care about the cash."

"Yes you do," Paul says. The space between an assistant's salary and union rates on an hour-long drama are massive. Olivia will earn more in those six weeks than she's made in the last six months.

"You have to let me negotiate something," she says.

"You're not gonna say no, and I've got nothing else to give," Paul says. Again, he sees why Victor liked her and made her promises, but he can also see how much she would have benefitted from the guidance he never got around to giving her. At least Paul can honor Victor's choices and give her this.

"Lunch," she blurts.

"What?"

"You have to buy me lunch. Somewhere nice. Where we can look important. Because I've done a deal, and I need some recommendations on finding a rep," she says. And then, because she's not done brazening it out, "Sometime in the next two weeks."

"You're fucking crazy, you know that right?"

"Sure," she says, tough and casual again. "But, like, who isn't?"

7

Olivia's question lingers. As the spring drags on, Paul has no idea what to do with the creative executor thing — he has the sneaking suspicion Victor made it up just to fuck with him, though God knows why Liam's involved in that case.

The network *M.A.R.S.* is on is completely onboard with the idea, however. Paul gets summoned to a mid-April meeting with the studio brass. Without so much as a by-your-leave Frank, Paul's least favorite network suit, announces that *M.A.R.S.* is bringing Paul on board as a co-showrunner. Paul hasn't seen a contract, and is perhaps less keen than he should be on saying yes.

Meanwhile, Mark's already been promoted from head writer to head writer *and* co-showrunner. There is no way, given the inside baseball of Hollywood, that this won't end in a mess of professional jealousy and disaster.

Paul also knows he's not allowed to say no. The realization, after the first vague horror of it, makes him chuckle to himself; Alex will be amused. Paul at least does have the good sense to hold up his hands, remind everyone that they need this on paper and insist they talk to his rep. Because he'll deal with Victor's files in memory of his dead friend, but solving the network's problems needs to come with a paycheck.

Unfortunately, it also gives him pause about the Olivia situation. Taking advantage of Victor's passing to hire her is one thing. Stealing her off a show he's about to have a professional relationship with, on a different network than *Winsome*, is ethically and legally a lot more dubious — even if she is just a writer's assistant to them and no one is likely to care.

As daunting as the assignment is — the network isn't really any more specific about what it wants out of Paul than Victor was — Paul knows it's a vote of confidence. With *Winsome* in its final season, that's a good sign for Paul's continued viability as a showrunner. It's also a good sign that something of Victor's vision will be allowed to stick around, no matter how many people he pissed off when he was alive.Paul is relieved; Victor may have made Alex's career in a much more visible way, but Paul owes Victor everything, too.

After the meeting, Mark pulls Paul aside in the hallway. "Look," he says. "I know you're Victor's pet and he was grooming you to take over his empire, but some of us here have a job to do and aren't actually thrilled that Victor's dead."

Paul stares. "Excuse me?" Mark's tone and body language are exactly the same as in the meeting — and the funeral. Paul is wary and also fucking confused.

"*M.A.R.S.* was Victor's show, not yours, and the last thing we need is you coming in and taking over."

"Okay," Paul says firmly. This has gotten so far out of hand so quickly he hardly knows where to start. "I'm going to be co-showrunning because the network asked me to. I *have* my own show. I do not want your job. I am here if you need me. I will go through Victor's notes, and I will give you what I find. That's it."

"Bullshit. Everyone's ambitious, and this is a perfect opportunity. I know what I'd do if the situation were reversed."

"I'm not going to complain if the studio wants to pay me to do work I'd have to anyway," Paul says evenly. "I know everything's fucked up for you, but you have no idea how tangled up Victor's life has been with mine and Alex's. This is more fucked up for us."

"Yeah, everybody knows how much Victor helped you and your boy and *his* boy," Mark says.

Paul realizes that Mark is talking about Alex and *Liam*; in the same instant he realizes his hands are shaking. There's a ringing in his ears and everything in him wants to punch Mark. Paul has spent years trying to restrain his more destructive impulses, and does his best to shove this one away.

"Crazy Hollywood power-plays aside, grief makes everybody insane." he says as he takes a deep breath and makes himself walk away. He needs to call his sister.

♦

Paul checks in at the *Winsome* offices, then heads home to work. He's still jangly from the confrontation with Mark and it feels like bad luck to bring that energy around the show that is actually his — and a little bit Victor's — baby.

Alex isn't home, and Paul assumes he's gone out climbing. Even with so much of it to do in Australia, he had little time and confessed to Paul that he missed "his" rocks. It's both weird and adorable.

He debates setting up camp at the dining room table. They bought this new, bigger house so he could have a proper office, isolated from everyone else in the basement. But when he can stand mild distractions he tries not to lock himself away from Alex. It's one of their mostly unspoken coping mechanisms for Paul's tendency to overwork even by Hollywood standards.

But he doesn't want Mark's bullshit settling into his home with Alex any more than he wants it at *Winsome*, so he trudges downstairs to his office and hopes Alex will be persistent in retrieving him later.

He opens his social media dashboard mostly out of guilt. He hasn't had time to deal with any of it since Victor died, and he has a lot of messages of condolence and support. Many of them are from industry acquaintances and folks in the business he hasn't met but professionally flirts with online about hypothetical future projects. It's probably about time to say thank you.

Of course, Paul is an idiot, and he tracks way too many social media tags — about himself, about Alex, about their shows, and about the people they work with. That has always, very much, included Victor.

Paul knows he shouldn't be surprised that the Internet is animated and deeply down in the anger stage with Victor's death. After all, Mark is, and if Paul weren't so exhausted he supposes the rage would have found him by now too.

Some of the anger, though, isn't because Victor's dead, but because it took him so damn long to finally achieve that state. There's a massive number of people retweeting exclamations of joy, as if Victor had been the Wicked Witch of the West. Victor would have probably laughed. After all, his Twitter handle is — was — @TheShowYouHate, and he used it relentlessly to antagonize the viewing audience, critics, colleagues, and sometimes even his friends. Fans never knew what to make of it whenever he and Alex went at it, mostly playfully, on Twitter.

But it's still miserable to see people celebrating the death of someone who made everything from Paul's career to his marriage possible. It all feels very, very personal, and that's before a random scan of his Twitter mentions turns up way too many tweets speculating that the only person who might be happier about Victor's death than them is Paul.

He can't get his head around it — this idea fans have that people who create shows also ruin them and are to be despised. Paul discovers he also can't convince himself these people are wrong, though he knows, or at least should know, that Victor died neither alone (Ellen's phone call was a testament to that), nor unloved.

It's sad, and it's terrifying, and Paul finds himself unable to look away, reading through days and days of messages, many of them awful, many roping in him and Alex and their whole social circle. He wants Alex but needs Victor right now — he was the only person that could ever talk him down from his anxieties about the consequences of his work.

When Paul realizes he's never going to have that again and the Internet is probably happy about that too, he chokes out his first tears about Victor until he cries for real in the way men — especially men from places like Marion, South Carolina — are never supposed to. Somewhere in the middle of it all, he realizes with a wet laugh that at least now he knows what the fuck Mark was talking about.

◆

Paul takes a run and a shower and is settled back at his desk by the time Alex gets home, sweaty and chalky and content. He's grateful when Alex hauls him back upstairs to make food together. Recent tragedy only sharpens his awareness of the happiness in their admittedly strange lives. Paul listens to Alex's account of his day on the rocks while they move around the kitchen and imagines the two of them in five or ten years and the shape of the lives he desperately hopes they'll have.

Alex is unkindly amused about the network asking Paul to co-showrun on *M.A.R.S.* until he realizes it's not actually a joke. He's even less amused that Paul and Mark are already at odds.

"Is Victor going to haunt us forever?" he asks.

Paul isn't sure how careless his choice of words is. "The entirety of our professional lives are linked to his. This isn't going to go away overnight, and you should probably get used to that idea."

"I'm still not used to the idea that he's *dead*. But since he is, some distance from him would be great."

"Well, that's not going to happen particularly soon. We still have to go through all his things," Paul points out.

"Whoa, whoa whoa. *You're* the creative executor. When did that become 'we'?" Alex looks alarmed at the prospect of spending any amount of time in Victor's house ever again. Not that Paul can really blame him.

"I can play the 'have you got anything better to do,' card, the 'Liam's going to be there and will need moral support card,' or, the 'I'm asking nicely because you're my partner and my life is about to get stupid' card."

Alex laughs darkly. "Victor really is a bastard."

"You keep saying."

"It keeps being true."

"While we're on the subject of what to do with Victor's legacy — "

"I can't believe you just used that word unironically."

" — we should talk about what this next year is going to look like for us. Because you're finally back home, and we probably shouldn't put it off any more."

"Okayyy," Alex says with trepidation. "Should I be nervous that you look like you're getting ready to make a pitch?"

"Well, when *Winsome*'s done...I was thinking about us having a baby."

"Excuse me?"

Alex's face is not exactly encouraging, but Paul plows ahead anyway. "I'm going to have the year off. Whatever I do with *M.A.R.S.*, it won't be a full-time gig, so you can stop freaking out about that. And you're between major projects."

"You know, the let's-have-a-baby-because-we-have-a-year-off thing only works if we have the baby at the *beginning* of that year," Alex says with increasing speed and franticness. "Not spending nine months waiting and then getting the kid right when we have to go back to work. Why don't we wait until your next break?" he concludes almost desperately.

"Because I'd like to have a kid before I turn forty."

"It's Hollywood. Guys have babies, like, in their seventies," Alex says. He's waving his hands around now, which is not one of his usual ticks.

"Yeah and that's kind of gross. Also Victor *died,* and he wasn't even sixty."

"For the hundredth time, you are not Victor. Like, it's a battle, but you actually sleep. And this is not a reasonable response to whatever crisis of mortality is going on in your head."

"Okay, well, there's another reason time is a factor," Paul says. He takes a breath and lays out his plan.

Alex stares at him, boggled. "You want me and *your sister* to have a baby?"

"Via a surrogate," Paul says defensively. He's a little irritated that Alex is being so deliberately childish.

"Have you talked to Sarah about this?" Alex asks, switching gears in a state that might be approaching panic. "Because you have a track record."

"Yes."

"YOU TALKED TO YOUR SISTER ABOUT OUR BIOLOGICAL FUTURE WITHOUT

ASKING ME FIRST? HOW LONG HAVE YOU BEEN THINKING ABOUT THIS?"

Paul crosses his arms over his chest and refuses to take the bait. "Admit you were going to yell at me if I hadn't talked to her too, just so we can move on," he suggests.

Alex maintains his glare but eventually deflates. Apparently, Paul isn't wrong.

"Besides, we've been talking about this for ages."

"We have not!"

"All the time you were in Australia?"

"I thought that was hypothetical!"

"It's *me*," Paul says, though he's aware that's not really a legitimate defense.

"And it most definitely did not involve Sarah," Alex presses.

"Well, that was a more recent addition."

"No shit!"

"We don't have to do it this way," Paul says because that's what fairness requires. "But I want to, and you should think about it."

8

"I do not need the gory details." Gemma interrupts Alex's monologue about how America will be obsessed over whether he or Paul is the biological father of their still very hypothetical child. They're in Paul and Alex's kitchen, Alex making popcorn while Gemma perches on a bar stool.

"Well, kids kind of come with gory details. Even when you get them with science and not sex."

Alex gives a dramatic shudder mostly, but not entirely, for comedic effect.

"Why are boys so bad at coping with biology?" she teases when Alex pushes the popcorn bowl across the island to her.

"It would be less dumb if Paul weren't making plans without me again."

"No he is not, and we are not going down that road again. You did not make me drive all the way over here so you could whine at me about your hot, talented, successful husband's overeagerness to have kids with you."

"I didn't make you drive over here," Alex protests.

"Well, you get weird when my neighbors take pictures of you coming and going so yes, you did."

"I'm freaking out that 'abstract plan' became a timetable overnight."

"Which is fair. But, Alex, seriously, you're being an asshole. Not everything in your life is out to get you, and it would be nice if you called me over here for something other than for me to give you advice about really expensive babies. I am not your therapist. Ask me how my job is going."

Alex grins. He and Gemma don't hang out as much as they used to, because both of their schedules are hard, but he appreciates her ability to call him on his shit. It was grounding the year his life went crazy, and it's still reassuring. "How's your job going, Gemma?"

Gemma launches into a monologue of her own about the struggles of trying to find her way into development without a bachelor's degree to her name.

Alex tries to listen, but he drifts off into his own head, wondering with a small bit of horror what their lives would have been like if Victor hadn't plucked him out of obscurity. Would he and Gemma still be living together? Who would Alex be with, if not Paul? Or would he and Paul have crashed into each other no matter what? After all, Paul noticed him before even Victor did. Would Alex be an A.D. by now? Or would he have had to go back to Indiana, without any of his excuses — first, no money, and now, no time — not to?

Gemma flicks his shoulder. "You're not listening."

Alex startles. "I am totally listening."

"What's the last thing I said?"

"Blah blah something about development blah?"

Gemma kicks his stool, but she's laughing. "Asshole."

Alex shrugs, mostly because he doesn't know how to apologize or how to be better. Sometimes, he feels like he doesn't know how to do anything at all. Certainly, that alone should disqualify him from being a parent.

"What the hell is up with you?" Gemma asks. "If the baby stuff is freaking you out, *talk to your husband about it.* You do not need my permission to have a family."

Alex is quiet for a long moment. Then he says, "I thought you said you weren't my therapist."

9

Paul tends to keep more reasonable hours when Alex is home but he's still often one of the last ones on the lot, which is why he's surprised to see a light on in the writers' office late one night at the beginning of May.

He sticks his head in the door to see Olivia, laptop open, typing furiously and, until he knocks on the doorframe, not remotely aware that he's there.

She jumps and then glares at him. "You should wear a bell."

"Not a lot of people around on a Friday night to scare."

"Nope," she says and goes back to typing. She gives him an annoyed look when he wanders further into the room and sits down in the chair across from her.

The *Fourth Estate* offices are long gone. It's been years since Paul was on a writing staff, but rooms like this still feel like home even if he's now on the other side of the desk, dispensing guidance instead of being lectured to — kindly or otherwise — by Victor.

"What do you want?" she asks.

"Friday night writers' bonding," Paul says. "Tell me about yourself. Your hopes, your dreams, how much *M.A.R.S.* is going to suck now." He's no Victor when it comes to wrangling people and forcing them to grow. He also knows he's kinder, and if people aren't his avocation the way they were Victor's, he still cares for them all. In Victor's now eternal absence, it's even more crucial to connect.

Olivia laughs and waves a hand at him before going back to typing, again. "Don't you have work to do? Or go home, stop bugging me."

"You're here," Paul asks, and it's leading.

"I'm working on new spec."

"Why?"

"You only gave me six episodes, and your show is ending."

"The specs you gave me will get you a job anywhere," Paul points out.

"Mmm, I wish," Olivia says. "Except I am neither white nor in possession of a dick, so Hollywood is doubly gross for me. Also I don't want a job anywhere, I want my own show. Go away."

"No, talk to me," Paul says, fascinated now. Dedication is one thing and is certainly admirable, but Olivia is working like a woman possessed. It reminds him more than a little of himself and the first year he'd spent writing for Victor, spending eighteen hours a day telling stories because the rest of his life was fucked up beyond belief. Olivia certainly seems better-adjusted than Paul was at twenty-five, but he still wants her stories, and not only the ones she's putting on paper.

"Paul, *I am working.*"

"Tell me what your deal is and I'll go away," Paul gives her his most charming smile.

"Okay, this is where I explain that I am not here to entertain you or explain myself to you, and shouldn't have to bargain with you to be left alone to do my work. It's also a good thing you're gay or you would be not just rude but also creepy." Olivia hits save and folds her hands in front of her keyboard.

"Sorry."

"Thank you. Now, since you've been useful in the past… I want to tell stories. Victor was a bastard and a genius, and the world is never going to appreciate how much it's going to miss him and that pisses me off. You're crazy too, and I'm not sure how that's going to blow up yet but you are and it is; but you're not an asshole like Mark and can probably be trained. Also, if you think you're going to be my mentor, just stop now and save us both the grief."

Paul stares at her. "What makes you think I'm going to be your mentor?" he asks, a little stung but mostly amused, because Olivia is sharp and delightful and completely not wrong.

"You're in here at ten o'clock on a Friday night asking me what my deal is."

♦

Alex, to Paul's weary dismay, is still incredibly irritated that, after Victor has been buried, his house still exists and Alex is getting dragged into dealing with it. He badgers Paul about it the entire ride over.

"Why can't Nigel do this?" Alex asks as soon as they get in the car.

"He's in New York."

"Jackson?"

"Not what he signed up for."

"Right, Liam?"

"That's cruel, Alex."

"I don't understand why it's us."

"You're being a brat," Paul says with a sigh. "And as charming as you are — "

"Not charming?" Alex asks.

"Nope," Paul says almost cheerfully. "Not at all."

Alex's dread makes a lot more sense when they get there. Carly is annoyed that they're late, and Liam is sitting cross-legged on the floor by a bookcase running his hand along the tops of the books on the lowest shelves.

"You're going to get paper cuts," Alex says.

Liam stops. Which actually seems to piss Carly off more.

"Can we get this over with?" she says.

"Woman after my own heart," Alex mutters.

Paul looks around the central core of the house's public spaces and sighs. "Does anyone think this isn't going to be days of work?" he asks incredulously.

"Don't feel sorry for yourself until you see what's on my to-do list," Carly says darkly.

"Why, what?"

Carly jerks her head in the direction of the kitchen. Paul follows her, mystified and already tired, while Alex crouches down next to Liam.

"Given the nature of fucking dead Victor's relationship with Liam, what's the last thing you'd want either of those two to stumble across while we're sorting through Victor's intimate effects?" she hisses once Alex and Liam are out of earshot.

Paul frowns at her, thinking. And then his jaw drops. "Oh my God."

"Yes."

"So you're going to — ?"

"Look for Victor's hidden stash of sex toys so Liam doesn't break down if he finds them and Alex doesn't blurt something idiotic if *he* finds them? *Yes.*"

In light of Carly's mission, Paul is grateful for his relatively straightforward, if herculean, task of going through Victor's office for whatever *M.A.R.S.* information he can find. The place is ruthlessly organized, but there's tons of material — desk drawers and filing cabinets and bookshelves — that he's going to have to come back for.

He assigns Alex the task of searching Victor's den for anything possibly useful to the whole creative executor thing. Paul's sure Victor didn't keep everything in his office and wants to stick his husband somewhere he's not going to come across any of the dreaded sex toys. Hopefully the den is free of them.

◆

Liam still hasn't said anything, but he drifts into the den after Alex and sits down on the floor again. Alex folds his arms and sighs, regarding the crammed bookshelves lining the wall. Victor really was a bastard.

He tries to be methodical, but there's too much here. Some of it is books, not that Alex ever once saw Victor read anything that wasn't a script page or on a screen. There are rows and rows of DVDs. One bookcase is given over to binders and notebooks, which he pokes over at random.

Alex expects Liam to say something when he starts monologuing at him about Paul and babies, but

Liam lets it all wash over him. It's unexpectedly soothing, to talk into the air.

When he kneels down on the floor to deal with the bottom shelf, Liam leans against his shoulder. It makes it kind of hard to move without jostling him, but Liam doesn't seem to mind so Alex shrugs and carries on. Liam is one of the few people he's easy sharing space with. It's unusual that Liam's still so quiet, but then, they are basically ransacking his dead lover's house. Alex doesn't want to think about ever having to go through Paul's office like this.

At least, if the unspeakable happened, Alex would get to keep the house. Though between the alternatives, Alex isn't sure which one he'd prefer. Mostly, he wants not to think of the possibility ever.

"Lee, I'm gonna move over," Alex warns him before he shifts to get a better access to the shelf. Liam picks his head up to let him, then starts playing with a bracelet — Victor's, Alex sees when he looks over. Alex is glad for the company, but the soft clink of the dead man's jewelry as Liam toys with it is completely unnerving.

The next book Alex puts his hand on is heavy, black, and leather bound. When Alex opens it, he's expecting a fancy dictionary or maybe some *Readers' Digest*-like series.

When he sees not printed text but pages full of precise penmanship, Alex snaps the book closed. Liam looks up at him curiously as Alex opens the book again, slowly.

It's definitely a diary, and, going by the dates on the entries, it's at least a few years old. The thought of Victor having a diary — not to mention one written on expensive paper and not a hard drive — is so bizarre Alex can't quite process it right away.

Alex checks the shelf; sure enough, there is a whole row of the books, all identical. He starts pulling them onto the floor. The dates go back decades, though most are from the last ten or fifteen years.

"What are those?" Liam asks, once Alex has them spread around himself in a circle.

"Victor's diaries." Alex runs a hand across a cover. "Do you want them?"

Liam thinks about it and then shakes his head. "No. Books can't bring him back."

Alex has no idea how to respond to that. "Is it okay if I take them?"

♦

Alex tucks his bag close to his side as he holds the door for Paul, who's carrying a brown cardboard file box that looks like it's from 1960. He's filled it with notebooks, a laptop, and multiple external drives. Paul hopes none of it is password protected, though he knows how likely that isn't.

Carly locks the door, and Liam doesn't give Alex their usual hug on parting; he still isn't on his usual touching terms with anyone. Paul watches, box balanced on his hip while Liam and Alex look at each other for a long moment before Liam follows Carly.

"What was that about?" Paul asks once they're in the car.

"Liam and I are gonna hang out this week." Alex carefully arranges his bag at his feet.

Paul looks sideways at him, but Alex doesn't say anything else; apparently Alex and Liam are having psychic conversations again. Paul shrugs and starts the car. He's learned life is easier when he doesn't poke too hard at whatever weird thing exists between them.

◆

As soon as they get home, Paul pulls Victor's laptop out of the box and plonks it down on their kitchen table. Alex has to resist the urge to tell him that he doesn't want it near where they eat; like bare feet in a restaurant, it's not actually unhygienic, but it still feels unseemly.

For a moment, they both stare at it.

"Are you expecting it to open by itself, cast an eerie glow, and convey a terrible message?" Alex asks, still not looking at Paul.

"Are you?" Paul asks, amused and hostile that Alex is including him in his own discomfort.

"Maybe? A little? Yes?" he finally turns to Paul.

"I wasn't 'til you said it," Paul grumbles before sliding into a chair and opening the thing.

Alex tries to leave him to it, not wanting to fret about it further. Certainly the diaries can wait. He's not going to give them power like Paul has the Magic Computer of Showrunner Godliness. Also, they really need a Victor quota.

"Can we, like, have a rule?" he asks as he stares into their refrigerator. He wants something to eat, has no motivation to cook, and can't imagine what's interesting enough to order in. That's the horror of not being on a project: he has to make mundane decisions all by himself.

Paul makes an inquisitive noise.

"That laptop never, ever, *ever* comes to bed with you."

Paul actually flinches at the thought. "Yeah. God. No."

Alex chuckles darkly.

"Fuck," Paul says.

"What?" Alex says, finally pulling out a bottle of water and hipping the door closed. Paul is staring despondently at the screen.

"Password."

Alex arches an eyebrow. "Were you expecting it not to be locked?"

"Are you going to be obnoxious, or are you going to help?"

"You know I can't read Victor's mind, either. Especially now that he's dead."

Paul sighs. "Is the sense of humor about dead Victor your way of coping or just you being thoughtless?"

Alex shrugs.

"Do you think Liam would know?"

"If I can't call him to see how he's coping with Victor's death, you can't call him about Victor's *password.*"

"Why not?" Paul asks.

"Because you're co-creative executors, and Victor was his lover, and you took the laptop without so much as a by your leave — "

"Liam doesn't seem interested — "

"What would you be interested in if I were gone?"

Paul shoves back from the computer likes he's been burned. "Whoa. Don't do that."

"What, put mortality issues on the table because dead Victor makes you want to have a baby?"

"Seriously, Alex. Computer password. The sooner I go through it, the sooner I can get it out of here."

"I don't know. Call Nigel."

"No."

"Why?" Alex asks.

"Because it's weird."

"It's Victor. Nigel is not unfamiliar with weird."

"I don't want to call him with the first problem we have, okay?"

Alex rolls his eyes and shakes his head. There is nothing unfamiliar about this iteration of they-both-have-issues-but-Paul-likes-to-pretend-he-doesn't. There is, however, only so much of Paul having bursts of password hacking inspiration followed by sighing petulantly at Victor's laptop that Alex can take.

"Give me that," he says, grabbing it and spinning it toward him on the table.

He leans over it, punches in four letters and triumphantly hits enter.

For a moment he stares at it blankly. "That actually worked."

"What was it?"

"*LIAM*, you idiot. That actually worked," he says again.

"That's a terrible password," Paul says.

"Foiled you long enough," Alex says, staring at the computer still. "Fuck." He picks up his water bottle and heads for the glass door onto their deck. He needs some air. And possibly a drink.

10

Cracking the password turns out to have been the easy part. Victor's notes are simple enough to find — his computer is as ruthlessly organized as his office — but they don't make much sense to Paul or, he guesses, anyone who wasn't Victor. Ultimately, after a few days of adding notes and being as useful with them as he can in between everything he has to do with *Winsome*, he makes copies of it all and brings them in to Mark.

Mark is less than thrilled to get it.

"Fuck this," he says when Paul hands over the drive. "Like I didn't have enough notes from the network already."

"Oh God," Paul says, the penny finally dropping.

"What?" Mark says, annoyed.

"I am the network." In the last six years he's often been at odds with the powers that be over *Winsome*, and the prospect of being put on the other side of that equation is horrifying. "Victor was an *asshole*."

"Fuck, you don't have to tell me," Mark says. "He died and now I have you hovering, collecting a network paycheck, and waiting for me to fuck up."

Paul sighs. "I get a network check because, if you do fuck up, I get a call at three in the morning and have to write you an entire episode by six. No matter where I am or what I'm doing."

"Or who?" Mark offers.

Paul stares at him for a moment. Then he cracks up. It's as much tension as anything, but after a shocked second Mark joins in.

The moment ends quickly, though, and Paul is left repositioning the hard drive on Mark's desk. He's more than a little concerned Mark isn't going to look at any of its contents.

"Good luck making sense of it. I made notes where I could, but you know how he was. I doubt I was able to make out anything you couldn't."

"Then why'd you bother?"

"To piss you off?"

"Better than going through the porn on his laptop?" Mark snarks.

"Don't," Paul says.

"You ask Liam to take a look?" Mark asks. Paul understands they've cycled back to Victor's notes, but the way they've gotten there is appalling. And it makes him — only somewhat to his surprise — damn fucking protective.

"He's got enough on his plate right now, don't you think?" he says sharply.

"Heyyy, no offense," Mark says, lifting his hands from the arms of his chair defensively. "Relax. I'm not going to barge in on him in his hour of grief, or whatever. But if neither of us can translate Victor into human, I need his expertise and I don't need to go through you to get it."

Paul is unimpressed with Mark's plight. "You had some pretty choice things to say about him and my husband."

"Yeah, well, you leave me notes on my show, I leave you notes on the harem you inherited from Victor. What the fuck is going on in your life, dude?"

Paul throws his head back and laughs darkly at the ceiling. "You have no fucking idea."

"Well," Mark says with a shrug, "at least you're getting laid."

◆

Paul calls Liam as soon as he turns the corner down the hall from Mark's office. He wants to do something useful and not stew on the pit of despair that *M.A.R.S.* is, but he also wants to give Liam fair warning in case Mark actually does try to get in touch with him.

Liam, though, does not pick up. After his calls ring through to voicemail twice, Paul calls Carly instead.

Carly is not amused at Paul's implication that she might still be screening Liam's calls.

"Liam's a big boy who is, by the way, currently in possession of his phone. If he's not answering, that seems pretty fair to me considering his partner fucking died."

"I didn't know you thought of it that way," Paul says softly.

"Tell me how I'm supposed to think of it."

"I thought you were cool with it."

Carly makes a noise of frustration. "The part I'm not cool with is the part where he's dead. Now, would you like me to see if Liam wants to talk to you, or shall

I continue to play his secretary so that you can be arbitrarily pissed at me?"

♦

Alex closes the journal and stares at it. Victor, at nineteen, unsettles him more than the Victor he'd known. Alex knows that's less a reflection on Victor, than on his own biases. But Victor honest and Victor angry and Victor thwarted, is fucking strange. There was never, as far as Alex had ever heard, any struggle in his narrative. One day he just showed up with stories everyone wanted to tell. Alex doesn't know what to think of someone who spent most of his life pretending he was too good for anything to ever be difficult.

Considering his own role in that is more difficult to examine. Victor was a magician who was always careful to make sure Alex — and everyone else — was looking at the wrong hand. Now that he's dead and Alex can look anywhere he wants, his gaze is starting to feel like a violation. Which, Alex supposes, is why he hasn't told Paul or anyone besides Liam he has the diaries. Eventually, he knows he's going to have to confess. He also knows it's going to be terrible.

He's also not sure why he's reading them. Grief, or a search for understanding of the very difficult man who changed his life would be reasonable — even noble. But Alex knows he's being selfish. He wants secrets or power, wants the relief that Liam's loss is not his own. Or, somehow, he wants an answer he can give Paul about babies and science and the massive space between wanting things solely because the world doesn't wish them for people like him and the relief at not having to make everyone else's choices.

Alex is almost on his way out the door to head over to Carly and Liam's when he gets a text from Liam. His phone's autocorrect has clearly had a field day with it, and while Liam isn't generally the best typist, Alex can usually make out most of what he's saying. This time, he has no idea. He hits call while he digs around in his bag for his keys.

Liam doesn't pick up, though he must be right next to his phone and Alex calls twice more before leaving a voicemail. It's enough to make him worried, and he finally just texts, *What did you say?*

Can't do lunch, he gets back after what seems like an inordinate amount of time.

Why? Alex asks, confused but also disappointed. He misses Liam and was looking forward to seeing him. It's maybe a selfish impulse considering the loss Liam's facing, but aside from the funeral and cleaning Victor's house, Alex hasn't seen him since he got back from Australia. That may have been his own choice, because he wanted to go nowhere and see no one except Paul in the first few weeks home, but it doesn't lessen his longing for Liam's company.

Can't, is all Liam replies.

Alex sighs and tosses his phone back on the counter. He could still get in his car and drive over there and make Liam talk to him, but that seems like unwise choices for any number of reasons. Liam could be in the middle of a grief-stricken breakdown or Liam could have company of the sort Alex tries really, really hard not to think about (polyamory is fine, but he *never* wants the details). Also, it would be rude, but his and Liam's relationship is such that considerations of social niceties are irrelevant. In any case, there's nothing that he can do. It's immensely frustrating.

◆

Carly is surprised when she gets home and there's no extra car in the driveway. She assumed Alex would stay through dinner as well as lunch. She already prepared a speech for Paul in case Alex ended up passing out with Liam and Paul decided to get jealous, although he doesn't really do that anymore.

Ali's still at preschool, and the house is unpleasantly silent. She finds Liam upstairs on their bed, sitting against the headboard and scrolling listlessly through his phone.

"Where's Alex?" she asks, flopping down on her side of the bed and kicking her shoes off. Barely four months in, pregnancy is already gross and annoying. Carly could do her sound editing from home most days in the blessed comfort of her pajamas, but working at the office gets her out of the house and around other people. Being attached at the hip twenty-four/seven is not part of the structure of her and Liam's life.

"I told him not to come," Liam says, still scrolling through the contact list on his phone. Carly wonders if he's actually looking for anything, or if the clicking noise the phone makes with every name he scrolls past is soothing.

"Why did you do that? You were looking forward to seeing him." It's reasonable for Liam to want to stay in familiar surroundings, but he also needs human contact other than just her and Ali.

Liam shrugs.

"Liam, I can't read your mind."

"It's complicated."

"Why is it complicated?"

"Because he's going to want to hug me."

"And that's suddenly a bad thing?

Liam frowns and finally manages to put the phone aside. "Victor's the last person who touched me."

It makes Liam-sense, but doesn't make Carly feel better. She's never been Liam's second choice, but it pisses her off that she and Ali apparently don't count as people who have touched Liam. She is right fucking here, and Liam is still looking somewhere past her.

"Words are really hard," he says, after a long pause. "And I can't tell if it's because of my brain or if I'm too sad to be alive in the world right now."

"Good thing you and Alex don't seem to need the words," Carly says lightly, but only to cover her own sense of horror. Liam's ability to function is, reasonably, crumbling in front of her, but she has no idea how much worse it's going to get, or how many of their relationships it's going to take down with it.

♦

Paul is relieved to find Alex's car there in the driveway when he pulls in at their house. Alex's presence in combination with the conversation with his sister feels like a good sign. Liam in crisis is going to be disruptive to their lives at some point, and while Paul is resigned to the fact that Alex is, sooner or later, going to fall asleep at Carly and Liam's, he's glad he's home now. Alex hasn't been back from Australia long enough for Paul to be used to the idea he's going to be in their bed every night. Dead Victor makes it feel dangerous to get used to the idea he's going to stay there. It's a terrible feeling.

Alex is asleep when Paul gets up to their room and mumbles groggily when Paul runs a hand down his back to wake him up.

"Mm, you're home. Workaholic," he says, pulling the covers back up around his shoulders.

Paul smiles. "Are you awake?"

"No."

Paul chuckles. "How was Liam?"

"Fucker bailed on me," Alex grumbles.

Paul frowns; that's unusual, but given the circumstances, perhaps, not remarkable.

Alex doesn't offer any further information. Paul finally says, "I talked to Sarah again today, and we did some research. Want to look at it?"

Alex blinks his eyes open at that. "Okay, when did I say yes to this baby?"

"This isn't going to be like the time you signed the *Fourth* contract without reading it. Research, Alex. Like, this is your *thing*." Paul pulls up his email on his phone and tries to hand it to Alex.

Alex squints his eyes and bats it away. "Paul, at what point did you decide that our hypothetical offspring had to be genetically related to both of us?" he complains sleepily. "Is this because the Internet is going to be obsessed over figuring out which of us is the biological father? Because they will, and that pisses me off, but my masculinity isn't going to be threatened if they decide it's not me."

"Okay, there was a lot going on in there, including the thing where you've been stewing over how we each feel about our masculinity."

"There is a lot going on, and you are asking me to father your sister's baby!" He doesn't sound angry, but baffled and irritated.

"It would also be nice if you would read what I'm giving you instead of talking about this like a child."

"Paul. It's *midnight.* I was *asleep.* Your phone is glowy and it hurts. I am pretty sure this is a violation of consent."

"Okay," Paul says resignedly, dropping his phone on the nightstand.

"If you're going to talk at me anyway, at least take off your clothes and get in," Alex grumbles, closing his eyes again.

Paul chuckles, and does. He really loves Alex.

"We were going to do surrogacy anyway," he says as he slides under the covers. "This way, we get to keep it in the family. As much as possible."

"Is this about you wanting a ridiculously freckled baby? Because let me tell you, freckles as a kid are not fun."

"You know, you can tell me I have masculinity issues, but I don't hear you saying no to the part about being the bio dad."

Alex rocks back a little. "So?"

"So, you don't know your father, and I want to know if this is something you want. Because I think it is, and I am *trying to have a conversation with you about it.*"

"Your timing is atrocious."

"Blaming you for that," Paul says fondly.

"Let me sleep on it?" Alex says. He sounds, for once, thoughtful and not petulant.

"Are you saying that just to make me go away?"

Alex rolls over and pulls the covers up again. Paul wraps an arm around him and chuckles when Alex snuggles back into him. Paul is so not the only one who's missed sharing a bed.

11

Carly and Liam come over for dinner with Ali in tow one evening toward the end of May. Carly is clearly still not sure how good an idea this is, but Paul has been cajoling her to get Liam to come to their house because Alex has been sulking at him about Liam's continued absence. Dragging Liam to dinner will at least get the pressure from them off of her and, hopefully, do Liam some good.

Liam is certainly still quieter than usual, although they all manage to chat about something other than Victor being dead over the course of the meal. It feels like moving forward, or at least a collective attempt to figure out what it's going to look like when they all finally do.

After dinner, Paul takes Liam downstairs to his office; it feels more appropriate to have this conversation there than over the dinner table. He surprises himself when he only narrowly resists the sudden impulse to lead him there by the hand. Whatever Carly might say about it, it has nothing to do with seeing Liam as a child. But what it has to do with instead, Paul isn't entirely sure. He bites at his lip as he considers both how to ask Liam about Victor's notes and ask Alex about everyone's desire to touch Liam.

Liam settles himself a little uncertainly on the couch, while Paul decides to keep things simple and rolls his desk chair over.

Paul says, "So there's a thing you might get asked to do for *M.A.R.S.* I wanted to talk to you about it first, so you're prepared if anyone decides to be an asshole to you."

"You mean Mark," Liam says.

Paul blinks and thinks about hedging, because he's really trying to back off from the open warfare situation, which will only come back to bite them all eventually. "Yeah."

"That's okay," Liam says. Then, "Wait, what does he want?"

Paul can't help but chuckle. "Help making sense of Victor's notes. They're a vague and confusing mess, and I'm sure they made sense to him, but I can't figure all of them out. You knew his brain and how he worked better than any of us."

"Do *you* want me to help?"

"That's... It's Victor's legacy. It's your call."

Liam nods thoughtfully. "I will. I mean this is probably why Victor put my name down," he smiles, a little watery. And then he says, "What's Mark saying?"

Paul blinks. "Um." He's not sure how much he should reveal about that, but Liam plows on anyway.

"Let me guess — you're fucking me to get ahead in the business?"

"Something like that."

"Don't feel special," Liam says with a smile that reminds Paul unnervingly of Victor. "He does that to everyone."

"He's infuriating."

"Victor thought he was hilarious."

"I don't know what to do with that."

Liam shrugs and smiles cryptically.

◆

"So that's new," Alex observes to Carly, staring warily at the door Paul and Liam have disappeared through. He's not sure which of them he's more nervous for.

"What, you didn't think they were going to fight over your honor for the rest of their lives? They're big boys, Alex. They grew up."

"The growing up is fine. The conspiring worries me."

"What's conspiring?" Ali asks.

"It means Alex is being paranoid. They're *working*. Let it go," Carly says irritably.

"This is ridiculous," Alex says, rinsing plates and handing them to Carly to stack in the dishwasher. "Our husbands are discussing business while we clean up the kitchen. Which makes us 1950s housewives, you know."

"Your little crusade against being treated like a girl got a lot less interesting somewhere around the thing where I got pregnant and then you and I fucked to Paul's enthusiastic narration," Carly says blandly.

"Carly!" Alex hisses, scandalized.

"What?"

Alex jerks his head toward the five-year-old who is currently attempting to lure Todd down from his regal perch on top of the refrigerator.

"She doesn't know what it means."

"It means you get in *People*," Ali pipes up.

Alex stares at her in horror.

"The *magazine?*" she says, like he's being obtuse. It doesn't make Alex feel any better.

He turns to Carly. "Your child terrifies me."

"She's not necessarily wrong."

"Why do you think I'm scared?" Alex digs the dish detergent out from under the sink. "So apropos of you to mention pregnancy."

"Ahhh yes. Paul's thinking about kids?" Carly says breezily. It only confirms Alex's suspicions that Paul's been talking to her about this, probably long before he started discussing it with Alex. Behind them, Todd jumps down, and Ali scampers off after him.

"Yes. With pamphlets." Alex is still irritated by the whole thing.

"Tell me you two discussed this before you went and got married."

"Yes, but in Paul's world 'sure, we should have kids someday' meant I agreed to a timeline and he asked his sister for her eggs."

Carly lets out a low whistle.

"Thank you."

"Oh honey, I didn't say I was on your side. I was enjoying your discomfort saying *eggs.*"

"Stop."

"Eggs," Carly repeats again, clearly finding it hilarious. "*Eggs, eggs, eggs.*"

"I hate you."

"You hate everyone."

"Eggs!" Ali shouts, reappearing from the living room.

"Yes," Alex says, trying not to crack up, "I really really do."

◆

"So how are you?" Paul eventually asks.

Liam gives him a wan smile. "Not good enough that you want an honest answer to that."

"You know, if you need anything…" Paul says. He doesn't understand Liam on either of their best days, but he knows enough of his own psychology to be more than a little worried under the current circumstances. Victor's death has been hard enough on Paul, and he wasn't his lover.

"I need a lot of things. But none of that makes me dangerous to myself or anybody else. You and I are different," Liam says with a little tilt of his head and a look that is frankly unnerving.

"I can't imagine what you're going through," Paul says pathetically.

"Don't. Don't practice this. I mean, I'm pissed off because I have no idea what I'm doing, but …" Liam trails off like he's run out of words. "I'll be glad to get back to work. I think. Scripts, you know?"

Paul nods. "Alex yells at me when I try to cope by being a workaholic."

"Sometimes Alex is wrong."

Paul cracks up at how matter-of-factly Liam says it.

Liam turns the bracelet on his wrist and goes on. "I don't need the sixteen-hour days though. I just need a thing to tell me what to do."

"Have you guys started shooting yet?" Paul asks, grateful for a topic that isn't the death of partners, or the rather complicated mess Victor left them both to clean up.

He realizes, as he does, that whatever Mark thinks of Liam's potential to be useful, that's not actually why Victor named him creative executor alongside Paul. He's sure, now, from the way Liam is responding to him and even leaning slightly toward him, that Victor wanted Paul to fill his place in Liam's creative life. In a way, that's a much bigger responsibility than the safekeeping of Victor's legacy. Paul is simultaneously horrified at Victor's presumption and desperate to do right by him and Liam.

"Not really," Liam says. "A few camera tests, some reads. Apparently we're having a theatrical experience," Liam says, rolling his eyes and making air quotes. "Not that I'd know. They've been kind though, which I know is more than you're supposed to be able to ask."

Paul blinks at him, unsure of what to say.

"Principal photography begins next week," Liam says, like he's just realized that was the answer Paul was looking for in the first place.

"Do you want me to set up a meeting for you with Mark before you have to get into that?"

Liam thinks about it for a moment and then shakes his head. "No. I mean, he's fine, but can you give me copies of everything and I'll look through it on my time?"

Paul has a sudden unwelcome image of Alex sitting in a chair on the other side of a desk, being asked by someone at his own network to translate Paul's notes for them. Sometimes, he's not sure how Liam is upright.

"Of course."

♦

After the kitchen is cleaned up Alex, Carly, and Ali all go out on the deck, where Ali becomes instantly engrossed in dropping woodchips from one of their potted plants off the edge. The sky in the distance is hazy with smoke from the wildfires that are still burning; Alex has almost gotten used to the pervasive tang of burning things in the air.

"I'm twenty-eight," Alex says, petulantly enough that he knows he sounds younger. He leans over the railing to make sure the woodchips aren't ending up in the pool, then lets her at it.

"You're not as young as you used to be," Carly says with a raised eyebrow. "If you're not ready, that's one thing, not that anybody is actually ever ready for kids, but don't blame it on your age."

"What is having kids even like?" Alex asks. The idea of having little people to teach things and play with and love with Paul is appealing, but Alex's life since he left Indiana has been one long lesson in the consequences of having the things everyone thinks they want. It makes him wary.

"It's like someone burned down your house and then gave you wings," Carly says, settling herself into one of their loungers.

"What the hell?" It's the most Liam-like thing he's ever heard her say.

"Exactly."

"I think my mom was relieved when she realized I was gay," he says, after another moment of having no idea how to pursue Carly's line of conversation.

"Yeah?"

"Yeah. Kind of reduces the risk of pregnant teenage girlfriend."

"Not necessarily."

"Yeah, but I *really* hated people in high school."

Carly cackles. "So you don't want kids because you're fucked up over Indiana and think reproducing is fulfilling some hick-ass narrative destiny?"

"I'm not fucked up over Indiana," Alex protests.

"It's the only thing I've ever seen you afraid of," Carly says in a way that makes Alex wonder if she's going to point out that they've fucked again.

"Yeah, well, you would be too if your sister tried to stab you in the kitchen," Alex says like it's no big deal, even though it is.

Carly stares. "Jesus Christ, Alex."

"I mean, it could be worse. Paul could have wanted to be bio-dad, and use Delilah's eggs."

"I don't think I've ever heard you say her name," Carly says cautiously.

Alex shrugs. "Mostly I try not to think about my felonious relatives."

"So, Indiana, bad," Carly ventures.

Alex turns and stares at her for a second before he cracks up. "Indiana, bad. Now, tell me about babies?"

Before she can answer, Ali returns from her woodchip adventure and crawls up on the lounger next to her. Carly smiles and brushes Ali's hair out of her face as she snuggles into Carly's side, then proceeds like they haven't just had a very strange conversation. After all, Alex supposes, she's married to Liam.

"Being pregnant sucks but you don't have to worry about that. Oh the magic of renting a womb. Or is that going to be Paul's sister too?" Carly asks awkwardly.

"Okay, see, this is the problem. My mother's house is worth like twenty percent of what this kid is going to cost. That is fucked up, Carly."

"At least you're not doing some sketchy foreign baby buying."

"STOP TALKING. Believe me, I wish we could do this like normal people."

Carly purses her lips. "Alex, you and Paul have a lot of money. And you're going to spend it on your child whether that's private school or an adorable little rabbit fur coat, or, you know, science! So you should probably get over the fact that you're fucking rich and it's fucking weird fucking now."

"Sweet little Alicia is going to be swearing like a sailor by kindergarten," he points out. Ali makes a face at him from under Carly's arm.

"Yes, and we'll be paying enough that they still won't kick her out. Believe me, my gratitude is eternal."

"Carly, you're not helping."

"Yeah, well, neither is the fact that you don't think you and Paul are normal people."

♦

"All right, Mr. Crickets, give me science," Alex says, stretched out on top of the covers while Paul undresses for bed.

"What?"

Alex rolls his eyes. "I know you've talked to Sarah and I *know* you've talked to Carly, who is getting much better at covering up the fact you still tell her everything first. When you say 'baby' and 'sister' and 'surrogate' what are you actually talking about? Details, please."

"Are you pissed?" Paul looks prepared to be contrite, which Alex appreciates.

"Impressed. Tonight was one hell of a coup."

Paul ignores the almost-compliment and carefully sits down on the edge of the bed. "Are we having the conversation I think we're having?"

"We're having the conversation where I say, let's have a serious conversation about what it's going to look like if and when we have a kid based on the current plan you have in your head, which I haven't actually signed off on."

"I know."

"You do, huh?" Alex asks.

Paul at least has the good grace to laugh at himself. "I know you. Even if I'm never exactly sure what's going on in your head." He smiles fondly and pushes a hand through Alex's hair.

"Well, give me science, so I can figure that out too."

Alex listens without interruption while Paul lays out his plan: egg from his sister, sperm from Alex, a surrogate. All of it is expensive, and all of it feels like the involvement of dozens of people. Alex isn't sure which he's more freaked out by, and he tells Paul as much.

"I have a team for how I style my hair and, like, what breakfast cereal I can tell people I eat. I don't want a team for a baby too. It's strange and invasive and like America is watching us fuck," Alex says, lying on his back and gesticulating at the ceiling.

"It's not like if you give me a really good blowjob the ice-skating judges are going to give you three tens and then we get a baby," Paul says.

"What is that metaphor? You spent waaaaaaaaaaaaaaay too much time with Liam tonight, clearly."

"I'm just saying it's not that invasive. It's less invasive than the whole world knowing, every time they look at Carly, that Liam fucks her."

"And that is the magical line between your four on the Kinsey scale and my six, because I have *never* had that thought."

"You're being weird about this," Paul says.

"I'd rather be weird about it than tell you I don't know if I'll ever be ready to do this. I want to, and I think kids are cool, but they were never going to be possible for me."

"Everything in your life is unlikely. Why is this the one thing you can't deal with?"

"I never had to spend time thinking about not being famous, because nobody real is ever famous," Alex says. His voice has slipped into a cadence he almost never uses, a reminder of the past he will never be able to completely erase. "Had to spend time thinking about not having kids, though. And it's hard to stay in the closet in fucking Paragon, Indiana if you don't have a baby."

"But you were never going to stay?"

Alex laughs incredulously. "You say that like nothing ever goes wrong."

"But it doesn't," Paul says with a shrug. "Not for you. Not really."

Alex doesn't have the heart to point out that Paul is tracing his fingers over the faint scarring at Alex's shoulder from the climbing accident he still blames Victor for.

12

Liam doesn't have a dedicated home office space the way Paul and Carly do, so when he gets the files from Paul, he sets himself up with his laptop in the living room. He's at the right range from Ali and her toys that he can keep an eye on her without getting sucked into the vortex of playtime. He delights in his daughter, and she's used to and easy with his periodic silences, but his understanding of Victor's notes isn't going to be improved with interruption.

Paul may have been worried that the work would be too emotionally taxing, but really it's just that — work. Liam's relationship with Victor was rarely about Victor's words or who Liam was on-screen. It was so intimate and comfortable that they didn't usually need words to express their feelings for each other. It's only now that Liam has so little tangible evidence of their time together that, that seems like a bad thing.

Which means that on some level it's soothing to have access to Victor's thoughts like this. On another, it underscores the degree to which Liam misses his voice. Among other things, Liam will have to keep living with the fact that Victor was always clearer about his stories than his relationships with real, actual people.

Victor's thoughts on *M.A.R.S.* are easy to ascertain. Victor's thoughts about Liam now seem more uncertain. There are no scripts or storyboards to reassure Liam of the things he thought he knew about his place in Victor's heart.

♦

"I think I want to talk to Ellen," Liam says when Carly gets home from work.

"You want to talk to Ellen, or you *think* you want to talk to Ellen?" Carly asks.

"I want to talk to Ellen."

"You have her number," Carly points out.

"I know."

"Are you okay to use the phone?" Carly asks uncertainly. "It's not like you need my permission."

"Yes," Liam says irritably.

"So talk to Ellen."

"I want to ask her what happened when Victor died."

"Whoa. Whoa." Carly throws her hands up in the air. "*What?*"

"I mean I know Victor was alive in the morning when I left and then ...not, that night, and I don't know what happened in between and I want to. Ellen was there, and she told me to let her know if there was anything she could do for me. I think I need to know if he was scared. Or if it hurt," Liam says and looks down at his hands.

Carly is horrified. "I don't think that's good choices for either of you."

"What would good choices be?" Liam challenges.

"Not torturing yourself about how it ended," Carly says, undaunted. "That's not what you want to fixate on."

"Can you not use impersonal pronouns?" Liam snipes.

"What?"

"It ended. You mean how Victor died."

"Liam — "

"Please do not protect me from words when I can actually use them."

"If words were the only thing I had to protect you from," Carly mutters.

"I don't need protection. I am not *fragile*. Please stop deciding that's what how I interact with the world means."

"It may not feel that way to you, but as the permanent adult-on-deck in this house, I have to take your day-to-day ability to cope into consideration. So when you want to do shit that's going to put me in the position of being a single parent, when you're right here, you're goddamn right I'm going to protect you."

Liam takes a deep breath. Because this at least is a script he knows. Explain what he is. Explain what he isn't. Restate the situation. Say what he needs. He hates when he has to do it, and it's particularly upsetting when he has to do it with Carly. With Victor it was always awful, but Victor was difficult and they often existed on opposite sides of a very deep chasm; with him, it was easier to forgive. With Carly, these moments feel unfair.

"I am an adult; I am autistic; and I am grieving. While trying to keep secrets which control what I say to who when," Liam says carefully. "I do not know how to do this. There are not books about how to do this. And it would help if you could care about what is happening to me as opposed to how it inconveniences you."

♦

Alex is deciding whether he should swing by Paul's office on the lot to say hi or go straight to the terrible basement room *Winsome* uses for table reads, when he rounds a corner and runs into Darcy.

He catches a glimpse of her tear-streaked face for a split second before she wails "Alex!" and launches herself at him and buries her face in his shoulder. "I'm so glad you're here."

For an instant, his heart stops. "Darcy, is Paul okay?" he asks, hands not working right to hug her back.

Darcy sniffles and lifts her head. Her eyes are red. "Of course. He's freaking out about the read but he always does that. Why?"

Alex breathes again. "Holy shit. Given recent events, can you maybe specify your freakout before I jump to conclusions about your showrunner and my husband?"

"What? *Oh*," Darcy says, and sniffles. "No, he's fine. Sorry."

Since Darcy still isn't letting go, Alex pats her gingerly on the back. "What's wrong then?"

"*Everything*," she moans, thunking her head into his shoulder again.

Alex has to work not to laugh. The extremes of Darcy's emotions are not something he's ever sure how to deal with. "What happened?"

"My parents found out about Jackson and me," she says despondently.

"Found out what?" Alex asks cautiously, not sure he actually wants to know.

"That we're dating."

"You and Jackson are dating?" Alex gapes.

"Yeah. Didn't you know? It's on the internet."

"I don't go on the internet. Since *when?*"

Darcy wipes the back of her hand across her eye. "Since Victor's funeral. We hooked up. He's really cute."

"*What?!*" Alex is appalled, not by the hookup itself, but by what he can guess of the circumstances. "Darcy, did you fuck in the church?" he hisses.

"No!" Darcy looks offended. "I have propriety."

"Not that much," Alex mutters.

"We hooked up at your house."

"YOU DID WHAT?" Alex hustles her to the side of the hall.

"After the funeral. You and Paul were upstairs sad-fucking, so." Darcy shrugs.

"So you decided to fuck in my guest room?"

"Your bathroom, actually."

Alex stares at her.

"Aren't you going to ask what my parents said?" Darcy asks.

Alex throws up his hands.

"They said that if I was going to screw a black man the least I could do was find one above me."

Alex blinks at her a few times. "I'm guessing they didn't quite phrase it that way," he says carefully.

Darcy shakes her head.

"Okay, I know you know this, and that it's not my place to say, but Darcy, your parents are crazy, racist assholes."

"I know. I told them that."

"You did?" It's not that Alex doubts her, but he's continually stunned, impressed, and kind of frightened by her.

"Mhmm. Can we go downstairs now? Paul yells when I'm late."

Before Alex can get his bearings, Darcy disappears around the corner in a cloud of bouncing curls.

♦

Paul is not as horrified by Alex's reveal that Darcy hooked up in their bathroom with Victor's assistant after the funeral as Alex expects him to be. That Darcy's parents are awful, he's known for a long time.

"We've done crazier stuff than that," Paul points out after the table read, while Alex swivels back and forth in the chair on the other side of Paul's desk. "Fucking in your trailer was a particularly memorable experience."

"Unlike Darcy, we never scarred anybody," Alex mutters.

"Zoe?" Paul points out.

Alex shrugs, though he still feels guilty about the poor P.A. who accidentally caught them. "That was different."

"How?"

"I apologized for that."

Paul laughs. "I think fucking in a trailer ranks up there with hooking up at a funeral."

"They're both incredibly tacky?"

"And traditional."

Alex grins. "Liam gave me shit about that for weeks."

"Victor was furious."

There's a bittersweetness to Paul's laughter, and Alex leans his cheek on his fist. "God, I miss that."

"What, fucking in your trailer, or getting chewed out by Victor?"

It's a strange memory; Victor was, justifiably, livid at their stupidity and poor choices. But getting screamed at in front of the entire crew for having sex was not a pleasant experience. Alex was barely able to bite his tongue and not yell back that maybe Victor would be a little less pissy about other people's sex lives if he were getting any action himself.

Knowing what he knows now about Victor's struggles with his sexuality, he's glad he didn't. God knows what Victor would have done to him if he had.

Alex feels weird talking about any of that with Paul, though, so he shakes his head. "I miss being obsessed with you, instead of all the ways our lives are hard."

Paul's face goes soft. "Me too."

"We were supposed to get that, when I got back."

"I know."

"And then, dead Victor, and baby, and," Alex waves a vague hand. "That didn't happen."

"I know."

"Do you think we'll get to have that again?" They've already had the conflict over schedules, Paul's workaholic tendencies and Alex's skittishness, and they're good now, so good. But they have careers, Victor's dead, and things are different.

"Of course," Paul says. "But I miss not being able to take my hands off of you."

"Wanna go fuck in my trailer?" Alex teases, once he's able to catch his breath from Paul's words and the hungry, wistful look on his face as he says them.

"Do you even have your own trailer?"

Alex laughs and pushes himself out of the chair. "I have half a trailer on shooting days only, and it sucks. Also, you have to work."

"And you have to climb things?"

Alex leans over the desk to kiss him. "I'll see you at home."

13

"How's Ellen?" Carly asks Liam when she gets back from picking Ali and a crateload of end-of-the-year art projects up at preschool. He's been curled up on the couch, hugging a throw pillow and staring out the window, since he got home. He's glad to see them, but doesn't know how to respond.

Liam cranes his head up to look at her, but doesn't say anything. The polite response of *fine* is untrue, which Carly knows anyway. And without a script he has no idea how to begin conveying Ellen's state of being, especially now that he has all the details of what happened the night Victor died.

"How are you?" she asks.

He nestles his head back into the arm of the couch and returns to staring out the window. He has way too much going on in his head right now to be able to deal with Carly's questions too. She may be his partner in everything and way more used to his day-to-day life, but Victor was always better with rolling with it when all the input to Liam's brain shut down his ability to give expected output.

Carly sits down awkwardly on the couch and runs a hand through his hair. "Talk to me?"

"Why?"

"Because I need to know that you're okay."

Liam rolls his eyes. He's tired of having to explain this.

Carly sighs as she gets up and stalks into the kitchen. "I knew your talking to Ellen was a bad idea," she says, rummaging through a drawer.

Liam frowns when she plonks the pad of paper and pen onto the couch in front of him, but he picks it up anyway. Having to think about the mechanics of making letters forces him to organize his thoughts in a way he can't verbally right now. After a moment of concentration, he writes, *It wasn't a bad idea. This isn't bad. It just is.*

Carly reads the note upside down and then asks for the pen. *You're not talking. Explain to me how this isn't bad.*

Liam bites his lip, takes the pen back, and writes, *Explain what I'm supposed to do without him.*

You can't stay like this forever, Carly writes.

It's always been a possibility.

We have a child. Not an option.

Liam grabs the pen from her and slaps it down on the coffee table and turns his attention toward the window again.

Carly picks up the pen, scrawls *To Discuss: Skills Regression* across the paper, and then drops it and the pen onto Liam's lap.

♦

"Alex?" Paul pushes open the door to their bedroom. The light's on, but Alex is asleep on top of the covers with a book open on his chest. Todd looks up sleepily from where he's curled up on the chair in the corner.

"You're not supposed to be in here," Paul tells the cat. Todd blinks at him and then curls his tail more tightly around his nose.

Paul walks around to Alex's side of the bed. "At least you're staying busy," he murmurs, picking the book up off Alex's chest and checking the cover to see what obscure topic he's investigating this week.

There's no title on the cover, though, and when Paul flips it open his stomach jolts unpleasantly. He turns a few pages. There's absolutely no mistaking Victor's handwriting.

"Alex!" he says, scandalized.

Alex stirs and blinks up at him. "Oh hey. You're home," he says groggily.

"You stole Victor's diary!"

Alex rubs a hand over his eyes. "What?"

Paul tosses the journal back to him. "What the hell are you doing with that?

Alex catches it clumsily on his chest. "Ow. Careful. Why do you keep coming home in the middle of the night and waking me up with weird questions?"

"It's seven o'clock."

"Oh."

"The diary, Alex."

"I didn't steal it. Liam told me I could take them."

"*Them?*" The only thing that makes this situation worse, in Paul's opinion, is that there is more than one diary.

Alex nods. "There's like dozens. I only grabbed a handful to start."

"You're reading a dead man's diaries."

"It's not like he's going to mind."

Paul stares at him. "This is incredibly fucked up."

Alex shrugs. "Maybe. Maybe I'm finally finding where he kept his soul."

Paul points at him. "*You* are incredibly fucked up."

"Don't sound so surprised," Alex says smugly, setting the book on his nightstand and holding out his hands for Paul. When Paul doesn't move, he gestures insistently. Paul crawls onto the bed obediently, but the whole thing is still incredibly unsettling.

It doesn't get any less unsettling when Alex frowns up at him for a moment and then asks, "Do you remember when Victor and Liam got together?"

"Yes?" Paul says, not sure where this is going.

"How did it happen?"

Paul gives him a puzzled look, but goes ahead. "It was the *Fourth* pilot party. The pretty, flaky actor guy flirted, Victor didn't shut him down, and as far as I know the rest is history. I wasn't really paying that much attention, I was too busy with the sorry state of my own love life."

"Weren't you with Craig then?"

"Nooo, way before him. I spent the morning before the party at Carly's apartment moping because she wouldn't go with me and be my wingman. Like, this was years before she and Liam were together. She yelled at me not to hook up with anybody and shoved me out the door."

"Did you hook up with anybody?

Paul chuckles. "Of course I did."

"Dated for a week and then broke up when you wanted to get married and he didn't?"

"Do you want the story or did you want to make fun of me?" Paul asks.

Alex grins. "God, you really always have been a fucking mess."

"You make me less of one."

"Is that a come-on?" Alex asks, clearly a little disbelieving at Paul's choices, which is probably fair.

"Yes?"

"Oh my God," Alex laughs. But before he can make a start at getting Paul's clothes off, Paul's phone buzzes in his pocket.

"Oh fucking seriously," Alex mumbles as Paul tries to get to his phone. "Nobody else better be dead."

Paul gives him a *don't even* look, as if Alex has some sort of magical jinxing power of life and death.

It's Carly, asking if they can take Ali for the night. Which is concerning, though Paul can tell by Carly's tone that this is not the time for too many questions as to what, exactly, is going on. He agrees after a quick check with Alex, and tells Carly they'll be over in forty-five minutes. Liam and Carly's house isn't horrifically far away by L.A. standards, but it's not particularly close either.

"Are they okay?" Alex asks after Paul hangs up. Paul shrugs, then shakes his head.

Alex slumps onto his shoulder. "Ali is fine and I love our friends and want to help them — "

"But you really wanted to fuck tonight?"

Alex nods morosely.

"We can after she's asleep," Paul offers.

"Not like I wanted to fuck."

♦

Carly is clearly relieved to hand a drowsy Ali over to Paul and Alex when they come to the door. Ali is cranky over the ordeal but she gets to wear her pink fluffy robe outside, which is apparently an event.

"She'll stop fussing as soon as she loses me as an audience," Carly tells Paul. She sounds exhausted. "And I hate that I'm probably supposed to feel like a bad mother for pawning my kid off on you, but she is five and loud and cannot understand that demanding Liam pay attention to her is making him worse."

Alex hovers in the doorway, clearly wanting to ask after Liam, but Carly stares him down and he backs away. Paul thinks, apprehensively, that the last time anyone particularly tried to keep them apart was when Victor banned Alex from the *Fourth* set. He has no particular urge to relive the sequence of events of that day, even if Victor's now dead.

Ali falls asleep in the car on the drive back. Paul has to carry her into the house and upstairs to the guest bedroom they've always put her in when she's stayed before. Alex follows with her bag packed with the requisite toothbrush and doll, and waits in the hallway 'til Paul is done settling her in.

"See?" Paul says when he emerges, leaving the door open a crack. "If we had kids it wouldn't be just us. We've got friends who would help."

"You do understand it's a certain degree of fucked up to say that on a night that we have Ali because Carly and Liam are the ones who need help, right?" Alex asks in a whisper.

Paul steps away from the door and heads back to their bedroom. "Not every night is going to be like this one."

"Nooo," Alex says, following. "Our current issue seems to be that nobody knows what any given night is going to look like."

"All the more reason to have each other's backs."

Alex raises his eyebrows as he shuts their own bedroom door behind them.

"What?" Paul asks.

"Did you set this up?"

"What?"

"You and the baby."

"Are you asking me if I manufactured a crisis with Liam and Carly so we could get their kid for a night, and I could woo you with baby feelings?" Paul asks more kindly than he could.

"Well, when you put it like that, it sounds like I'm the crazy one."

14

Gemma, one leg tucked under herself on the couch in Paul and Alex's living room, listens to Alex's complaints about having to clean out Victor's house with rapidly diminishing sympathy. "You have the time to do it yourself. Or the resources to pay other people to do it. Also, isn't this kind of Jackson's job?"

"I've been informed it's not fair to add 'packing up spatulas' to the list of bullshit Jackson has to deal with as assistant to the dead. And I'm not going to let other people into Victor's creepy house." Alex picks at the corner of a book on the end table. June sunshine pours in through the windows, and Todd basks in a beam falling across the rug.

"You know, for someone who claims to have hated him, you're being immensely protective."

"Not of him. Of anyone else he might suck into that pit of eerie creative horror."

"Victor's *dead*. He loved his work, and it's a house. You're the one being creepy."

Alex shrugs and gets up to hunt through his and Paul's liquor cabinet for the tequila.

Gemma folds her arms and sits back further on the couch. "So do you not want me to help, or are you being passive aggressive about asking and want me to volunteer?"

Alex looks over his shoulder. "I'm not being passive aggressive."

"So you don't want me to help?"

Alex grabs the bottle and two shot glasses and returns to the couch, handing one of the glasses to Gemma without saying anything.

"You never even thought about asking me," she says accusatorily.

Alex shrugs.

"Alex!"

"What? You hated him too, and you escaped his clutches. Be happy about that."

"You mean be happy you found another family I'm not a part of?"

"I've had this family almost as long as I've known you!"

"Not *nearly*," Gemma protests.

She's not sure if Alex is being deliberately obtuse or just a stupid boy when he doesn't follow her argument, and it leaves her more pissed off than ever. If Alex doesn't want her in Victor's house because of whatever fucked up feelings about the man he's still dealing with, that's fine, but Gemma really would like to feel like she's not being written out of Alex's life. For all he continues to rely on her, she can't help but feel like she's been chasing him lately. It's an unattractive revelation.

"Do you want to come to the science education dinner thing Victor was making people do for *M.A.R.S.*?" Alex asks.

"What?" Gemma blinks.

"It was one of Victor's pet charities. I have to go because Paul has to. Only now there's an extra seat, because, well..."

"Are you inviting me to a dinner to fill a dead man's seat?" Gemma asks, somewhere between appalled and amused.

"Yes?"

"And *that's* not creepy."

"Well, somebody has to. Otherwise it's gonna be empty and that's just depressing. And Paul's been bitching at me about it all week."

"You are so weird."

"Do you want to go or not?"

Gemma laughs and grabs the tequila bottle from him to actually pour them shots. "Yes. But you're still on the hook for forgetting about me."

◆

Victor's funeral aside, the charity dinner is the first time Alex has been out at a public event since he's gotten back from Australia. He hasn't particularly missed carpets and photographers and all the intrusive staring.

He's particularly irritated because he's here mostly in support of Paul. Paul isn't doing anything wrong, but when Alex stands next to him at events like this he becomes the pretty arm candy of the older, mad creator. While Alex finds Paul's beard and graying hair as hot as most of the internet does, he could really do without the damned narrative.

Victor's diaries make him look at the event differently though. The entries from Victor's college years painted a picture Alex doesn't recognize, of someone who struggled with school because both because of his grand ideas and because of institutional bias. It makes Victor's support for something like science education seem like something beyond, perhaps, merely a *M.A.R.S.* tie-in.

At least there's plenty else here for people to pay attention to. All of the network brass is there, probably happy to be in the limelight and let everyone know that *M.A.R.S.* is doing fine. So is most of the *M.A.R.S.* cast, who are being charming and fittingly subdued in respect for their fallen captain. Darcy is in attendance, and has brought Jackson along as her date — Alex isn't sure if this outing is going to mitigate the way in which his life has turned entirely upside down lately. There's also a large number of people more or less associated with Victor, who only ever come out of the woodwork for events like this.

Liam and Carly are there too. Liam works the carpet and the fans with the same seemingly effortless poise and enthusiasm he always has, but Alex can see Carly keeping a closer eye on him than usual. Alex can hardly blame her; as far as he knows, it's the first time Liam's been out since the funeral. This would be a lot for anyone.

Paul and Alex are seated with Carly, Liam, and Gemma. Nigel is also there, and while Alex has no qualms about reading the diaries, it is immensely awkward to shake hands with him while knowing far more than any non-involved party should about all the times Nigel and Victor spent without clothes on before Victor sorted out his asexuality.

But Nigel is also, apparently, one of the first people who helped Victor make sense of himself. Alex is only beginning to fathom how massive an undertaking that was, and how confusing Victor was

— not just to everyone else in the world — but to himself. It makes Alex respect Nigel. It also makes him wonder all the things Nigel's figured out about *him*.

At least Raphael is there, and his wife Irina, for which Alex is grateful. Rounding out the cozy little family group is Frank Pearson the VP from hell and, to Paul's very evident horror, Mark.

"Behave," Alex has to whisper in Paul's ear more than once.

Almost no one at the table is really on the same team, and everyone makes practiced small talk that hews a line between polite and calculatedly needling. Alex is charming, because he has to be; Darcy is talkative, which is always a blessing now that she's learned to be a little less of a loose cannon in front of the execs.

"How's *The Parrot Tree* going?" she eventually asks Liam.

"They've been really good about giving me time," he says softly. While it's a coherent answer, it isn't really the right one, even if everyone at the table knows at least some of the impact Victor's loss has had on him.

Darcy rolls with it, though, nodding with a sad smile. "We've missed having him around for *Winsome* too."

"Hopefully you can do something interesting with *M.A.R.S.* now," Frank chimes in.

Alex blinks and turns his head slowly toward Frank. He laughs at the man's sheer mustache-twirling ridiculousness. It's never been a secret that the guy has hated the *M.A.R.S.* concept from day one, insistent that serious drama can't involve "spaceships and laser guns" when *M.A.R.S.* isn't about either. That a guy can be that senior and be working against his own network's interests, Alex has never understood. He's glad that whatever level of open animosity that existed toward *The Fourth Estate* was only exhibited amongst other industry people and kept well out of the public eye. Apparently it's a new era.

"The body isn't cold yet," Alex says. Several people at the table give him dirty looks, and it only occurs to him belatedly that perhaps that wasn't the best way of putting things in front of Liam.

Liam toys with his fork and says nothing.

"Maybe," Mark says graciously. Alex has half a second of thinking they're going to get out of the sudden awkwardness unscathed when Mark follows it up with "It'll be hard to do anything if I keep losing writers."

"People are bound to look for other opportunities when things get uncertain," Frank says to Mark, not expending much effort to sound sympathetic.

"That, and *Winsome's* poaching my staff." Mark says it jovially. "I should sue you over Olivia."

"You're welcome to try," Paul says. "Don't think our lawyers didn't go over that bogus non-compete with a fine-tooth comb."

Mark shrugs. "Might be bogus, might not."

"Seriously, Mark, I don't even know if you're joking, but if you were that vindictive I'd put my own money behind defending Olivia, and newsflash, I have more of it than you do."

"Thanks to your husband," Mark clarifies.

"Yeah, I hear alimony is a real drag," Alex chimes in, as much to shut up Mark as to convey the depths of his displeasure to Paul. Mark's messy divorce a few years back is no secret in their overlapping Hollywood circles and Indiana made sure that Alex is never above fighting dirty when he has to. L.A. really is the smallest of towns.

Liam whistles softly, impressed. Mark shoots both him and Alex dirty looks, and Paul winces.

"Ahh, Victor's legendary family of artists," Frank says, with the air of someone watching Rome burn and loving every moment of it. "I wondered how long you'd last without him."

Liam turns to stare at him. "We," he says, and then blinks but doesn't say anything else.

Frank looks at him. Nigel and Carly exchange looks across the table.

"You?" Frank prompts, after the silence has stretched unreasonably long.

Liam looks pleadingly at Alex; Alex shakes his head. The situation is tense enough without him helping Liam egg the disaster on, but that just makes Liam look more insistent about it.

Finally Alex shrugs. It's not like tonight can get particularly more terrible than it is right now. "We know what Victor thought of you," he says.

"And what's that?"

"It doesn't matter," Alex says, with another prompting look from Liam. "Because he was better than you, and his work is still here."

"Okay. Paul," Carly leans into everyone else's space, hands on the table as she levers herself to her feet. "Will you come with me?"

Alex hides a grin behind his fist at how quickly Paul agrees. In the flurry of movement that follows, Alex thinks he hears Nigel groan.

♦

"I swear to God, not smoking is the worst part of pregnancy," Carly says as she stalks away, Paul hurrying to keep up. "Has the table gone up in flames?"

Paul looks back over his shoulder. "Not yet."

"Alex and Liam are terrible," Carly huffs. "Like, I know you two are monogamous and you are over the whole jealousy thing but thank God they are not together. They would alienate everyone."

"What was up with that?" Paul says, standing to the side in a doorway where they can keep an eye on their friends but stay safely out of range. "I've never seen Liam like that."

"Yeah, well, welcome to the hell that is my life," Carly says. "I do not know what to do with him. He's not okay at home, he's clearly not okay to be out in public although he seemed fine on the carpet. Liam's life is not one he can live from our bedroom, and I am running out of cope."

"Carly?" Paul says gently. Carly is one of the most resourceful people he knows. Her life and her relationships never have been easy, but she's always mastered all of them. The note of helplessness in her voice is disconcerting.

"Yes?"

"What's going on?"

Carly sighs. "Do you mean the shattering grief of his losing a partner or the exciting adult autistic regression? It's so hard to choose."

For half a second, Paul thinks she's joking. But he knows how Liam numbers his points in conversation and highlights his scripts in multiple colors to note not just emotion, but tone, intonation, and pitch. He remembers, also, Victor's ongoing war with *The Fourth Estate*'s wardrobe department because they kept giving Liam's character oxfords but Liam would never tie the laces. Suddenly every flaky or vain thing Liam has ever done looks remarkably different.

"I have a lot of things to say about that," Paul says carefully. "I'm not sure any of them are useful or fair."

"I shouldn't have told you," she says.

"Hey, no," Paul says. "I mean, probably not, but… wow, autism makes me like him a lot better than the whole manic pixie dream boy thing."

Carly shakes her head and laughs, tilting her head back to the heavens.

"What do you need?" Paul asks.

She brings her head back down to look at him darkly. "Anything you can give me."

♦

"Life with you people is never boring," Gemma says drily into the tense silence that follows Paul and Carly's departure from the table. Raphael and Irina exchange horrified glances, Frank looks delighted, and Liam is staring at his plate so he doesn't have to look at Mark, who is staring at him.

"At least you didn't bring a date. We'd scare him off forever," Alex says to Gemma. He means it as a tease, but Gemma glares at him.

"Can we actually not bring my dating life into this conversation? Or any conversation in public, ever?" Gemma says, sharply.

"I said *date*, you said dating life."

"Okay." Gemma tosses her napkin down and pushing her chair back. "We are not talking about this or anything here," she says, stalking away from the table.

Alex watches her go miserably. The obligations of long friendship probably require him to go after her. It's a horrifying prospect, but getting yelled at by Gemma would probably be more pleasant than staying at the table any longer.

Alex looks at Liam, who seems unaware of the entire unfolding drama, and then at Nigel.

"It's fine, I've got it," Nigel says.

"Me too," Raph says, which is more encouraging. It's not that Alex doesn't trust Nigel or his good intentions, but the history between him and Liam is anything but smooth. Liam at least likes Raphael, and he was never a rival for Victor's affections.

Alex grudgingly stands up and trudges after Gemma.

She's waiting for him by the rest rooms. As soon as Alex appears, she grabs him by the elbow and hauls him into the women's.

"Gemma, what the fuck," Alex says, pulling out of her grasp as soon as they're inside. Gemma takes a cursory look around to make sure it's empty.

"Okay, I understand that the success and the fame of your magic life comes with some shitty downsides, but can you not fucking make fun of my relationship status *in front of a network executive?*"

"I was teasing!"

"They don't know that! Jesus Christ, Alex, it is bad enough that I have to deal with not having my own dreams come true, but, you know what? I am making my life awesome even if it doesn't look like what I used to think it would. But that be much easier to do if you weren't humiliating me in public."

"I'm sorry," Alex says contritely. "I can go fix it."

Gemma rolls her eyes. "No you fucking won't. I am a big girl and I don't need you to smooth shit over for me. But this whole forgetting that I am actually a person thing is getting increasingly fucked up."

"I actually have no idea what you're talking about."

"*Darcy?*" Gemma hisses, like it's a curse. Alex almost takes a step back.

"What the hell are you talking about?"

"We have been best friends for years, through some relatively screwed up shit, except now you never call even when I can actually be fucking helpful to you. You've replaced me with some younger prettier more famous *and white* version of myself, so you can pretend that we've all actually succeeded!"

"THAT'S NOT WHAT I DID!" Alex yells when he can finally get a word in edgewise.

"YES IT FUCKING IS!" Gemma yells back. "I am not being a jealous bitch, but you need to fucking deal with whatever shit it is that makes you think a white me is necessary, because, *God,* Alex you are a fucking moron."

"You're also jealous."

"Of course I am. Jesus fuck, Alex, we ran away from home to move out here together. Like we actually have this life, whatever it is, because we spent too much time in high school emailing each other about television shows. What am I supposed to be when we never hang out anymore?"

"Pissed at me in the women's bathroom at the Beverly Wilshire during a very prestigious public charity event?"

Gemma glares at him.

Alex offers her his arm. "Truce?" Right now he can't start to unpack what Gemma laid out for him. Her criticisms aren't unfounded, but it's also the last thing in the world he wants to spend any time examining.

Gemma gives a disbelieving laugh, but she takes it. "For now. You are such a fucking asshole."

"At least I'm better than Mark."

"Not by much."

As they leave, a toilet flushes behind them. They had not been, as they thought, alone. Gemma buries her face in Alex's shoulder and moans. This is all going to be so stupid.

◆

"That night could not have possibly gone any worse," Alex says. He tosses his jacket over a chair and tugs open his collar before collapsing onto the couch.

"Yeah, you were a real force for calm and civility there." Paul follows him into the living room.

"Mark is a terrible human being, Frank was being horrible, and you took their bait and used me to do it. Fuck calm and civility."

"You and Liam were lighting fires," Paul points out. "And to be fair, I did steal Olivia." He taps Alex's knee. Alex lifts his feet so Paul can sit down, and then stretches his legs over his lap.

"No, Olivia quit and was smart enough to do it in such a way that got her on a better team," Alex says. If there's anything worth rehashing in tonight's disaster it's not the petty accusations of people they don't even like. At least Paul doesn't know about the scene in the bathroom with Gemma.

"I think I'm flattered?"

Alex snorts and rubs his hands over his face. "Your possessiveness is always charming, yes."

"And you're trying to talk your way out of your own bad behavior."

"Are you scolding me?" Alex raises his eyebrows at Paul over his own hands.

Paul gives him a look.

"Fine. I'm sorry," Alex says. "But, fuck, all of our friends are insane. And so are our enemies."

"We should get used to that one of these days."

"Mmm." Alex looks at Paul thoughtfully.

"What?" Paul asks, when he doesn't say anything else.

Alex grabs for one of Paul's hands. "So. I thought we were gonna have a nice night and then I could say this," he says, both intent and playful. "But then it was a car crash. Which given all the players involved I should have expected."

"What were you going to say?" Paul asks curiously.

"Our friends are crazy and our jobs are terrible. Coming back from being away is always hard but this reentry has been something else. I want something that's not a part of that, and I want something that's just for us."

"Yes?" Paul says carefully.

"I want to talk to Sarah and do some research on my own," he says. "But I'm sort of starting to like the idea of a family we choose as opposed to the one that keeps choosing us."

"Really?" Paul asks.

Alex nods. After all, kids were always the plan. Paul jumping the gun from hypothetical to schedule is annoying but not surprising or unprecedented. Now that Alex has recovered from the shock, the idea is actually appealing. He is beginning to understand that their lives will never be big enough to hold everything they want to do, which is all the more reason to do what they can when they can. After all, as Victor's diaries remind Alex daily, nothing lasts forever.

"Please tell me this isn't just to apologize for being a brat tonight."

Alex laughs and shakes his head. "Take the yes and be happy, Paul."

"Okay. Well. *Wow*," Paul says, adjusting.

Alex hums smugly.

"Well, okay." Paul still sounds a bit dazed. "There was something I was going to ask you, actually."

"What's that?" Alex asks.

"Liam."

"Oh God, don't — "

"How long have you known?" Paul interrupts Alex's assumptions.

"How long have I known what?"

"About the autism, and why didn't you tell me?"

"About what autism?" Alex asks, confused. "I mean, Ali's weird, but — "

Paul stares at Alex. "Not Ali. *Liam.*"

"What the fuck?" Alex says.

"Oh my God," Paul says.

"Liam's autistic?" Alex asks, trying to make sense of this new — and vague — information. "Did you just out my not-boyfriend to me?" he continues incredulously.

"I assumed you knew," Paul stammers. "And I am not processing *not-boyfriend* right now. I mean, I assumed you two talk — "

"Noooo," Alex shakes his head. "*What* the fuck? And don't assume things about me and Liam."

"I don't know what to say."

"He's, like, *normal* though," Alex protests into the lack of further information. "I mean, not normal-normal, he's Liam, but — "

"It's a spectrum," Paul says.

"But don't autistic people not talk and obsess on weird shit and, like, not live alone?"

"Okay, none of that is strictly true," Paul says carefully. "But you also just described Liam. And if you keep describing him, it's not going to be less of a match."

Alex stares at Paul. Aside from Paul, Liam is the person Alex knows best in the world. Now suddenly it feels like he doesn't, not because anything has changed, but because it all means something else now.

"Why am I *still* the last one to know anything? Seriously."

"I thought you knew!"

"Well, I didn't."

"You're seriously going to be pissed about this?"

"Yes, I'm pissed about it! Jesus, Paul, this isn't some little historical nugget. This is like, a thing that's happening. Is this why Carly won't let me talk to him?"

"I think you'd have to take that up with Carly," Paul says cautiously.

"How do you even know this stuff?"

"Older mothers have a higher chance of having autistic kids. I've been researching it."

"Bullshit."

"Well, that's true, but Carly told me when she freaked out at dinner."

Alex gives a strained, disbelieving laugh and turns back to look at Paul. "I think I need a drink."

◆

Liam's phone goes off while he's standing in the living room with Carly and Carly's long-time girlfriend, Risa, who's been watching Ali. He's trying desperately to figure out when the conversation is at a point where it's socially appropriate for him to leave and go to bed. When he finally manages to fumble the phone out of his pocket, he sees that it's Charles. He gives Carly and Risa apologetic looks before slipping off to take the call.

Charles is drunk and chatty, just home from celebrating with fellow cast members from his current show. It's funny and it's shockingly normal, Liam teasing Charles about his latest fling with the latest pretty actor boy who has caught his eye. They were each other's firsts, way back when they were still in high school together. Now they date whenever Liam is in town. It's not a serious relationship in terms of time commitment, but the history is long.

While Liam has Carly — and had Victor — and still has Alex to some strange and mostly unspoken extent, as far as he knows he's Charles's only long-term lover. Charles has always seemed perfectly happy without the web of relationships that are so vital to Liam's existence. But, now, having never really had one, he's intensely curious about what the loss of such a relationship means to Liam.

Liam goes quiet when he asks, but it's not the wave of despair and panic he's felt so often lately — mostly, because Charles has actually asked, which forces Liam to actually think about it.

"Do you remember junior year when Jamie and Sam were cheating on their SOs with each other and complaining to us about how hard their lives were?"

Charles chuckles. "They were doing that senior year too."

"Yeah but, early on. And Jamie kept wishing someone would die because then everyone could use grief as an excuse to talk about their big fucked up love?"

"How the hell are you poly after all their bullshit?"

"I keep thinking about that," Liam says, ignoring him. He fidgets with the edge of his nail. "About Victor being dead, and Jamie being wrong."

"He's dead," Charles says. "You can say whatever you want. No one will blame you. And Victor can't even yell. I know there's nothing good about what's happened, but you do have the freedom to speak."

"I really don't." Liam wishes Charles were correct, but what his friend and lover doesn't understand is that anything Liam says will have consequences for everyone else in his life.

"Why not?"

"You mean other than Carly, Ali, future baby, and the press?" Liam can't shield his family from all the consequences of who he is, but he sure can try.

"Yeah."

"Because Victor didn't belong to anyone. That doesn't change now that he's dead. And with him not here to tell me, I'm not even sure I was his."

15

Now that he's committed to it, Alex throws himself into the research process about *baby science* and *baby law* and *baby contract* with the enthusiasm he has for every subject that piques his interest. Paul's grateful, even if he knows that part of why Alex is taking this on is because he doesn't trust Paul's attention to detail. Alex isn't wrong; running a show and a half doesn't leave him a lot of free time.

They find a surrogacy agency, and Paul is insistent about selecting a woman who has been a surrogate at least once already. Alex agrees. Knowing that this is something she has done before and is willing to do again makes it not actually repugnant.

The day Alex gets the call from the surrogacy agency saying they've found a candidate, Paul finds him at their kitchen table. One of Victor's diaries is sitting on the chair next to him, and he's staring blankly at his laptop screen.

"What's up?" Paul asks him.

"I'm nervous."

"About what?"

Alex gives Paul a look.

"Hey, I'm trying not to assume here. Specificity. Please."

"I don't know if I can. It's everything. Like, science and hi, I'm going to be a parent, and there's going to be a person running around in the world that has my genes and Sarah's genes and I'm kind of freaking out about all of that?"

"Do you not want to do this?"

"Okay Paul, the thing where you ask for specificity and then get defensive and decide what I mean without waiting for me to explain? You should stop with that."

"Sorry," Paul says, and then, as instructed, waits to say more. Alex's energy is jittery and strange, and Paul can't blame him. He's nervous, too. This is entirely uncharted territory for them both.

"I want a kid," Alex states slowly and clearly. "So please take that off your worry list."

"Okay."

"But I need to go out to South Carolina."

"But everyone will be out here for the procedure. The surrogate's here," Paul says, confused.

"It's not about that."

"Then what is it about?" Paul asks. Alex likes South Carolina, but they've only ever been there for vacations, and this doesn't sound like Alex looking for a holiday.

"I've been on the phone with your sister a lot but I mean — your family's doing a huge thing for us. I want to do right by them, and me, and Sarah especially, and I need to spend some time out there before all this starts to happen so I can feel okay with it."

"I wish I could go with you," Paul says. Alex's sense of responsibility surprises a little, though that feels unfair to Alex whose family structures and loyalties have never quite looked like anyone else's.

"I'll be all right."

"I'm not worried about you," Paul says with a tired smile. "I could use a fucking break."

"Well *somebody* was supposed to take a year off..."

"I still will," Paul says, but it's reassuring, not defensive.

"Does it ever bother you that I don't have a degree?" Alex asks idly.

"What?" Paul is baffled by the topic and the lack of any segue, although it probably makes sense in Alex's head.

"You went to college. Carly went to college. Liam didn't, but he went to an actual school for the arts. I have a high school diploma from my shitty, *shitty* hometown."

"Is this about you not being like other people or wanting to go back to school or thinking this has something to do with how you'll parent?"

"All. None. I don't know. Victor wrote about film school a lot. It sounds interesting. And I want to be smart for our kid."

Before Paul can investigate further, Alex closes his laptop and asks what he wants to do about dinner.

◆

Alex has no idea what to expect the first time they meet with the surrogate on a hot, smoky afternoon in July. Alex is afraid they're supposed to be friends, and he's relieved when that doesn't seem to be the narrative, saving him from being the star of his own one-season sitcom.

Some days he feels like he already is; Liam has retreated from the world entirely, and Alex tries not to be pissed or hurt at being shut out. Alex hasn't heard from him at all since the terrible charity dinner.

Predictably, Alex's snarling match with Gemma in the bathroom of the Beverly Wilshire turns up on the internet. Alex just can't decide whether the best or worst thing about it is the suggestion that they're ex-lovers. But that Gemma feels the need to leave him several irate messages about it, and its potential impact on her current professional quests, is decidedly not funny.

But there's nothing Alex can do about it, and he's not going to apologize for blinds on the damn internet. Gemma made his life this way when she insisted he say yes to Victor's offer; she can live with the consequences of being his friend now.

As far as his messy friendships go, Gemma is not his biggest concern, though perhaps she deserves to be. But Alex doesn't know what he's supposed to do about Liam. He has questions and confusion. More than once Paul takes Alex's phone out of his hand while he's angry and ready to call Liam to demand answers.

"If he wants to talk to you he knows where to find you." Paul sets the phone down on his desk before resuming his typing.

"He's my friend. Why won't he talk to me?"

"Victor died, Alex. It's not a conspiracy."

He continues to protest and gripe and worry until Paul snaps that it's not all about him.

"I don't understand how you can have the bond you have with Liam and not get how deep that thing with Victor went." Disappointment evident in Paul's voice.

"I'm not questioning that," Alex says with frustration.

"Then what is your shit? I don't mind you being moody but I do mind you refusing to examine and take responsibility for your own emotions."

"I want to help," Alex says petulantly. "No one is letting me help."

"You can't fill those cracks for him for the same reasons you two aren't together," Paul says. There's no bite to it because there doesn't have to be for it to land hard.

Alex gives him a level look and then stalks off toward the door of the deck. "Fuck you for being right," he says, before wrenching it open.

♦

Paul gives him a couple of hours to cool off, but once the sun goes down and the temperature drops and Alex still hasn't budged, he joins him in staring out at the dark landscape.

"I'm not pissed at you," Alex eventually says.

Paul nods.

"I don't know who I'm pissed at."

"Victor's been working out as a plan for you," Paul's joking, but it wouldn't kill Alex to examine his persistence about that.

"Right now," Alex says, "Victor is an angry, scared, and very brilliant asshole trying to figure out how to do life when he's not like any other people. He's not the person I knew. I'm fairly sure he's not the person you or Liam knew either. Nigel did, which is just weird. Every time I'm angry at Victor, my life blows up, so mostly I'm trying not to do that. It's starting to feel unfair."

"Will it piss you off if I say I approve?"

"Probably. If we're having a kid, you can't treat me like one anymore."

"I don't."

"No withholding information."

"I told you about Liam within hours," Paul protests.

"Because you thought I knew. And if you hadn't, you wouldn't have."

"I — "

"You know how Carly didn't tell Liam 'til morning?"

Paul nods.

"Don't ever do that to me," Alex says wrathfully. When he retreats into the house, Paul doesn't let himself follow, although it is cold and lonely in the dark.

♦

Children, no matter how dramatic and demanding, are more resilient than Carly would prefer. Because it's not that Ali doesn't notice her father's moodiness, nor is it that she doesn't care. It's that she makes it a game. Who looks prettier staring out the window, who can not react to Carly the longest, who can come up with the most complicated pattern of taps the other can still echo back throughout the day.

Abstractly, it's fascinating. Practically, it's sort of annoying. And intellectually, Carly finds it faintly terrifying. She can't be entirely sure Ali is mimicking

Liam as opposed to rewiring her own brain to fit more tightly into his world.

It's definitely something she and Liam are going to have to talk about. She waits until Ali's in bed, because Ali doesn't need to overhear any of this and Carly doesn't need her here being her charming and demanding self.

She pushes a notepad and a pen at Liam, and says, "We need to talk."

Liam spins the pad around and writes *About what?*

Carly holds out her hand for the pen. When Liam gives it to her, she scribbles, *About the things you have the capacity to do, and what that means for what we're going to do.*

Too tangled, Liam writes back.

She sighs and tries to simplify. No matter how hard she tries to get it right, this always where they have the most trouble. When he needs her to clarify, it's it far too easy for her to accidentally speak to him like a child instead. Actually having a child hasn't helped that.

How we try to get your skills back. What happens if we don't.

Not a switch, Liam scribbles back. *No off/on.*

I know. Can this be our job right now?

Why is talking better than this? he writes.

Faster, she scribbles.

He snorts as she drops the pen after the word, and they look at each other, smiling. They did this, passing notes back and forth, the night they first slept together. She thought he was being whimsical, and mostly he was trying to convince her that he was. But it kept that night small and close and funny, and made him trust her. She was as not like other girls as he was not like other boys. It's bittersweet now.

Fair, he scribbles back, after he thinks on it for a moment.

You also talk for work. These words she writes more slowly, having learnt long ago that there is cadence in talking this way too.

He doesn't reach for the pen when she puts it down, but he also doesn't drift. She watches as he goes to speak. While his hands move, the words won't come. He tries twice more before writing, *I don't want to write it.*

"What? Why?" she asks, even though it's an incredibly unfair question. The potential answers are too big and vague.

He sighs and averts his eyes, proving her point.

"Okay," she says, kissing his knee before getting up from the couch. If she gives him space, there's half a chance he'll come back to the conversation, and at least it's on the table now.

She spends a few hours in her office, grateful for a to-do list that needs attention and for tasks that only involve one form of communication. When she returns, he's written *The Parrot Tree* and drawn a deliberate line through it.

◆

Alex is sitting on the couch in their darkened living room when Paul finally goes back inside. His inability or his unwillingness to use words to express himself has always been frustrating to Paul. When Alex was in Australia, however, words were all they had, and as Paul regards Alex's still and silent figure he can't help but feel that they've turned back the clock, and not to anywhere useful.

"Talk to me?" he asks.

Alex flicks his eyes up to Paul but doesn't say anything.

"Other than the fact that you're pissed off, I'm not sure what's going on in your head. Can you find some words before you decide to be pissed off at me, too?"

Paul keeps his tone light, but Alex doesn't smile, looking at him with an assessing gaze. It's unsettling, and Paul is uncomfortably reminded of why Alex keeps getting cast in roles where his characters die. His eyes are not entirely of this earth.

Alex lifts a hand and beckons Paul over. When he takes it, Alex pulls him forward and tilts his face up for a kiss. When Paul bends down to give him it, Alex turns his head to whisper in Paul's ear instead.

"Come and see." His lips brush Paul's ear, and he slips out from between Paul and the couch. Before Paul can get his bearings, Alex vanishes out of the room and up the stairs.

Paul follows. Their bedroom window is open, and the room is cool and smoky-smelling from this season's perpetual wildfires. Any thought of making Alex talk has disappeared. If he wants to deal with whatever is going on in his mind by losing himself in sex, Paul is more than on board.

Alex sits on the edge of their bed, waiting. He's nearly thirty now, but he knows how to hold his body to look younger as well as older, and it feels like the most appealing of time warps when he looks up at Paul from under his lashes.

When Paul approaches he doesn't wait, but stands up and pulls him into the kiss in one fluid motion. It's all tongue and teeth, and Paul loses his breath as Alex spins them around and pushes him down on the bed.

Getting naked is a mess of tangled sleeves and limbs, but Alex is insistent about getting to skin and growls when Paul gets distracted running his hands over Alex's back. Paul lifts his hands and Alex catches them, pinning them to the bed on either side of Paul's head.

Paul gasps and lets his head fall back on the pillow, breathless. Alex hovers over him, keeping his weight on Paul's hands. He groans in anticipation.

Alex has to let go of one of Paul's hands to reach for the lube. He immediately wraps his free hand around the back of Alex's neck and pulls their foreheads together while Alex slicks himself and starts to push in.

Like in the club when Alex shoved him against the wall, and in this bed after Victor's funeral, this is not how they usually have sex. Paul can't do anything but dig his fingers into Alex's hair and pant his name while Alex fucks into him. He stares at Paul with a gaze that's far too intense.

The orgasm, when it hits, is overwhelming. Alex doesn't stop, and Paul lets his eyes fall halfway closed and drifts while Alex continues to fuck him. It's clearly fascinating to him, to have Paul this out of it under him. When he does finally come, Alex sounds as stunned as Paul feels. He stays, shoulders bowed, over Paul while they both come down from it. It's a long time before they can get their limbs coordinated enough to pull apart and get themselves cleaned up, only to collapse onto the sheets next to each other.

"What was that about?" Paul asks, reaching for Alex's hand.

Alex laces their fingers together. "I think I missed you."

◆

In the morning, Carly is unsurprised to find Liam at his laptop, hunting and pecking an email to his manager about needing to drop out of his project. It's the opposite of any sort of solution, assuming there is one, but it's movement and choice, and it at least makes her sure they're not dead too. He's interrupted by Ali running into the kitchen for breakfast chittering about the nightmare she proudly tells everyone she put herself back to sleep from. To Carly's surprise, Liam actually picks her up and uses his voice to tell her she only has to fight monsters alone if she wants to because he's always happy to help.

Despite the email, extracting himself from *The Parrot Tree* takes the better part of the week. Andrew, the director half of the writer/director team in charge of *The Parrot Tree* actually takes time out of his schedule to come over for lunch and is concerned and understanding. And then the legal and PR wrangling begins. When the announcement goes out, Carly finds herself relieved for the first time that Liam is too lost inside his ongoing grief to pay much attention to the public fallout.

16

Alex's hopes that Victor's house and the rest of his possessions will magically box themselves up are dashed when he gets an email from Nigel, reminding him that, for Nigel's own sanity and the legal process, they really do need to get everything itemized. Nigel offers to help, since he's back and forth between New York and L.A. for work so much, but that's an easy offer to decline. Nigel doesn't need the extra work and Alex doesn't want to deal with Liam and Nigel in the same room. Particularly when that room belongs to Victor.

And so another day gets sacrificed to Victor. Even with all four of them there — Carly and Liam come too — the house feels eerie and empty.

"Why did we have to do this on your one day off?" Alex grouses as he hauls boxes and his tablet into the living room. Liam trails behind him with an armload of newspaper and bubble wrap he scrounged from the basement when Alex refused to go down there.

"There's nothing stopping you from doing this alone whenever you want," Paul calls from the kitchen, where he and Carly are regarding Victor's multitude of cooking implements with something approaching despair.

"Only the ghosts," Alex shouts back, though it doesn't feel like there's anything at all here anymore. It freaks him out. He had expected Victor to linger.

♦

Alex starts a list of all the things on one of the bookshelves while Liam stands next to the piano, frowning.

"What's wrong, Lee?" Alex asks eventually.

Liam picks up the metronome that's resting on top of the piano. "This doesn't go here."

"Okay?" Alex says. "Don't metronomes go with pianos?"

"Victor didn't play." Liam shakes his head and sets the metronome down on the floor before sliding onto the bench of the piano. Alex decides not to question him further. At best, he'd probably just get more Liam-logic for his trouble. He's also not sure he wants to find out why Victor owned a piano if he couldn't personally use it.

Now that they're actually in the same room in relative privacy Alex wants to ask Liam any number of things instead, with *why the fuck didn't you tell me* right at the top of the list. But the degree to which Liam isn't acknowledging Alex's presence is spooky. Alex is afraid of asking questions and not getting responses, as if Liam's lack of engagement would mean that Alex isn't actually here.

After a while Liam starts plucking out notes on the piano. What is at first tolerable noodling becomes a hellish repetition of a single note, over and over and over again.

"Liam? Can you stop that?" Alex says irritably first and then with more aggravation when he gets no response.

It goes on until Paul appears in the doorway, Carly close behind him. "If you want to learn to play, Liam, we will find someone to teach you, but if you keep plinking the same damn random note I am not responsible for my actions."

Liam stops immediately and tucks his hands contritely in his lap. Alex stares.

Paul blinks in the sudden silence and then turns to Carly, who raises an eyebrow at him. "I didn't need that information," he says.

"Add it to the list," Carly says and turns back for the kitchen.

♦

It's almost lunchtime, Alex's stomach informs him with a rumble, as he stares down at the pile of folders and notebooks perched precariously on the arm of the sofa in Victor's den. "I found more stuff for *M.A.R.S.*, do you want it for Mark?" Alex asks, leaning out of the doorway to shout down the hall to Paul.

"Official answer or dream answer?" Paul yells back.

Alex grins. "Just tell me what to do with the fucking stuff."

"Bring it. And then Mark can shove it up his ass for all he's using it."

Alex stacks the pile carefully in his arms — this day does not need the hassle of trying to re-organize mysterious Victor paper if he drops them everywhere — and makes his way down the hall to Paul. "Why the fuck did Victor put up with him for so long?" Alex asks when he reaches the kitchen, setting the stack down on the counter.

"He's good," Paul responds.

"He's not that good," Alex snorts.

"I know. I'm better."

Alex cackles. "Yes. Yes you are."

♦

It's by chance that Paul glances into Victor's den while he's yelling down the hall to Alex about bringing more boxes next time. He stops short at the sight of Liam huddled into the corner of the couch with his arms wrapped tightly around his knees.

Liam turns his head toward him when he walks in, and his blue eyes are huge and pleading and completely magnetic. He looks so vulnerable that Paul immediately wants to help, whatever help might mean in this case, but when he approaches, Liam pulls more tightly into himself and shakes his head.

"Okay," Paul says soothingly, taking the armchair instead. With the data he has from Carly and everything he knows about the night he and Alex took Ali, he thinks he at least has some idea of how not to make anything worse.

Eventually Liam lifts his head, shuffles his shoulders and says, "Sorry."

"Hey, hey, hey, it's fine," Paul says gently. "Are you okay?"

Liam clearly thinks it through and then nods, unwinding his limbs so that he's actually sitting with his feet on the floor and his hands in his lap. "Yeah. It's hard sometimes. Embarrassing."

Paul regards Liam for a long moment.

"You know about these, right?" He raises a hand to show Liam the scars he doesn't bother to cover and also doesn't ever really talk about.

Liam nods. "Carly."

Paul isn't surprised that Carly is the vector of that particular piece of information. That Liam has some of Paul's secrets makes the balance of the universe feel a little more even.

"You've got nothing to be embarrassed about. I had to spend a summer in the loony bin over them."

"Why did you do it?" Liam asks, gesturing at Paul's wrists.

Paul has to smile at Liam's blunt inquisitiveness. "Because most people don't understand what it's like to make entirely reasonable choices in entirely unreasonable circumstances."

Liam sits up straighter and leans forward a little. "I could have ended up so many places not L.A.," he says. "And I don't mean everyone doesn't make it in the business. My parents could have been so much less patient."

"People with good intentions can make decisions about your life in ways that are really scary," Paul says carefully. He's a grade-A asshole if he guesses wrong anywhere in this conversation.

Liam nods slowly. "Carly's pissed because I'm regressing."

"Has this happened before?"

Liam nods. "Never this long."

"How did you get out of it?"

Liam shrugs. "Time. Therapy. Victor. There's too much going on. No one is more freaked than me about what happens if I can't learn to talk on command again."

"You're doing okay right now," Paul points out, not necessarily wanting to look too closely at Liam's word choices.

"I don't have any feelings for you, so it's just words. You're easier to talk to than Alex."

Paul blinks at what he thinks is Liam's consideration for the awkwardness of the situation. When he chuckles, Liam actually cracks a smile.

"Is there somewhere else you could go? Like, if things are too much for you here," Paul suggests. Certainly his own escape from South Carolina, albeit under different circumstances, had gone a long way to letting him sort out his own shit. Considering Victor was instrumental in that process too, it's hard to know how any of them are supposed to get on with their lives in his absence. "I know it feels like being close helps, but it might not," he adds.

Liam tips his head back and forth, considering it. "Maybe. Maybe New York. But like, one, the baby's due in four months, two, I don't want to leave Carly and Ali, three, it's a lot to ask of my parents, and, four, what if I don't come back?"

At that, Paul can only shrug. "One of your partners just *died,* Liam. Anyone who's telling you you're supposed to be able to think about more than the next five minutes is probably wrong. The timing sucks, but when wouldn't it?"

♦

Alex finds Liam and Paul in Victor's den, side by side on the couch. Paul looks up a little guiltily, and god knows what that is about, but Liam seems more present than he did earlier. Alex has no idea what he's interrupted and almost feels like he should back out the door again, but Paul says "Hi," while Liam blinks thoughtfully at him.

"Carly's ready to go," Alex tells both of them, and then waits while Paul unfolds himself from the couch and then turns to offer Liam a hand up. Liam twitches the corner of his mouth up but doesn't take the hand, standing up on his own and slipping out of the room.

♦

"So. You and Liam." Alex says once he and Paul are home and in bed.

"This is a strange role reversal," Paul jokes. He's glad they're talking about this, even if he's sure that significant awkwardness is about to ensue.

"I've never seen him look at you like that."

"Believe me, you are not the one most freaked out by that," Paul admits. "Although I feel like I can see now in him what you do and maybe what Victor did."

Alex pushes back from Paul slightly. "Okay, please don't compare my relationship with Liam to Victor's."

"Why not?"

"Because Liam overshares, and they're not the same thing. No. Don't ever."

"But — "

"You're about to say something terrible, aren't you?" Alex asks.

"Maybe he needs something like that."

"Like what?"

"Like where someone's willing to exert a bit of authority with him. He seems to look at me that way, and I know he trusts you that way."

"Worse than I imagined." Alex sits up. "What is wrong with you?"

"You've been whining at me for weeks about wanting to help him," Paul points out.

Alex gapes. "I want to *talk* to him."

"Really?" Paul doesn't believe him. Even when they haven't been having sex, whatever Alex and Liam are about has never seemed like just talking.

"I thought you had put the whole jealous asshole thing to rest. Don't start again now."

"I'm not!" Paul protests. "I was fine with you two making out that night at Victor's."

"How is this conversation happening?" Alex boggles. "That was a year and a half ago!"

"Alex," Paul chides. "Would it really be that unreasonable?"

"Yes!"

"Would you stop flipping out and actually listen to me?"

Alex gives Paul a long look and then tucks his feet in to sit cross-legged under the sheets. "Okay. Fine. I'm listening, but I strongly suspect this is a worse idea than having a baby."

"He told me that whenever this has happened before Victor helped fix it," Paul says a little helplessly.

Alex rolls his eyes. "Let me spell this out for you in tiny words. Liam and I fucked because we were sort of the same age and it felt like having a boyfriend. The fact that I had no idea what I was doing with him was okay in a way it wasn't with you. You are way overstepping right now."

Paul makes a sound of protest at Alex's probably fair assessment of their early relationship, but Alex holds up a hand before he can interrupt further.

"No, listen," Alex says. "Whatever power games you think will fix this — and Paul, come on, you are not Victor — I have no interest in them. That's also why Liam and I aren't together, because I don't want that responsibility. So fuck you, okay? Like I know you're trying, but just stop, all right?"

Paul pulls back. Whenever he thinks he has a handle on Alex and Liam as a unit, he gets another piece of the puzzle and has to recalibrate. "Okay," he says, willing to drop it. Alex's tone doesn't brook an argument.

"Where is this coming from?" Alex asks.

Paul considers that. "We talked about my wrists. Which makes Liam the second person I've told about them who I wasn't dating or related to."

"And how did you get from there to sex?" Alex prompts.

"Because things are changing, and I thought maybe it could help us, too."

"Whoa. What?" Alex asks. "What about us needs help?"

"I'm hardly home and we're planning for a baby, and on top of that stuff is changing with us and sex. I'm not sure what's going on with that."

"We're having a lot of it?" Alex offers hesitantly.

"Yeah, but the vibe is different. I don't know what's going on in your head about it, but if things are changing it seems like something worth discussing."

"Okay, look, Paul, if you want to address how we fuck, *talk* to me about it, don't try to bring Liam into it. This is sloppy even for you."

"I was trying to kill multiple birds with one stone?" Paul says weakly.

"And his big sad eyes were really pretty?"

"Alex — "

"I know, okay! Ugh. But still, involving Liam in any part of this is not good choices right now. Or ever. You and I can't fix every one of our issues with sex. You can't fix everyone else with sex either. Like seriously."

"I know. But — "

"But *what?*"

"But sex is this really central thing for us. It always has been. We have a lot of it. It's incredibly important in our relationship. And it's caused problems for us in the past."

"I remember," Alex says dryly.

"Something's going on with it now, with you, and I don't understand. Given everything else that's changing I thought we should maybe have a conversation about it before anything gets out of hand."

"That's reasonable, but framing this discussion as 'Let's fuck Liam!' so you can reassert your dominance or whatever is profoundly not."

"Whoa, okay, so not what was going on there, but point taken."

"Really?" Alex asks skeptically.

"Really. Whatever we do is fine so long as it's working for us. I just want to make sure it's working."

"Well, it is for me if it is for you," Alex says with fond exasperation.

"So that's a no to the threesome," Paul says in an attempt at a joke. He wants to put this topic to rest now, if only to hopefully keep Alex from bitching at him about it forever.

"You know how you get possessive of me? I get possessive of that time I had with Liam. I'm happy with it on a shelf, but please don't try to touch it," Alex says.

"So that's no to a threesome with *Liam*," Paul clarifies, still going for levity.

"Correct," Alex says firmly. "And to the rest of it, at least for now. Focusing on the shit going on in our lives isn't the worst thing in the world."

"You mean like asking you what's going on in your head?"

Alex gives a disbelieving laugh. "Then next time just come out and fucking ask."

"Fine. What are you doing?"

Alex sits up abruptly, and swings a knee over Paul's waist to straddle him. "Trying new things. Feeling good. Making you feel good. Expanding this *big central thing* we have."

"Don't tease," Paul chides.

"I'm not. Although you're one to talk," he says, pressing his fingers to Paul's lips with a smirk. It fades into something more serious, and Paul finds himself arrested by the way Alex's eyes dart over his face and then lock with his.

"I like our adventures," Alex says quietly, like he's trying to make sure Paul hears him. "But I want them to stay that way — adventures, that we get up to, together, sometimes, when the time and place is right. I don't want an open relationship. I don't want a triad, with Liam or anybody else. I want *you*."

Paul is too overwhelmed to be able to respond to any of that properly. Alex shifts off of him and gets him to roll over on his stomach, kneeling behind him and then hesitating, pressing his hands almost gently into Paul's waist and ass.

"Sometimes I get so nervous doing this," he confesses as he reaches for the lube, and his voice is different, again, gone somewhere Paul still doesn't quite know how to follow.

Paul groans and folds his arms under his head as Alex lines himself up and starts pressing in. "You've been doing this a lot lately." After all, that's part of what he'd been trying to get an answer on.

"Yeah, but I can never quite believe I get to."

Alex digs his fingers into Paul's hips while he pounds into him. It's aggressive in a way that, hot as it is, Paul still isn't used to. And for all they've talked about it now, Paul still isn't sure what Alex is doing, or what it means for them.

When Alex's hands creep into his hair and pull, it's glorious. It's also a little exhausting, because even after all their talking and all this feeling, Paul still isn't sure what Alex is actually chasing.

17

Despite the weird conversation about sex, and the conversations about the baby, and all the lingering effects of dead Victor on their lives, Alex at least tries to keep up a semblance of normalcy as the summer passes. On his day off, he takes Darcy shooting. He hasn't been to the range in ages, and she should brush up her skills before the *Winsome* finale, not that she needs the excuse to spend a day out with Alex where they might get photographed.

Paul's grateful Alex has something to occupy himself while he has to work. It makes him feel less guilty for spending time at the office when Alex is about to take off for South Carolina so soon.

He does his best to moderate the time he's at the office, but that means taking work home with him. When he and Olivia get caught up in a discussion about her latest spec script, he glances at the clock and tells her to pack up and come back to their house with him.

"If I keep talking about pilots with you here I'm playing favorites. Come over and it's off the books," he tells her. "Also our kitchen is somewhat reasonably stocked." Olivia agrees readily.

It feels like an extension of what Paul's job was like when he worked for Victor, hosting parties and keeping everyone human and healthy. Victor did it too, for his inner circle, with meals and gatherings at his house. With Victor's house soon to be gone from their social landscape, Paul and Alex's is a logical successor.

Once there, laptops and notes spread across the kitchen table, the conversation turns from Olivia's script to the network notes from the latest table read. Paul's been pissy about them and hasn't yet brought them to the writers' room at large. When Olivia asks why, he gives her a considering look before he passes his laptop over to her.

The notes are irritating, and mostly about Alex's character, and while Paul will take some of them because it's the network and he has to, he'll fight for others. Doing this work in front of Olivia is one thing, but he really does not want to discuss any of them in a room full of ten people who all work for him.

"This is appalling," Olivia says, scrolling down the page.

"Mhmm."

"How do you not go crazy with shit like this?"

"Mostly I go crazy," Paul chuckles, although it's not really a joke.

Olivia has her hand clapped over her mouth, half in horror and half because she can't stop laughing, when Alex and Darcy come in.

"What is going on?" Alex drops his bag in the doorway.

Olivia gives Paul and then him a look.

"The network sent back notes for the episode with the love scene between you two. Specifically, they sent back notes about your love scene," Paul says.

"Oooh, let me see," Darcy says, crowding around Olivia's shoulders.

"How on earth do they have notes on that? It's not like it's chock full of dialogue," Alex says.

"Yeah, well, it wasn't the dialogue they had issues with."

"'Don't put woman on top for love scene, lest audience remember actor is gay,'" Darcy reads from the screen.

"*Seriously?*" Alex says, coming around to see for himself. He sounds more incredulous than \pissed.

"Okay, both of you need to not breathe down my damn neck," Olivia protests.

"But Melissa has to be on top," Darcy protests. "She's so much better than Jason, and my tits will look better."

Everyone turns to stare at her.

"What?" When no answer is forthcoming, she can't help but dig in deeper. "They will," she says, cupping them. "Gravity. I hate that side-boob thing."

As sarcastically as possible, Olivia types, *Actress says no due to side-boob concern* in response to the note.

◆

After Alex drags Darcy out to the back deck with beer and to *discuss your top and bottom bullshit, oh my God*, Olivia can almost see Paul slide into a funk.

"What's going on with you?" Olivia folds her arms on the island when Paul fails to talk about anything constructive. She watches as he wanders in circles, complaining about *Winsome* and the fucking network, and *M.A.R.S.* and fucking Mark. She is not Paul's therapist, but he's also not being useful to anyone at the moment, which makes her more inclined to help him sort his shit out. She's starting to understand that Paul is one of those people who needs to talk out anything and everything that's bothering him.

"Our jobs are idiotic," Paul complains.

"Our jobs are actually awesome. You've been doing this way longer than I have, and you worked for Victor. This cannot be the worst you've ever see."

"Maybe not, but Victor being dead makes it a special sort of hell. The network is giving me homophobic bullshit, the ratings have been slipping which is so not where we want to be going into the end of the series, we're not even going to talk about *M.A.R.S.'* ratings, and Alex is going to be gone for two weeks now and then a month in the fall when he has to do the media junket for his movie. Also, I have no idea what he or I are going to be doing in a year."

"You should, like, get on that," Olivia says.

Paul gives a tired chuckle. "Last time I pitched a pilot I had Victor over my shoulder the whole way. And now he's gone. I don't think I can replace him."

"In terms of needing someone else over your shoulder or in terms of being him?" Olivia asks, curious. His response has the potential to impact her own strategies and tactics.

"Both. I'm not good at working alone, and God knows I can't keep everybody functional."

"Well, you can work with me, and Alex can keep you functional."

Paul side-eyes her. "Did you just appoint yourself my new creative partner?"

"You could call Mark," she says, like that's any sort of option.

"You're really fucking manipulative, you know that?" Paul's voice is good-natured, but he's reminding himself of what she is too.

Olivia shrugs. "So was Victor."

◆

Alex could probably get more of Victor's journals while everyone is at the house in their ongoing and incomplete task of putting his life into boxes, but it seems wrong. Whatever Alex is learning about Victor feels tender and private and somehow intentionally just for him. He's not ready to share it with anyone else. Or face their reasonable outrage at him rifling through desk drawers not to organize, but to steal.

Paul keeps his set of keys to Victor's house — on loan from Nigel — hanging by the door to the garage with the rest of their keys. He seems reluctant to put them on his own key ring, which Alex can hardly blame him for. This reluctance also makes it easy for Alex to take them one afternoon while Paul's at work.

He drives to Victor's house alone. He's leaving for ten days in South Carolina soon. A trip to do right by Paul's family before they start the medical part of the baby procedure seems a fitting time to read more of Victor's journals.

At this point, Alex doesn't really need the rest of them. He knows how the story ends. He was there for a lot of it. And as much as he's learned about the man who was so often his own private villain, Victor is dead. Alex can't actually do anything with his growing empathy or possible regrets.

Somehow, though, he still wants to know the story, as Victor chose to tell it to his diary, the intended audience of which Alex still can't figure out. But Alex has known there is magic in story since he left his doomed life in Indiana to come to Los Angeles with a girl he didn't even know but somehow expected to keep him safe.

Despite all the years he has worked in TV and film now, Alex is still learning how stories work, not on his heart, but on the world. They are machines of haunting beauty and houses of the heart. Victor's diaries make him care, in a way he never has before, about the technology of language, of arc and of cadence. It would be wrong for Alex to stop reading and let this particular story's task, whatever it is, go unfinished.

◆

Liam does his best to keep Carly in the loop about what he's considering doing with his life. That endeavor would be easier if he didn't feel guilty every time he thought about leaving her alone with Ali and the pregnancy while he goes back to New York to try to remember how to drive a car and use the microwave. Carly deserves a less complicated life than the one he's able to offer her. While that's always been true, it feels more unfair now than ever. There are no lists anyone can give him that will solve it.

He's still not sure if being at Victor's house makes it better or worse. Since he can't figure it out, he tags along when Carly goes to meet Paul and Alex. As distressing as it is to see Victor's belongings packed and removed, the house, like the man who once owned it, will not be there forever. Liam wants to be able to say goodbye for as long as he can.

Alex is grumbling about being tasked with boxing up Victor's den for no reason anyone can ascertain other than that he's pissed about being there again. Liam finally has to walk away from him; he doesn't have the ability to explain to Alex all the things he wishes his friend understood about Victor. What makes it worse is that Alex may never actually understand why that's such a tragedy.

"What the hell?" Paul says as Liam wanders into the kitchen. He's reacting to his phone, though, and not to Liam, so that's nothing to worry about.

Liam drifts on to where Carly is sitting with her laptop and making a list of the kitchen contents. She'll send it to Nigel, so he doesn't have to send them polite but increasingly insistent emails every week.

Paul still has his phone in hand as he walks to the front door. Liam peers at him curiously as he opens the front door and finds Darcy on the doorstep.

"What are you doing here?" Paul demands.

"I need to talk to you guys."

Alex, as if drawn by her voice, rounds the corner from the den. "What the hell is so pressing you had to come here in person?"

"Don't be sharp," Darcy retorts. "Even though there aren't going to be blinds about you and me fighting in the women's restroom."

"Oh my God, no," Alex says. Before Paul or anyone else can react, he grabs Darcy and hauls her back outside.

◆

"The blinds were really funny," Darcy protests, as Alex makes her walk the long way around to the backyard and the pool deck.

"Yeah, Gemma was especially pleased to be the subject of internet ponderings regarding my possible bisexuality, and whether I'm suddenly dating the chick I lived with for three years."

"I used to think you were a couple."

Alex stares. He doesn't want to think of Darcy as someone who was once a fan. He feels awkward enough straddling that divide himself; he doesn't want to contemplate anyone else doing the same.

"Before I met you! What?"

"What do you want, Darcy?"

"So speaking of the internet, it's being really gross about Jackson."

Alex groans. It really only was a matter of time. While Alex is aware the internet is *always* gross about something he has no desire to be pulled into Darcy's dating drama. No matter how much he likes Jackson.

"Everyone's being really racist and saying awful things," she states. "I don't understand, it's not like we're in the fifties anymore."

"It's Hollywood. It's always the fifties."

"But everybody thinks you and Paul and your awesome gay romance is awesome."

"Are you actually listening to the things coming out of your mouth?" Alex is aghast, and if it were anyone but Darcy saying these things, he'd be yelling right now.

"What? Your awesome gay romance *is* awesome."

♦

Packing is interrupted twenty minutes later by a rustle, thud, and a sharp "Fuck!" from Paul. Alex looks across the kitchen to see Paul at the table, staring disconsolately at a stack of papers he's accidentally knocked to the floor, scattering them everywhere. Alex moves to help him pick the papers up but to absolutely everyone's surprise, Liam appears behind Paul and, very gently, puts his hands on his shoulders. When Paul doesn't shrug him off — just cranes his neck around to see what the fuck Liam is doing — Liam starts massaging his shoulders.

"What the hell?" Paul says, more confused than anything.

Liam shushes him and digs his thumb in. Paul's shoulders slump with obvious relief.

Alex understands instantly what's going on even as he finds it unsettling. Liam and Victor's negotiations regarding how Liam was allowed to touch him are, after all, a recurring topic in the diaries. Victor's solution had been massage classes for Liam so he could have the touch he needed while Victor maintained the more clinical distance he needed.

Darcy looks as confused as Paul does, but Carly shoots a look at Alex and then moves to the next cupboard. Alex continues with his work too. Paul doesn't need know that Liam has decided he needs to be cared for the same way Liam used to do for Victor.

Darcy eventually goes on her way after extracting a vague commitment from Alex that he'll do drinks with her and Jackson at some point. Liam ends up on the couch in the living room, curled up small and hugging a pillow to his chest while Alex marks the boxes of books to be donated to charity.

"I'll miss you," Liam says suddenly. Paul looks up from where he's working on itemized lists for Nigel.

"Where are you going?" Alex asks, looking over at Liam.

Liam doesn't say anything, but Alex nods after a moment, and then they don't break eye contact for minutes.

"What the hell?" Paul asks softly, when Carly walks in the room again.

She waves a hand in their general direction. "Ignore them, they're being witchy."

"No but seriously." Paul is convinced someone should be discussing this. Whatever is going on, it's unnerving. It's also not coming from Liam but rather seems to be something Alex brings out in both of them.

"Is there an explanation that exists that actually makes you feel better?" Carly asks.

"Alex was right about this house. It's creepy."

"The house is not always the problem."

18

Paul hates coming home after dropping Alex off at the airport. Alex is only going to be in South Carolina for ten days, but Paul still feels like he's just gotten back from Australia even though it's July now and that was months ago. The empty house feels entirely wrong.

He puts off calling Carly to see how she's holding up until after Alex is gone. He doesn't want to start more drama about what Liam hasn't told Alex and how much of Liam's everything Alex is — or is not — entitled to.

When Paul does finally call, she sounds exhausted. "I thought breaking up with you would have reduced your dependence on the lonely late night phone call thing."

Paul doesn't know whether she's joking or not. "How are you?"

"Six months pregnant with a five-year-old who is being even more of a brat than usual because she misses her father and a full slate of work tomorrow, whether or not I get any sleep at all tonight. How are you?" she asks with a sharp sweetness that makes Paul wince.

"I can take Ali tonight if you need a break."

"If I thought she'd go, I'd walk her there myself." There's the muffled sound of Ali negotiating to sleep in her mother's bed that night. "Just a minute, Ali, I'm on the phone," Carly tells her.

"I do not know how people do this single parent thing," Carly says when she comes back.

"Not what we expected our lives to look like in college, is it?" Paul feels guilty at the question. Usually he means all the ways his life is better than he'd ever thought possible.

"Nobody ever expects their life to look like this. I still can't believe he left," Carly says angrily.

Paul winces. Her phrasing sounds so final. "I thought you wanted him to."

Carly sighs sharply. "My husband went home to his parents because he needed a quiet, safe place to learn how to do the world again. A place that was not with me because our child and my pregnancy are apparently burdens for him. That it was the right thing to do does not mean I am not pissed that I get no support system."

"Do you both want to come over? Or me to go over there?" Paul offers, though he is aware that it's, at best, a stop-gap solution.

Carly laughs darkly. "Thanks, but let's save the exploration of the family-that-almost-was for nights more dire than this."

Paul is horrified to realize such nights might actually plausibly exist. It's an unsettling thought, not because he can see it happening but because he can see it happening whether Alex and Liam are involved or not.

◆

Alex doesn't realize how accustomed he's become to the pervasive smoke from the wildfires outside LA until he steps outside at the Charleston airport. The air is heavy with the scent of oversaturated earth and vegetation as he tosses his bags in the back of the rental car. The change is dramatic but doesn't feel like relief from either the fires or the situation he left behind him in California.

He's glad to do the drive alone, and flips through radio channels as he speeds down now-familiar roads. Eventually he lands on a country radio station all but identical to the one he used to listen to on the shitty radio in his shitty car on his way to school and his terrible jobs in Indiana. He's surprised he still knows enough of the songs to sing along. Some things don't really change.

When the sun sets, Alex flips on the headlights. He feels isolated from the world in a way he almost never does on the opposite coast. In L.A., someone is always watching, and someone always knows where he is. Here, he's just a guy in a car on a highway. He feels small in a way he hasn't in a very long time.

It's almost dark by the time he gets to the house. Beth waves to him from the verandah as he pulls up the drive and hugs him tightly when he makes it up the steps. For that moment, Alex feels like he has stepped through a portal into an entirely different life.

◆

Being back in New York is hard. On some level, it's a relief. To a certain extent Liam's systems for navigating the world kick in as soon as he can see the city from the air. This is where he learned everything that has let him have the life he has. Knowing how to get home in a crisis was one of the things drilled into him from the beginning. He never thought it would look like this.

Neither of his parents meet him at the airport when he lands on a hot, humid morning. JFK is far, and Liam doesn't want to subject them to whatever attention it might attract. But Liam knows to look for the guy with the sign and follow him to a black car. As he watches Queens and then Brooklyn pass by the windows in the dark, he realizes he doesn't feel particularly sad about being in New York. At least, he's no sadder than he is about anything else. At a given point, all loss is one.

It's a nice night, and his parents are sitting on the bench in the small courtyard in front of their brownstone when the car pulls up. He lets them hug him, but it's awkward and reminds him too much of the line of condolences he had to endure at Victor's funeral. His parents hadn't been there, because he'd asked them not to come. He heads inside without comment when they say how sorry they are.

For the first few days, everything feels much worse. Therapy doesn't really feel much better, not that it should at this point. It's all so practical. There's a soul-deep horror to realizing that even if he can learn to do things again and say words he's decided on independently, Victor will still be dead. Liam will still be completely unable to talk about it in most places or times, not because of his brain, but because of the world he lives in. It's not a particularly motivating circumstance.

It takes almost a week before Liam can muster up the will to invite Charles over.

They've known each other since they were eight, since before Liam was ever on TV, and since before he became so good at seeming like other people, more or less. Which means Charles not only understands when Liam mostly isn't talking, but that he doesn't find it particularly exceptional. They've been sleeping with each other on and off for years out of what has gone from friendly boredom to an actual, serious — if long-distance and tertiary — relationship in Liam's complex web of companionship.

Charles is loud and effusive in filling in the space that Liam's silence leaves. Liam finds that a little uncomfortable. He's also bluntly curious about what it's like to have a dead lover and how Liam is navigating this. The conversation that sparks is far outside the realm of things Liam can talk about with most other people, which is a relief. Everything is still miserable — and Liam has to think too hard about the right steps to accomplish most basic tasks right now — but not having to police himself is a definite bonus.

Charles invites himself to the house for dinner, checking in only to make sure Liam isn't too tired. Some days are better than others, and exhaustion isn't exactly the problem.

Sometimes he feels like he's everything the internet said he would — and wouldn't — be when he Googled autism when he was ten. Still, being like this feels less dishonest than so many years of passing and pretending that "high functioning" is something real or even valuable.

But Liam can tolerate Charles's presence. Possibly, more importantly, Liam can tolerate Charles touching him — a hand covering his, a touch to the shoulder — because he knew Charles long before Victor. Charles erases nothing.

Liam kisses Charles, which would be completely unsurprising in any other circumstance. Liam would happily do more, but Charles wants to have a conversation about that and Liam isn't up for one. So they wind up making out. A lot.

"This is so surreal," he tells Liam.

"Why?"

"Because I feel like we're kids, and about to get caught, and like you're a regression vortex we're all getting sucked into."

Liam frowns.

"You have a whole life you're supposed to be getting home to," Charles notes.

Speculation about the Campbell family splitting up has been all over *Entertainment Tonight*, Liam knows, because he overheard his mother watching it. He's sure Charles knows about it too, but no one has had the nerve to mention it to him directly. It's a hot mess of upsetting, but so much is wrong right now Liam is not sure how to prioritize his distress.

Liam shrugs. "I know. That's what I'm doing."

"Really?" Charles asks. "Here or there?"

"Does it matter?"

◆

Sarah, as far as Alex can tell, is taking the whole baby situation in much better stride than he is.

"It's drugs, a trip to L.A., and half a day at the doctor's office. And then you and Paul get a baby," she says, while she and Alex shuck corn.

Beth has banished them to the verandah, because they were getting the corn silk everywhere in the kitchen. It's the kind of handwork that Alex never has the time or need to do any more, unless he's here. It reminds him both of the childhood he tries not to think about as well as the vacations he's taken here with Paul. He feels young in a way that's not entirely useful given the circumstances.

"There's an appeal to keeping this in the family," she says.

Alex nods, and tries to explain that he doesn't know who his father was, and that Delilah is, as far as he's ever been informed, his half-sister. "This whole genetic continuity thing was never part of my life."

"Well, lots of things were never going to be part of your life," Sarah says with a smile.

Alex gives a thoughtful far-away hum in response.

"What are you going to do about names?" She changes the subject.

Alex chuckles. "Paul is forbidden from picking up a baby name book until after the first trimester. And I told him the kid can have his last name."

"He must have been all over that."

"It's only fair, I won the bio-dad thing." Alex doesn't think it matters either way. Alex himself has his mother's last name and Paul doesn't have any contact with his father anymore. Neither Beth nor Sarah talk to the man either. Alex doesn't blame himself for that situation, though he and a great deal of drama around their wedding was largely responsible for it. But Paul's name is Paul's name, whoever else's it may be, and if it matters to him, Alex can respect that.

"Is it really a competition?" Sarah asks.

"I'm just relieved Paul didn't want to procreate with my felonious sister."

But as awkward as Alex feels at first about discussing the topic with Sarah, it's way weirder talking about it with Sarah's husband, Mike. There is absolutely no gracious way Alex can find to open the topic.

He and Mike are on the verandah steps after dinner, left alone deliberately, Alex suspects, by the women of the house, when he finally blurts "I'm sorry I'm having a baby with your wife."

Mike stares at him for half a second while Alex wishes he could crawl under the porch. Then Mike cracks up.

"It's weird!" Alex protests.

Mike claps him on the back. "Look. It's weird that my brother-in-law writes TV, and married somebody famous, and at one point I would have thought it was weird that you're a guy, but you and I both married into a family that has a creepy farm house and a cricket barn. The baby is weird too, but everything here is weird."

"Oh my God, the crickets." Alex laughs to himself in nervous relief that he's found an ally on that particular point.

"They're horrifying, aren't they?"

"Paul acted like it was normal!"

"Yeah. No. It's really not."

◆

Paul talks to Alex almost every day. Even with the calls — and the texts and pictures Alex sends throughout his day — Paul misses him desperately. It's only ten days, but travel is always hard for them. In all of the upset their life has been for the past four months, Alex's absence is a misery.

When a new batch of completely asinine notes comes through from the network, Paul groans out loud in his office and reaches for his phone. It's late enough that Alex has to be asleep. Paul could wake him, but what he actually needs is to freak out at Victor and get a dose of sanity and tolerant exasperation in return. The call rings only once before it rolls over to a stock voicemail message.

Paul jerks the phone away from his ear and drops it on his desk as he realizes what he's done.

After a moment he buries his face in his hands. The chaos Victor's death has thrown into everyone's lives into has left him no time or space to deal with his own grief. Paul really fucking misses his friend.

◆

The pace of life is different in South Carolina. While Alex still gets up early as a courtesy to Beth, there's also a pleasure in coffee over the misty sunrise of the mornings. He spends his days rambling around the house and the property, which somehow seem less forbidding without Paul's ominous stories at his side. There are no demons in the barn, no creatures in the lake looking for children to drown, and the knives in the kitchen and the guns on the range are all just tools.

In the late mornings, with everyone he's come to see at work, he gets in his car and drives. Marion and the surrounding towns shouldn't seem as different from Paragon, Indiana as they do, but the land is lush and the strip malls aren't any uglier than the ones in Los Angeles. Alex can see, certainly, how it would have been a hard place for Paul to grow up; it probably wouldn't have been kind to Alex either were their situations reversed. But it seems like a place where people at least have the right to dreams and the possibility of getting out. Paragon never did. Alex wonders if he'll ever stop feeling like it's waiting to claw him back into the dirt.

Even with long conversations out on the verandah after dinner, bed comes early in a place where work doesn't creep on toward midnight and later, and restaurants close at nine. Alex spends the nights reading Victor's diaries.

The Liam first introduced therein is a stranger. He's so young, and Alex is fascinated by Victor's clinicalness.

Liam is just a tool in the story, not of Victor's life, but of *The Fourth Estate*. Until he asks Victor out. The entry that follows is pages of confusion and frustration at a young man who is both willing to break into Victor's bedroom at a party in the hopes of seducing him and happy to talk for hours over dinner and at least wait out his asexuality, if not accept it. Both the narrative and Victor's sudden uncertainty is fucking bizarre. And that's before Alex gets to the part where Liam wants Victor to watch him jerk off.

'I don't need you to do anything, but if we're going to be together however we're going to be together — we're together, right? — I need you to see me like this.'

Alex's brain breaks on the asexuality thing, not for the first time. Victor was enraptured by Liam in a way that feels distant to Alex. Yet it was clearly anything but. Just different from how Alex experiences people. Whatever it was, was some sort of uncomfortable for Victor.

The power dynamic is also unnerving.

Liam's discovery of pain is an accident, Victor gripping his wrist too tight in the kitchen to save him from the results of an ill-advised attempt at teaching him to cook. The image is strangely hot to Alex: Liam surprised and eager; Victor, after so much literary agony over what pleasure he can and can't stand to give Liam, suddenly gifted with permission to hurt.

There are so many names of desire.

Alex reads of everyone's weary amusement during Liam's disaster with Natalie. Watching Carly morph from Paul's girlfriend to Liam's partner to Victor's friend is particularly surreal. Alex learns to recognize that Victor at times lies in his own journal, omissions indicating a grief or anger he suspects he felt he had no time for. Victor was born both ambitious and resigned.

Alex's own story is shocking. Victor's first entry about him is a single line.

I ruined someone's life today.

Alex is only sure it's about him because of the date. It's not one he can forget, and it's not one that could possibly belong to anyone else.

The other entries are mostly a wall of puzzlement, which Alex is starting to understand as Victor's way of offering praise. If he couldn't understand something and it was still interesting to him, he tried to solve it by dragging it into America's light: television.

While the diaries linger in the back of Alex's mind during the day, they particularly haunt him at night after he's closed the cover on his latest readings. Attempts to convince himself it's because he's away from Paul and not getting laid don't particularly assuage the weirdness.

For all the things Victor omits from his entries, he's incredibly detail-oriented. Alex feels as if he's read about dozens of Liam's orgasms but none of Victor's own.

In some ways Victor's relative absence from the diary makes it easier for Alex to allow himself an interest in its sexual content. Some that is his history with Liam. Liam is beautiful, perhaps most especially in Victor's prose, which narrows him to a finely focused instrument. But a lot of it is the sexual content itself.

He and Paul may fuck often, fuck well, and have their adventures, but the two things that figure most prominently in the journals — bondage and sex toys — aren't things they've experimented with much. Alex's ropes are for rocks, and buying sex toys is eight kinds of complicated in their ridiculous lives. He thinks of the blind items that could result and can't help but giggle.

But Alex also can't help but think of what it would be like to do all those things to Paul. What would it be like to make Paul beg with his own mind clear enough to just watch it happen? Alex knows he wouldn't deviate from the plan or grant unearned mercy.

Alex huffs out a little laugh at the twists his mind takes in his already complicated life and shoves a hand into his pajama bottoms. After all, without Paul here, the only plan he has is the narrative in his head of Paul bound and waiting and impatient.

Paul wouldn't be good the way Liam was for Victor. For Alex, that would be even better. Alex smiles slyly as he jerks himself harder. There's an appeal in showing off, even if it's just for the people in his head. And even if one of them is dead.

19

Paul doesn't particularly want to go to Frank's birthday party and suspects that given delicate network politics and his own unhappy headspace he probably shouldn't. Mark and the entire M.A.R.S. team will be there, however. Paul will need to be there to defend his and Victor's territory.

At least he recognizes that's one of the more fucked up thoughts he's had in a while.

"I could go with you," Darcy offers that afternoon as they're wrapping up on set.

Paul shakes his head. "I don't need a date. Especially not my starlet. Especially not at this event. Aren't you having enough fun in the tabloids with Jackson?"

"Let's not talk about that and yes you do. Alex is out of town and, like, probably being a hermit somewhere in the mountains because he didn't tell me where he was going, but you really don't want to go by yourself, Paul."

"I'll be fine."

"You're moping."

"I'm *fine*." Paul stalks away shaking his head. He has things he needs to finish in his office before he deals with this damn party.

"Don't say I didn't warn you," Darcy calls brightly after him. It's been a bad enough day as it is, and Darcy's cheerfulness and general habit of inappropriately camping out in his office is, at this point, just grating.

♦

Frank Pearson's house is as large as Victor's but much more annoying. Victor's place may be hideously modern, but there was a sly self-awareness to the way Victor inhabited it that made the overabundance of corners and excess of white paint bearable. This place is just ugly and Frank doesn't know how to decorate.

The company doesn't particularly improve it. The room is full of people from *M.A.R.S* who didn't like Victor, or have decided they don't like Paul or, for the sake of appearances, are acting as if they don't like Paul when they're not sucking up to him. He drinks too much, because taking another sip keeps being preferable to opening his mouth and giving his honest opinion on anything.

He ends up in conversation in the corner with one of the production guys he's known vaguely for years; Eric was part of the crew Victor kept on *The Fourth Estate* when he reshuffled half of his people to Paul in *Winsome's* first season. In hushed voices, they cautiously talk far too much shit about Mark and the direction he's taking *M.A.R.S.*

The whole conversation is hilarious. Also, Paul feels ridiculously vindicated to have someone else on his side. As the evening progresses and they both get drunker, Paul gets more pissed about everything being done to Victor's legacy, especially since he's the one entrusted to uphold it. When Paul realizes that they've somehow wound up pressed together nearly against the wall in the crush of people, ducking outside seems an entirely logical suggestion to make.

Paul doesn't really register when they start making out. Eventually they wind up in the backseat of Paul's car getting hot and heavy in a way he'd be aware was a bad idea, if he weren't so angry about Victor's death and confused about his own place in the world. Right now, though, he can forget that Victor is dead and his place seems simple enough.

There's not enough room to slide down on the floor between the seats but Paul manages to fold himself up small, get Eric's pants unzipped and down, and start sucking his dick while Eric swears and pants above him. Paul feels fragile and barely there, tethered to reality only by the scent and feel of sex.

After Eric comes, they shuffle around awkwardly on the seats so he can go down on Paul, both of them too drunk to care what a mess they are. Paul is digging his fingers into his hair and encouraging him on with half-formed words and moans when someone raps at the window.

"*Shit*," Paul hisses. Between his legs Eric jolts back. The sun has set, but the light from the garage is more than bright enough to make out Mark, waggling a phone at him from the other side of the glass. Paul can make out the pictures he's taken.

Mark blows a kiss and then saunters away. It takes every ounce of self-control Paul has left — as well as the knowledge that his life is about to get very stupid and it is entirely his own fault — not to burst out of the car and deck him right there.

♦

Jackson is still mostly asleep in bed at his apartment when Darcy reaches for her phone to start scrolling through the internet and anything interesting that may have happened last night.

"Do you have to do that right now?" he mumbles, rolling over and pulling a pillow over his head. Weekends are for sleeping in, not dealing with more of the industry bullshit his life has been since Victor hired him. Jackson's still not sure if saying yes to that job offer was the best decision he ever made, or the worst. That he's still getting paid from Victor's estate to be a dead man's assistant until everything is finally taken care of is definitely strange.

"If it's bothering you, I can stop," Darcy says, snuggling closer so she can use his chest as a pillow.

"Nope, as long as I don't have to do anything about anything that's happened."

"Promise. You're off-duty."

Jackson laughs. Darcy goes back to happily scrolling through her feed of social media and gossip sites.

"OH MY GOD THERE'S A PICTURE," Darcy suddenly shrieks. She drops the phone as if it's bitten her and scoots away from it.

Jackson, startled, flails and almost falls off the bed. "Darcy, what the hell?"

"THERE'S A PICTURE!"

"Of what?"

"OF PAUL!"

"Okay...." Jackson tries to get a rein on the sudden jolt of adrenaline while simultaneously trying to figure out how to get Darcy, who is clutching the sheets with a look of abject horror, to calm the fuck down.

Darcy takes a couple of deep breaths. "There is a picture of Paul Marion Keane in a compromising position in public with a man who is not his husband," she says with what is clearly a superhuman attempt at decorum under these trying circumstances,

"Paul cheated?" Jackson asks warily, although he does actually want this piece of information. His job, and now his relationship, put him in the way of knowing more than he ever wanted about the complicated lives of various public people.

Darcy looks like she's going to cry.

"Darce, internet gossip sites are bullshit, you send in blinds once a month."

"There's a *picture*," she wails. She fishes around in the sheets until she finds her phone and shoves it at him.

"Whoaaa, okay, more of him than I ever needed to see," he says, passing the phone back as quickly as he can. Dark, blurry, and shadowed for sure, but that picture, on not an at all reputable website, doesn't leave enough to the imagination.

"What's going to happen? Are they going to get divorced? What's gonna happen to *Winsome* if they get divorced? Is this why they thought it was a bad idea for Alex to be on *Winsome*? I still have to work with both of them!" Darcy says with increasing speed and franticness.

Jackson gently tugs her back down onto the pillows. "Okay, you have no idea what happened, no idea what any of it means, and it is not any of your business. You promised I wouldn't have to deal with anything you found on the internet today."

"You don't have to deal with anything! Oh God how are we going to deal with this? I should call Alex — "

"By going back to *sleep*."

"But -"

"No. No calling anybody. No dealing."

"Fine," Darcy says sulkily, curling up next to him again. "But if they get divorced they're going to have to deal with *me*."

"I'm sure that's the biggest concern on their list right now."

◆

Alex notices the email when he's still in bed. He's been BCCed on it — it's addressed to one of the sleazier internet gossip sites — and Alex's mind immediately jumps to Darcy. But when he clicks on the attached pictures and then zooms in, squinting, his stomach sinks. Darcy can be ridiculous, sure, but this is more than a vaguely-sourced blind. And Paul is making far worse choices than Alex could ever have imagined.

Paul picks up his phone just before it goes to voicemail.

"I'm so — "

Alex cuts him off. "Are you okay?"

Paul laugh-sobs in response but doesn't form any actual words.

"I'm going to take that as a no," Alex says.

"Alex, I'm so sorry."

"Where are you right now?"

"What?"

"Where are you," Alex repeats, more slowly. If they're going to get through this, Paul needs to answer his damn questions.

"I'm home."

"Are you alone?"

"Alex — " Paul says, pleadingly.

"That wasn't an accusation. Give me data, Paul. Are you alone?"

"Well, Todd's here. But otherwise, yes."

"Okay." Alex sits down on the edge of the bed. He can hear Beth moving around downstairs. The absolutely last thing he needs is for this conversation to be overheard by Paul's mom, for everyone's sake.

"Are you angry?" Paul asks.

"I'm beyond angry. What should I be reading into this?"

Paul hesitates. "You know I've always had a tendency toward self-injury."

"I know," Alex says. It's why, on top of being pissed at his husband, he's scared. "But are you saying that so I won't yell, or because it's true?"

"Victor's dead, you're not here, and I am *fucked up*."

Alex flops backward on the bed. "I will take it as a marginal win that you're somewhat aware of how fucked up you are," he says sharply. "How much of this was because I said no to the threesome?"

"I don't care about that," Paul says. "Do you know what it means to me that you will say no to me?"

Alex reels from that a little. That's big and powerful and not something he has the bandwidth to touch more firmly right now.

"Then, I don't get it," Alex says. "Are you unhappy? Is that why you keep trying to figure out if I am?" It's such an inconceivable idea, that Alex might not be enough or quite right for him anymore, he can hardly put it to words.

"*No*," Paul makes that half-laugh, half-sob sound again. Alex's heart breaks even as he draws a relieved breath. "No. Not the way you mean."

"Okay," he says more softly. "In what way then?"

Alex has spent so much time reading about Liam through Victor's eyes, and now has a clearer sense than ever before how much Liam has always needed the world to tell him where to go, what to do, and how to feel about it. The things Alex hated about Victor were kindness to Liam nearly always, and the diaries have only served to clarify for Alex why he and Liam could never be together.

That said — and this is the part Alex hates, the part that makes him resent Victor even as Victor is dead — Alex hasn't been able to avoid seeing his own abilities in the man. That's been unsettling, and sometimes frightening, but right now with Paul silent and seemingly unable to answer him, it's really fucking useful. Paul wants to make things better, but he needs to be told how.

"I am starting to understand that this is just how you are," Alex tells Paul, his voice steely. "But when this happens, I need you to not pick up a knife or run twenty miles or go to some party. I need you to call me so I can interrupt you."

"Oh my God," Paul says. He sounds so relieved.

"Paul?" Alex asks, and it's softer and a little uncertain now. All of this is new, and even Victor made mistakes.

"How are you so calm about this?"

"Because when I climb rocks, if I get emotional, I could die. As I have learned. Right now I'm making sure no one dies."

"What do you want to do?" Paul asks after an uncomfortably long pause.

"We're going to figure out how you're going to get through the next seventy-two hours of public humiliation for getting caught getting your dick sucked by a *M.A.R.S.* production dude." Alex is often surprised by his life, but this moment is a realm of unpleasantness previously unanticipated.

"Are you coming back?" Paul asks with equal parts hope and dread.

"No. I mean, yes, I'm coming back, but on Monday like we planned. Not today. We are getting you in a place where you're not a danger to yourself but, Jesus, Paul, I need some space from this."

"Okay," Paul says.

Alex takes a deep breath. "Also, we are going to postpone the baby."

"Alex — "

"We need to take a step back and decide whether this is really something our lives can handle right now. Or ever."

"But we already decided," Paul protests.

"We did, and then you went and hooked up with a random at a party. Carly's pregnant and alone with Ali while Liam's in New York *at your suggestion* because he can't do life. Your issues are not his issues, but that's feeling like a cautionary fucking tale right now, especially considering how entangled we all are. Before you and I have a baby we need to deal with the fact that having responsibility turns you into an asshole because this is now officially a trend."

♦

By the time Alex hangs up, he and Paul have come up with a plan — or rather, Paul has gracefully submitted himself to Alex's decisions. Paul will call Alex twice a day until Alex is back in L.A.; he will not pick Alex up at the airport; and Alex will smile and wave and be friendly at the paparazzi that will inevitably be waiting. Neither of them will comment publicly, and there will be no official statement. If anyone asks Paul about it at work, and they will, he will behave as though this is part of their agreement and there is no relationship drama.

Alex has envied Liam's ability to keep secrets from the public for as long as he's had access to those secrets. As he contemplates his strategy for returning home — and for the coming weeks — Alex is horrified that this is the sort of secret he needs to hide with that same level of skill. It makes everything feel worse.

He emails Liam while Beth is at work and the house is empty. He's not used to having to convey this type of information in writing, and once again perhaps draws too strongly on his recent reading material, in the hopes that something of Victor can help him be clear in a way Liam will get.

Lee —

This email is about three things. None of them need a response from you.

1. Because Paul is terrible, Mark got a picture of him getting a blowjob from someone in his car and now it's on the internet. Yes, not me, and no, that's not in our rules.

2. Strategy is we're going to pretend it is in the rules so maybe the media drama will go away faster. Thank God it was his dick and not mine. But when that happens, which it will as soon as I land at LAX on Monday, the internet is going to go back to wondering about you and me. Be aware.

3. I'm still reading Victor's diaries. A lot of them are about you. I feel weird about that, and I'll stop if you want. But Victor puzzling through how to be with you may have just saved my marriage, which is fucked up and I'll explain if you want me to, so I wanted to say thank you, and I'm sorry I'm always such an asshole about him, even though I am not taking back the part where he was a jerk to me a lot. I'm glad you got his wisdom and his affection; it seems like it was a good thing to have.

Please surface soon. I'll be angry if New York becomes the only way I can see you.

Alex stares at the message for a long time. He hopes it's clear enough for Liam to digest right now and not insulting for it.

He also has no idea how to sign it.

Love seems like a disaster waiting to happen. The situation with Paul makes Alex superstitious, and saying something like that to Liam without clarifying it is either perfectly fine or the worst idea in the world.

Alex sighs and decides this isn't the time for gambling. He signs his name with nothing more than a dash and hits send. From there there's nothing to do but wait, and hope that everyone he has ever known, but right now most especially Beth — and her coworkers — goes nowhere near the internet. He's glad she and Sarah don't ever really go after celebrity gossip online or elsewhere. He feels guilty for not planning to bring it up with them, but *your son cheated on me* is too terrible a thing to say when he's standing under their roof.

After he emails Liam, he calls Margaret to discuss the situation and what the fuck they're going to do about it. After Margaret is Gemma, not because Alex particularly wants to talk to her, but because calling her is much preferable to waiting for her to call him, and she will.

"Are you okay?" she asks.

"I have no idea," he says. "But I'm managing."

"I'm sorry, the internet is terrible."

"Gemma, I seriously don't want to know."

"I'll leave it to your imagination then."

"Oh God, don't do that!" Alex gives a despairing sort of laugh.

"Do you want to do lunch?" she offers, more softly than she's spoken to him in a while.

"Yeah, but in a couple weeks," he says. He has so much more to do before he can brace for that.

20

Alex drives back to the airport on a clear, blindingly bright day. He fumbles his sunglasses on one-handedly as he pulls onto the highway and away from the peace of Marion in the face of Paul's poor choices.

He spends the flight with his headphones on but not listening to music. He reads one of Paul's intro-to-film textbooks he'd grabbed from the shelf in his old bedroom. Reading the diaries in public is entirely out of the question. Given the current circumstances he doesn't want to go anywhere near the internet.

Once they land Alex, waits until everyone else has gotten off the plane then tugs the hat lower on his head, not that it's going to help him. The waiting might, however, marginally shorten the time he has to spend at baggage claim.

The strategy is sound — there are paparazzi crowded just outside the door by the carousel taking pictures and shouting obnoxious questions at him almost as soon as he gets there. Being LAX, even with his own late arrival, it takes more than a few minutes for his bag to surface.

Finally, the suitcase tumbles down the chute. Alex snags it as quick as he can. He flashes a brilliant smile at them all as he strides out the door. He pauses for effect before letting himself slide into the accent of his childhood to ask, "Haven't you boys ever heard of the zip code rule?"

♦

Alex lets himself into the house. Before he has time to even lock the door, Paul appears from the living room to stand awkwardly in the foyer, hands in his pockets.

"Hi," Paul says.

"You look like shit."

Paul chuckles weakly and looks at his feet.

Alex drops his bags by the door and goes to stand in front of him. When Paul finally brings his head up, Alex kisses him dryly. "Come talk."

Paul nods, looking scared and grateful and lost. When Alex leads the way down the hall, he follows.

"Can I say I'm sorry now?" Paul hovers uncertainly by the kitchen island while Alex opens cupboards.

Alex puts a pan down on the island and smiles tightly at Paul. They've had to deal with more crises in the near-decade they've been together than Alex cares to think about.

"Apology accepted. But it would be more useful if you told me exactly what set this off. You don't do this, not like this. At least, I don't think you do. Do you?"

Paul shakes his head. "No. I don't know what it was." He slides gingerly onto one of the island stools.

Alex gives him an unimpressed look. "Bullshit. You may be a jerk, but you're a self-aware jerk. What was it?"

Paul shrugs helplessly.

"Paul." Alex says patiently.

"You know I don't do well when we're not together. And then it was a bad day. Just, ordinary shit.

Network notes and crap like that. I forgot Victor's dead."

When Paul tells him about trying to call Victor, Alex pauses with his hand on the handle of the refrigerator. "What is it with you and ghosts?" he asks.

"What are you doing?" he asks instead of answering the question.

"I'm starving and I don't think you've eaten today." Alex turned the stove on, all brisk efficiency, because one way or another, they have to get to the end of this conversation, and he has no desire to drag it out. "Now tell me why you went to the party."

◆

Getting grilled like this is intensely uncomfortable for Paul. His discomfort increases when Alex gets the chili simmering on the stove and pulls up the barstool next to him. Paul has to stop himself from physically squirming when Alex turns the unrelenting gaze on him that he usually reserves for the camera.

The discomfort of it scratches whatever self-destructive itch that got Paul into this mess in the first place. It's pain, yes, but in Alex's careful hands it makes things better for him — and them. He's grateful.

Paul recounts the story, all the way through Mark tapping on the window, his awkward extrication from Eric, and the miserable drive home he barely remembers.

"Okay," Alex says. "We need to talk about fluid risk. And you need to tell me exactly what you did, and if it was just you getting your dick sucked because you were drunk and horny and have terrible judgment."

"I already told you it was," Paul says.

"Yes, on the phone. To be fair, if the situation were reversed, honesty might not have been my first choice." Alex clearly thinks the worst of him.

Paul looks at him for too long.

"Whatever you tell me right now is the final version of the story," Alex says slowly. "I will not hound you about this. So if there's something I need to know about for our safety or our relationship, this is your moment."

Paul nods, more to acknowledge having heard Alex than anything else. When he dips his head in affirmation the second time, it doesn't come back up.

Alex takes in a sharp breath.

He doesn't look at Alex as he speaks. "I went down on him and then he sucked me off."

There's an awful silence. Paul lifts his head only to see Alex draw himself up on the stool, his spine straight and his shoulders back. It's a small movement physically, but it feels like Alex has gone somewhere miles away.

◆

All Alex can hear is Paul's breathing. He feels like his own lungs have forgotten how to work.

"Are we getting divorced?" Paul finally asks. His voice is small and quiet in a way Alex has never heard before and never wants to again.

"*No*," Alex says fiercely. And then again, "No."

Paul closes his eyes in relief.

"You are going to get tested though," Alex says, his voice distant in his own ear. Logistics are easier than how much bigger this wound feels than he expected when he was in South Carolina and just wanted to be sure Paul was all right.

Paul nods.

"Once now. Once in three months," Alex adds.

"What about the baby thing?" Paul's voice is still too small but at least there's breath behind it now.

Alex can't quite believe the segue. If there was ever a moment to lay into Paul, this is certainly it. He takes a deep breath and continues to work the conversation like it's the side of a mountain. He needs to be calm and steady and full of acceptance for the path presented, no matter how strange.

"We both need a little time and space from this particular event," he says. "The baby topic is getting tabled for the next three months. No decisions until we get your test results back."

"You were never really on board with it anyway."

"Excuse me?" Alex has no idea why Paul thinks it's a good idea to pick a fight with him right now, but it's damn annoying. He's also not interested in giving Paul the shouting match he seemingly desires.

"I just feel like this has become really convenient for you," Paul says.

Alex blinks at him. "You cheated on me. You got *caught* cheating on me. I am not threatening to leave you; I am not even making you sleep on the couch; and now you're pissed at me because I think your terrible judgment about cheating on me and lying about it is a good reason for us to reconsider kids?"

"You said you weren't going to punish me for this, and now you're punishing me for this."

"You do not want to find out what punishment from me looks like." Alex stands up, fully aware that he's channeling Victor and not giving a remote shit. "Right now I can't trust you with my life. Therefore, I'm not trusting you with a baby's."

♦

Alex ignores most of the notifications on his phone. He does the missed call from his mother after Paul retreats downstairs to his office for a couple of hours' work after they manage to eat dinner.

She makes small talk, but it's stilted. Alex's resolve to only answer questions he's asked eventually waivers. "Are you calling because of Paul?"

"I wanted to hear from you what's going on," she says.

Alex knows that means she's read every piece of gossip she can get her hands on. With dread he considers how everyone in his hometown will treat this drama; promiscuous gay Hollywood boys who deserve whatever end is coming for them, no doubt.

He hasn't been back to Indiana since he left. He has also never had any intention of letting his small town follow him here, especially not now. But trauma is often a monster with its own mind.

"We're fine," he tells his mother. If they aren't now, they will be. "But we've changed some of our plans."

Alex hadn't told his mother about the would-be baby yet. He wanted everything to be sure. Now that their plans are in turmoil though, he needs her support. The relief of talking about the whole fucking mess with someone who is not Paul is massive. But while Alex finds it soothing to speak his wariness out loud, the possible consequences of Paul's actions feel all the more awful for it.

His mom surprised. Alex understands that it's a lot to take in, especially under the circumstances, and her support is appreciated. But Alex wishes she weren't so startled at the idea of him having a kid. Alex tries not to feel guilty as they finally get off the phone.

Then he calls Sarah. That conversation is much harder, only in part because he only left her family's house that morning. Somehow, Sarah and Beth haven't seen the news yet. It's a small and terrible thing to be grateful.

He lays out the whole story for her and asks Sarah not to call Paul to yell at him. "If you're willing to tell your mom, I won't say no, but out of respect for her and your family I will call her myself. Just not tonight."

"What am I telling Mom, other than the obvious?" Sarah's measured reaction in the face of crisis reminds Alex of just how small this particular drama may be to her. God knows how many crises she's dealt with over the years, between Paul and their father and her own marriage and child, to sound this calm.

Alex explains how they're not going to make any decisions one way or the other until the three months are up.

"You get to back out too," he says at the end.

♦

When Alex pushes open the door to their room, Paul is already in bed, sitting up with glasses on and his tablet propped on his knees. He immediately sets the tablet aside and sits up straighter while Alex walks around to his own side of the bed.

Alex doesn't say anything right away. "How's your mom?" Paul asks. He's in contact with his own family far more frequently than Alex is, especially recently given the baby situation. Alex might talk to his mom once a month but whenever he does, the conversations can last hours. Paul never knows what to make of that, but it works for them.

"She's fine."

"How's Sarah?" Paul's far more worried about that.

"She's okay."

"What did she say about the baby?"

"Paul. We didn't have that conversation yet. She needs time to think no matter what."

Paul nods miserably. "How was South Carolina?"

Alex bites his lip. "I like it there. Sometimes I wish it were closer, but then it would mean something different. To both of us."

"I notice you resisted the urge to antagonize the internet with guns again," Paul notes.

Alex gets up and starts shedding clothes.

Paul's grateful that Alex isn't making him sleep on the couch, but he also has no idea what degree of intimacy he can look forward to in light of the situation. The lack of a real kiss upon his arrival home made Paul nervous — and clearly sex is not going to happen tonight — but Alex stripping down to his briefs is at least a positive sign.

"There wasn't anyone to take a picture," Alex says.

"You do the selfie thing at the range all the time."

Alex looks at Paul over his bare shoulder, the one with the faint scar from his terrible fall. "I was trying to find a nice way of saying 'I was too pissed to feel good about picking up a gun.'"

"Oh."

"Yeah." Alex tosses his clothes in the direction of the hamper and crawls into bed.

Paul rolls onto his side to face him. "How are you?" Paul asks, when the silence stretches.

"I'm glad to be home, and I'm pissed off I came home to this. I don't know what our future looks like, and I'm furious at Victor for dying and leaving us this mess."

"This isn't Victor's fault," Paul protests, though Alex venting at a dead man instead of anyone alive is useful.

"I am in this bed with you right now because of Victor. In a lot of different ways. If I have to deal with the consequences of that, he can at least take some of the blame."

"What do we do now?" Paul asks.

Alex tucks his arm under the pillow and stares at him. "I look at you and try to imagine you with someone else. And then I try to stop, because that's a very bad idea too."

Paul tries to interrupt.

It's not jealousy," Alex says, "I just don't get it."

"I've been with other people," Paul points out carefully, because historically discussions of their respective dating history — specifically, his reaction to Alex's — have not been constructive. "We've been with other people. Together."

"I know. But even when you were with Craig — and I guess I was with Liam when you and I were a fucking hot mess — me being with you was the only thing that made sense in my head."

"What does that mean for us right now?" Paul asks.

Alex doesn't answer. He puts out a hand and traces Paul's shoulder through his t-shirt, the line of his collarbone down to his chest. He's concentrating hard, like he's trying to memorize Paul. The touch seems good but the look on his face is a little terrifying.

"Alex," Paul says softly.

Alex drags his eyes up to his face and blinks at him, like he's coming back from somewhere far away.

"Where did you go?"

"Nowhere relevant."

21

Alex is surprised and relieved when Liam calls a week later. Liam explains that replying via email would be easier. Words are still hard, and Alex writing that intimately about Paul and about Victor is a lot for him to process. Ultimately, though, Liam wants to be able to call, so he did. Alex is touched and a little awed by the amount of effort Liam is putting into a reply he didn't have to make.

They don't talk for very long, and there are a lot of pauses in what they do say, but Liam is wise about fuck ups and forgiveness and the terrible decisions people in pain make. Alex knew of this, of course, but hearing it from Liam settles and reassures him.

"New York's been good for me." Liam admits. "I don't have to concentrate as hard, and it's left room for everything else."

Grief, Alex thinks he means. "I'm sorry I dragged you into my mess," he says. He didn't have to burden Liam with any of this.

Liam makes a sound that Alex thinks would be a laugh, if the last three months hadn't been so awful. "It's fine. You did what you needed to do, and that's all you gotta do. And go easy on Paul. He's a little broken, and he missed you."

"I can't even imagine him with anyone else."

"Well, lots of things happen in life you can't imagine."

Alex doesn't know how to respond to that. "When are you coming home?" he asks after a long pause. Maybe that's a dangerous question; he's not sure. Liam has always brought out a mess of conflicting emotions in him.

"Not soon, but...soon after soon?"

"Liam. Other-people timeframes, please."

Liam huffs. "Fine. A few months. Maybe more. I don't know yet. But I'm thinking about it, and that's new."

"I miss you," Alex says.

"I know."

"I should let you go." Alex wonders if he means right now or for always as he says it.

"Okay," Liam says, but doesn't hang up.

"Can I call you later?" Alex asks.

"Totally," Liam says. "Also, hey, thing."

"Yeah?"

"I love you."

Alex actually bangs his head down on the table, even though it doesn't sound like Liam is saying it with any particular intent. He wonders if this is Liam responding to the way Alex didn't say it in his email.

"Lee!" he moans.

"Don't be dumb. Why is everyone so obsessed with words?"

"I don't even know where to start with you! Fine! I. Love. You. Too. Words don't matter, and now I'm hanging up on you."

"Bye!" Liam says, almost brightly, before the line clicks off.

Alex stares at the phone in his hand as it goes black, and doesn't know whether to scream or

be grateful for all the relationships in his life that make no sense.

◆

Olivia doesn't comment on or ask any questions about the debacle that is Paul's personal life — at least not verbally. She does give Paul a long, unimpressed look over the top of her laptop the next time he wanders into the writers' room late one night in August before shoving a draft for the next episode at him. Paul finds himself oddly grateful. Victor, certainly, would have had his own opinions and he mostly tries to think about how, if Victor were still alive, Paul wouldn't want to put up with hearing them.

Now that they're into the final months of *Winsome* he needs to start worrying about what comes next. Which is how Paul ends up in his office too late one night, with Olivia in the chair on the other side of the desk, both of them staring at the whiteboard on the wall and praying for inspiration for whatever their new project is going to be.

"You know, finishing the script for the next ep might actually be easier than this," Olivia says when an hour of talking around in circles yields absolutely nothing.

"Please don't say that," Paul laughs.

"I still say the idea of the blended family with all the kids has legs for our next project."

"No. Absolutely not. We're not doing a Brady Bunch reboot."

"But what if the family was like, multiracial, and doing gay quad or poly parenting or whatever?"

"Still too much like a sitcom," Paul chuckles. "If you want to do it, have at, and I will support you, but not my thing."

Olivia twirls a pen across her fingers. "You say that, but have you actually looked at your life lately?

22

Carly is unsurprised when she gets a call from Paul in the middle of August inviting her and Ali to join him and Alex for lunch. At least he's waited a suitable period of time in which, presumably, he and Alex have gotten their shit together as well as they're going to for now. Carly's also glad for an afternoon of adult conversation and more sets of eyes to watch out for Ali.

Todd, curled up in the sunlight coming in the slider door to the deck, flees when Ali tries to pet him. He's suffered more than one pulled tail at her eager and careless hands, and Carly entirely cannot blame him. Sometimes she wishes she could deal with her daughter's excess energies the same way.

After lunch, Alex offers to take Ali to the neighborhood playground. Carly's pleased and grateful that now he's had a chance to catch up with Liam, he's giving her and Paul the opportunity to do the same.

"I won't get her dirty," he promises while she gets her shoes on.

Carly snorts. "One, I don't care. Two, you do not have anything to worry about there. Good luck trying to get her in the sandbox."

"The sand is gross. It *touches* me," Ali says, aghast.

"Then we'll try the swings. Come on, you." Alex ushers her outside.

Carly turns around from closing the door to see Paul staring at it mournfully.

"Yes, he'll make a wonderful father," Carly deadpans as she lowers herself into a chair. She kicks off her shoes so she can rub her ankles. Pregnancy seriously sucks, and if nothing else. she is very glad this particular ordeal will soon be over.

"Yeah, about that," Paul says tightly.

He deals with the lunch dishes while he lays out his and Alex's plan. The first test came back negative, but there's still another test — which will also likely be negative — and a lot of uncertainty to get through.

"Alex is good for you," Carly says when he's finished, and it's almost, but not quite, a non-sequitur.

"How's Liam?" Paul asks. "Alex said he talked to him."

"Liam is still in New York," Carly says with a viciousness now that Ali isn't around. She's talking about much more than obvious geographical location.

"And?" Paul prompts, glancing over his shoulder at her as he puts the clean dishes away.

"And he says he's thinking about coming back, but the baby's due in ten weeks and he is apparently not. I keep wondering if things would be easier if he just stayed there. I can't take care of three people, Paul. Not when one of them is my husband. Not by myself."

"He'll be better when he comes back," Paul says cautiously.

"Well, what if he isn't? Or doesn't. So he's talking on the phone with Alex. Great. How the hell is he going to deal with a newborn?" She's glad she doesn't have to hide her anger from Paul. They've been close for too long and he knows her too well to have any need to put on a front.

"What are you going to do?" Paul asks. "I mean, you always have a plan."

"I don't know. I don't know if I can stay with him. This sucks now, but if it doesn't get better, that's not fair to anyone. Especially me."

"Does Liam know?"

"I think he's scared of it. I assume he's asking himself similar questions. But we haven't talked about it. The stress would only make everything worse."

"I don't know what to say."

Carly sighs. She knows this whole mess makes her look heartless. "Look, Liam can't entirely live alone. Which means whoever lives with him is, whatever else they are, his caretaker."

"Wait… what the fuck was he doing before you?"

"Victor. Various other relationships. His 'team,'" she says with vicious air quotes. "He's very clever. His family is very clever." She shrugs. "To be fair, I did know all this going in, but the thing that sucks about love is the same thing that sucks about being with someone who isn't normal or healthy or whatever we're calling it."

"Which is?" Paul prompts.

"I don't get super powers just because he's fucked up."

"Alex apparently gets super powers because I'm fucked up," Paul offers more cheerfully than is really helpful.

"Yeah, I'm still bitter about that."

♦

Ali chatters on the entire walk to the playground. Her talkativeness is how she takes after Liam the most, aside from the wild dark curls, but even those she likes to keep tamed with sparkly purple hair ties.

She's also as fascinated with fantastical stories as Liam is, so long as they involve shiny things and princesses and attention from adoring crowds. Alex is fairly sure she doesn't get that trait from Liam, that it's Ali being a five-year-old kid, but he finds it hilarious nonetheless.

When they get to the playground, he offers to take her on an adventure.

"Where to?" She folds her arms and looks up at Alex with all the seriousness she can muster.

"Wherever you want, it's your story."

"Are there dragons? And a princess?"

"There can *totally* be dragons and a princess. There can even be a dragon princess if you want."

Ali side-eyes him. "Just a normal princess, thank you."

They set off. They have to climb the mountains of the jungle gym, and ford the mighty river that is the puddle left by the sprinklers. Alex tells her that the heavy ever-present smell of smoke from the wildfires have actually been set by the evil dragons, and Ali nods very seriously. Finally, they have to balance on magic light-beams to get to the castle.

It's the kind of play Alex did by himself, in the fields and woods of Indiana when he was a kid not much older than Ali. His games involved far fewer princesses and magic towers and more outlaws and violence but then, they grew up in a very different world.

He had started thinking about doing this with his and Paul's own baby, whenever it's old enough to walk and talk and follow a narrative. Only now he might not ever have a kid of his own. Alex is stunned that in such a short span of time he's gone from struggling to adjust to the idea of having kids, to struggling to adjust to the idea of maybe never having them.

He watches Ali with delight and also a strange sadness as she gets distracted by the game, asking questions and contradicting him proudly whenever the story takes a turn she doesn't like. She is absolutely not noticing how muddy her sneakers are getting or that her hands are dirty from climbing up and down the jungle gym.

Ali — and Carly and Liam's soon-to-be-born baby — may be the only children Alex ever really has. The terrible thing about Victor's death is the lesson that things don't stop going wrong once the worst happens.

He helps Ali up on the monkey bars and then is terrified when she hooks her legs in and hangs upside down. Carly and Liam will never forgive him if he breaks their kid. But when she seems steady enough, he digs out his phone to snap a picture of her grinning face and messy pigtails.

After a moment of deliberation, he sends it to Liam. *This isn't to guilt you, but we totally wish you could be here.*

A minute later, he gets a text back. There's a picture of Liam attached, in the backyard at his parents' house. He's got his sunglasses on, and he's smiling. It feels like an image from another life, which is eerie but also comforting. *Me too!*

♦

Paul flops down next to Carly on the sofa and puts his feet up on the coffee table. She kicks him affectionately.

"You know you and I have the same shit going on as Alex and Liam, right?" he says.

"'Cept, without the creepy psychic part."

"A little bit with the creepy psychic part. We're more vocal so we hide it better."

Carly rolls her head against the back of the couch and turns to look at Paul. "Yeah, so where is this going?" she asks.

"So you know the thing where Alex and I are kind of like Ali's other dads?"

"With an emphasis on 'kind of,'" Carly says, eyebrows raised.

"What if we made it more like actual other dads. Like, kids are difficult and exhausting, everyone has those friends who offer to help who are really enthusiastic until the kid barfs all over their guest room or whatever, right?"

"Riiiiiight," Carly says slowly, watching what's clearly going to be a train wreck of a conversation unfold with great curiosity.

"So then you feel guilty asking, and it's not really help because it's help that's about borrowing a kid not actually fucking helping or having any real skin in the game, right?"

"Also right."

"Well, you don't need that type of help."

"Why does this feel like more of your bad crazy?" Carly says warily.

"The four of us are practically family anyway. Why don't we use that to make all of our lives easier?"

"Paul, whatever you're working up to, spit it out."

"You've got Ali and a baby on the way. If I'm lucky, Alex and I are going to have a kid too. What if we raised our kids like siblings with traveling homes? I mean, if we help parent your kids, you'd help with ours. Why can't each of us handle three kids on the good nights? Alex would get to feel like he had a support network and a backup system that wasn't only me and our families in their shitty small towns. You'd get help with the kids and support whether Liam's here or not. Liam would get some space when he needs it. It might keep me from turning into the asshole Alex hates when I'm given responsibility. And all of us would still maybe get to have adult lives."

Carly blinks at him slowly.

"What?" he asks. "What are you thinking?"

"That you make some valid points," Carly says. "Which you haven't discussed with Alex, are contingent upon me not leaving my husband, may not work, and are arguably you trying to con your husband into having children. Also polyamory. Kind of. Without sex. Which, fine, but just wanted to point that out." This is certainly not the train wreck she was expecting, but that doesn't mean it's not a disaster waiting to happen.

"But other than that it sounds perfect, right?"

Carly leans down to the end of the couch, grabs an accent pillow and smacks him in the face with it.

♦

"Children. Are. Exhausting," Alex says, as he pulls off his shirt that night in their room.

Paul chuckles.

"I'm serious," Alex says. "They run fast, and they're short so you have to keep bending over to tell them things or pick them up. I ache in the weirdest places."

"You're getting old," Paul teases with a level of absolute glee that Alex finds charming.

"I'm not even thirty yet."

"The Tragic Life of J. Alex Cook."

"Ugh, don't even," Alex says, as he takes off the rest of his clothes and climbs into bed.

Paul closes the screen on his laptop halfway and asks if they're sleeping, fucking, or talking.

"I don't know," Alex half moans. "But get your computer out of this bed and turn off the light."

The second they settle into each other and the dark, Paul says, "Carly is thinking of leaving Liam."

Alex doesn't sit up and slap his hands against Paul's chest in outrage, demanding answers, which is a testament to how unsurprising this is. He goes very, very still instead.

"Do you think she will?" he asks.

Paul shakes his head. "I don't know. I don't think so. I don't think it's unreasonable for her to fantasize about a normal life sometimes though."

Alex blinks in the dark. "That's a shitty thing to say."

"Not Liam, just *everything*. They're not even thirty-five and she's helping Liam grieve a partner. She's pregnant as fuck, Hollywood's horrid, and look, I didn't spend the day with Ali but — "

"She talked about dragons."

"What?"

"You were going to say something about paparazzi or *People* or her *look*. She's five. She talked non-stop, and it was mostly about dragons. She's about as normal as I think five gets when everyone isn't expecting her to be the littlest diva on the lot."

Paul smiles. "You had fun. After totally being freaked out by her for *years*."

"We both have lives that don't make a lot of sense to other people. I mean, she still freaks me out, but Victor adored her and not merely because she's Liam and Carly's kid. She's trying to get through life and actually doing it really well all things considered. I sent Liam ill-advised pictures of her hanging upside down," he adds.

"I talked to Carly about her plans for after the baby's born."

"You did what?" This time Alex does try to sit up, but Paul pulls him back down.

"Shhhh," Paul says, "Listen to me for a second. Everyone offers to help, and then doesn't when the going gets hard. Right now, the only thing Carly and Liam have had for a while is hard, and long-term they need a better support system than friends who are willing to babysit once in a while."

Alex thunks his head against Paul's shoulder. Repeatedly.

"What's that for?"

"Wherever this is going, surely," Alex says.

"Look, whether we have a baby of our own or not, we have the resources to help them out. If we do have a kid, what's an extra baby or two on nights that are kid-focused anyway?"

Alex doesn't know where to begin. "I'm pretty sure kids are exponential in terms of headaches," he says. "I'm also pretty sure you just suggested we all mutually timeshare the collective children, of which ours may not actually exist because you are a delusional fuckmuppet."

"Kind of?" Paul says.

"Did Carly yell at you, or do I need to?"

"Carly hit me in the face with a pillow," Paul says blandly.

"And then she said what, that made you suggest we should all be one big happy platonic family in response? And by the way, you did this without consulting me, Liam, Ali, a baby that hasn't been born yet and a baby who may very well never be born." Alex sighs. "Jesus. I wanted you to turn the lights out so we could relax, not do freaky confession time."

"I'm sorry?" Paul offers.

"New rule," Alex says. "When Carly shoots down one of your terrible ideas, you don't have to tell me about it."

"It's not terrible," Paul says, and Alex is surprised at the clarity and confidence in his voice. "Our lives are hard. Babies are hard. We all trust each other a lot, and our lives are all fucked up and intertwined anyway. Why can't we share some of the responsibilities so we can all maintain some semblance of individual adult life?"

Alex squirms far enough away, though Paul keeps an arm draped over his waist, to roll onto his side. He studies Paul's face until his eyes adjust enough to the dark that he can see Paul searching his in return as well.

"We took the baby off the table for discussion for three months, Paul. The time's not even close to being up yet, and while I appreciate that you're trying to figure out how to do life in a way that works for everyone, this kind of feels like manipulation more than an actual solution."

"Hey, hey, no — "

"I'm not saying it's a bad idea, even though it is inexplicable. But it's a *lot*, and it hinges on a lot of variables that we don't have the answers to or control over. What if you're positive? What if Liam never comes back to L.A.?"

"Then we come up with a different plan," Paul says. "But why can't this be a start? At least to talk about?"

"Because it's crazy."

"Our lives are crazy."

"*Yes*, but," Alex says, and then gives a despairing sort of chuckle.

"But?" Paul presses gently.

"Explain to me why this isn't you having problems with boundaries and control."

"Because it makes sense?"

Alex does manage to roll out of Paul's arms then and onto his back. He laughs when Paul inevitably reaches out for him. "Don't touch me."

Paul pulls his hand back cautiously. Alex is fascinated by the gesture. It's not cowed, merely deeply wary.

There's a silence that draws on almost too long until Alex exclaims, "Fuck!" and starts laughing again as he presses his hands over his face. Then he kicks his heels against the mattress repeatedly. "Fuck fuck fuck."

Paul makes a careful interrogative sound.

"How do you actually make things worse when you make sense?" Alex asks, peering at Paul from between his fingers.

"Because normal is overrated," Paul grins.

"Oh shut the fuck up and come here."

"You just said — "

"Come *here*," Alex says reaching for Paul, who takes his hands cautiously.

Alex practically yanks him down into a kiss, and after all the hard conversations of the day it still feels strained, but it's also funny.

♦

For a while they make out and Paul assumes that's all they're going to do. What sex they've had since Alex got home has been limited in creativity and variety, but Alex's anxiety around intercourse given Paul's transgressions is understandable. Paul is just grateful he gets to touch him at all.

Eventually, Alex pulls back and blinks up at Paul from the pillows. "Do we even have condoms in the house?"

"There's sex we can have without needing those," Paul points out.

Alex rolls his eyes. "I've missed this, I want you, and I am not letting your bad choices fuck us up even more. Yes or no, Paul."

"I don't actually know?"

"Oh my God," Alex rolls his eyes and shoves at Paul's chest. "Everything in our lives is aggravating. Would you go *look*?"

Paul crawls off the bed and heads for their bathroom muttering under his breath. Alex cackles.

They do in fact have condoms, for which Paul is immensely grateful. By the time Alex gets him on his knees and starts pressing into him everything else in their too-hard, too-complex, involving too-many-other-people lives disappears. Whatever their lives are going to look like, in three months or a year or ten years from now, at least they'll be together.

23

Liam looks good when he picks up for his and Carly's regularly scheduled Skype call one evening at the end of August. He's been gone almost two months now. New York City has been good for him, and she tries not to resent that too much. Their lives work by the grace of all the systems they've perfected. It is simply a reality of their current situation that their systems, both individually and as a couple, demand adjusting.

"How was your weekend?" Liam asks her, curious and warm. He's got the laptop propped on his chest, and she can see the headboard behind him. The first night she spent with him there, not long after she learned the last of his secrets, they stayed up all night talking until long after the glow-in-the-dark stars faded again.

"Ali and I went over to Paul and Alex's for lunch yesterday."

"I know, Alex sent me a picture. Ali looks amazing."

"She's doing really well," Carly says. There are, after all, so many reasons why she shouldn't be, with her father gone and her mother about to have another child. "I'm not sure if she gets the resiliency from me or you," she adds. It's an easy, if cruel, opening.

Liam laughs ruefully and shakes his head. "You I think."

"I don't have to be resilient every day though. You do. And she does, right now."

Liam doesn't say anything for a long time. Which is fine. Not only has Carly gotten used to that in the current and ongoing crisis, the thing she misses about him most is being able to sit quietly while he pores over a script and she reads a book. The silence, when it's domestic and not frightened, is welcome. Right now, it's somewhere in between.

"Can you have this conversation now?" Carly eventually asks when Liam's hands, barely in the frame, turn fidgety.

"The one we're having?" he asks, but it's not guileless or unaware.

She shakes her head. "The one about us," she says instead.

He tips his head at her for her to continue, a gesture he always uses, even when he's glib and facile. It's sweet, decorous deference, and it makes her feel like she doesn't deserve him.

"You know I love you," she says.

"Love you too," he says, like the simple matter of habit and fact that it is. Carly smiles sadly.

"We have a baby coming. And we need to make some decisions about what our family is going to look like once that happens. Are you coming back here? Are you staying there?" Carly takes a breath, because she's rehearsed this line but saying it still feels impossible. "And what do our lives look like if our relationship becomes something more secondary?"

"Those questions are massive," Liam says.

"I know. But we need to talk about them, instead of being scared of the things we're not talking about."

"Mostly," Liam says, because words are not automatic for him right now. He's explained to Carly before how sometimes he has to remember that he is supposed to speak, understand what sort of thing he is supposed to say, find phrases that work, and then add to those.

Carly rests her chin in her hand and stares at him for a while. Then she just asks it. "Do you think you'll be able to get back to where you were?"

Liam shakes his head, but it's the slow one, that doesn't mean *no*, but that he's thinking about the question. He starts and stops his response three times before he can find a way for it to make sense.

"Charles was here for dinner last night, and I told him this story about Victor and it was...well, it was terrible. I did it, though. This is still going to be the worst year, but I was okay."

"That sounds good," Carly says carefully.

"It is. New York is good for me. You could come here," he says, too brightly, and Carly's stomach sinks. "I'd have more help. So would you."

"We're not leaving California," Carly says, only marginally shocked that she feels so strongly about it.

"Why?"

"Because our life is here," she says. "My friends and my lovers and my job and all of my support systems are here. I give up so much for you. Not for my job or this city, just you. Acting and fame and the hours, and you can't. You just can't. I lost someone too. He was a brother to me, and I have had no time to do anything but feel terror because he is dead."

"Can we name the baby after him?" Liam says.

Carly starts crying. "Look," she says, wiping her eyes while Liam stares at the screen, his expression heartbroken. "Victor was a massive part of our support group, and he was such a force for good in Ali's life."

"In all of our lives," Liam says.

"And I was talking to Paul today about his and Alex's plans for kids, and what our situation with Ali and the baby looks like."

"But we don't know what our situation with the kids looks like," Liam says. "Like that's what this is about." He waves a hand to encompass, Carly thinks, this whole not-quite-argument.

"I know. That's what we were talking about. And he kept coming back to this idea that is totally dubious but that is an option I think we want on the table, while you decide whether you can handle coming home."

"What is it?" Liam asks.

Carly sniffles and brushes back her hair. "He and Alex are kind of a mess, did you know?"

Liam snorts, and, to Carly's relief, smiles. "I talked to Alex."

"Well, they're looking for child support systems too. Or at least Paul is, to try to convince Alex to have kids with him. And what he suggested was the four of us raising whatever kids we all have together. Not just trading off the babysitting but like, surrogate siblings."

"Wow," Liam says.

"Good wow or bad wow?"

"A lot to process. Like that could be really good, but there are a lot of red flags."

"This isn't about being sexual partners with them," Carly adds. In their lives that's a completely reasonable thing to need to clarify. Also she knows what kind of relationship Liam and Alex would have were Alex and Paul not monogamous. "And they bring their own issues to the table. But having other adults around Ali and the baby would be good for them and for us."

Liam nods, slowly. "That's a good option," he says, and even sounds excited about it. "Until things go wrong."

Carly nods to encourage him.

"Well, one, Paul's kind of nuts, and I think he's manipulating Alex with all of this baby stuff, and I love them but their dysfunction is intense, and I don't know if I want to get that involved in it. Two, I don't understand why this is on the table at all? I'm happy that it is, but I want to talk more about it and who gets to make decisions about what, and how you all can't leave me out just because of how I am. Three," Liam says, and sighs, "We don't even know what's going on with us yet. It's not fair to make deals with anybody else until we know what ours is. Like, I want to say *yes* but the list of reasons to say *no* or even *I don't know* is really kind of long right now."

Carly wishes Liam were not on the other side of the continent. She very much wants to reach through the screen and touch his hand, or curl up with him on his old bed in the room under the glow-in-the-dark stars.

"So with that on the table. Can you tell me what you need to come home?"

"Or if I'm not."

She nods. "We will always be together Liam, but right now I need to know how. I am providing you with as many options as I can. But I need some feedback from you."

Liam nods. "I can't," he starts, but then corrects himself. "I'll need some time, to make some lists." His voice is almost a question.

Carly's heart clenches with the mix of hope and fear she feels. "I'll be here whenever you do."

◆

Paul and Alex's schedules have rarely overlapped so that they have to get ready in the morning at the same time, but Alex starts to make an effort to get up when Paul does. Seeing each other before everything that fills their days is pleasant and their relationship need all the pleasant they can get these days.

This morning, like most mornings, neither of them are fully awake as they move around each other in the bathroom after indulging in a joint shower.

Alex frowns and rubs the mirror with his fist to clear off the fog. "Okay, plan." He meets Paul's eyes in the mirror.

"Yeah?" Paul says with trepidation. He's not sure what, aside from baby and testing, Alex has been turning over in his head.

"The internet is continuing its field day with you and your terrible choices and its own fantasies about me and Liam. If we are going to consider your ridiculous co-parenting idea with Liam and Carly — and I am *not* agreeing to anything right now — we are damn well going to remind the world that we are actually a couple, that we are not breaking up, and that I am actually very happy with you. Also, that I am not pining over Liam because he's vanished from L.A."

"You are pining over Liam."

Alex rolls his eyes. "Paul." Paul knows he isn't wrong, but Alex apparently doesn't want to poke that particular wound right now.

"Sorry."

"So for the next little while, you and I are going to be as publicly adorable as we possibly can. Date nights out, holding hands in the park, whatever cute stuff you want to do on any carpet that comes our way."

"Okay," Paul says cautiously. It's been a long time since Alex has been skittish about being seen together in public, but the attention still annoys him, and he usually keeps a reasonable degree of distance between them whenever they're at events. Paul has learned to live with it — mostly because he doesn't really have a choice — but it's not his ideal and Alex knows it. "Is this a gift or a punishment? Because it's kind of feeling like both."

"Neither. It's just a thing that needs to happen," Alex says. "If it were a punishment, you'd know."

That Alex is being so clinical about it doesn't actually make Paul feel better.

◆

As the summer winds down Alex goes about being publicly cute with Paul with as much determination and grace as he pursues anything else in his strange life. He even consents to go to brunch, though that's less about the opportunity for photos and more so he can lean into Paul's side and snark back at Brian when he's an asshole about the cheating drama.

Paul is busy with the rapidly approaching end of *Winsome*, but whenever he has a free evening he and Alex go out for food or a hike. Sometimes they even go to the movies together. Paul's thirty-ninth birthday is the perfect opportunity to get caught at some hip place for dinner, even if he's kind of freaking out about being one year away from forty. Alex tries to be amused and not irritated with that particular concern.

For Alex it's the strangest sort of performance, doing the things they'd both do regularly if either of them ever had enough time. There's a lesson in here somewhere, he's sure. He just has no idea what it is yet.

Alex recruits Darcy to help in his *Mission: Public Cute* too.

"I know you read all those blinds." Alex tells her one day at work on *Winsome* while a shot is getting reset. "Put in one about us."

Darcy raises an eyebrow. "You and me? I thought the point of all this was to like, make you guys look good."

"No! Paul and me."

"That makes more sense," she concedes sadly.

Alex sighs. "Well?"

"Normally I have my people do it."

"Come on, you're like *on the pulse*, Darcy," he says, his tone mocking every shitty gossip website in existence. "Help me out here."

She considers that for a moment, then crosses her legs at the knee and clasps her hands over them. "Okay. What did you do?"

"I don't know. This is why I'm asking you."

"You can't just be cute. There has to be a scandal element!"

"Yeah, and Paul got his dick sucked in a car. No thank you."

"Like the time you two fucked in public!" Darcy says brightly, ignoring him.

"We did not!"

"You totally did. You could do that again!"

Alex rolls his eyes. "I would only go through that pain of that fallout again if I got to have the fun of it."

"So why don't you do that?" Darcy asks seriously.

Alex is saved from answering when they're called back for the shot.

◆

During one of what becomes their semi-weekly Skype calls, Alex offers to read Liam bits of Victor's diaries.

"Some of this you should read yourself, if you want. It shouldn't be in my voice," Alex says. "But seriously, the part where he's pissed at everyone because you and Natalie hooked up is *amazing*."

Paul comes home to the sound of both cracking up in the living room. Liam waves to him from the screen. And then offers them both tips if they want to get caught together in public more.

Sitting there, with his hand around Alex's waist, feels like exactly the life Paul wants. No less — and despite his previous inappropriate suggestions — no more. It's a strange unfamiliar sort of peace, especially when he now has to wait on everyone else, and only in part because of his own mistakes.

24

Paul and Olivia both look up from their laptops when Alex knocks on the doorframe of Paul's home office in the basement. Paul isn't sure how long Alex has been up; it's ten in the morning now, but he and Olivia have been at this since six. Printed pages are scattered across the floor, and the massive whiteboard that covers almost an entire wall is covered in scrawled notes in both of their handwritings.

"Sorry to interrupt. Hi, Olivia," Alex says, as Todd uncurls himself from a stack of papers on Paul's desk and jumps down to rub against his shins.

"Hey." She waves.

"Going climbing?" Paul asks.

"Yeah, I'll be back this afternoon. Brainstorming?" Alex asks, walking further into the room to examine the whiteboard and its scribbles.

"In a manner of speaking," Olivia says.

Paul chuckles when Alex leans forward to look at a line more closely and then frowns.

"Okay, this is a day I'm glad I just have to be in the damn films."

"It's harder than it looks!"

"Clearly." Alex laughs and is glad neither of them is offended. Alex leans down to pat Todd then kisses Paul briefly. "You two have fun revolutionizing the television medium. I'm going to go climb rocks."

"Be careful!" No matter how many times Alex has gone climbing in the intervening time, ever since he almost died Paul has a stab of fear every time Alex leaves.

"Always am." Alex disappears back upstairs.

Once he's gone, Olivia leans back in her chair with a sigh, regarding the whiteboard with an expression of doom. "We completely suck."

"We don't suck. We just haven't found the right idea yet," Paul protests. He's still slated to take a year off when *Winsome* is finished, which is going to be soon now, and his own imminent parental status is somewhat in limbo. But if he's going to keep making TV magic he and Olivia need at least a plan of what they're doing next, even if not a pitch.

"You wrote down *combat dolphins*," Olivia says.

"*Elite* combat dolphins. Drama, human interest, action."

"It's *Flipper* with a fucking AK-47. No."

"Also international geopolitics," Paul points out.

"Where the hell are you even going to hire *dolphins*? What do they get paid? What are the work rules? Also did you read that thing on the internet about how dolphins are *totally* rapists? This is not a good plan! Can you even get ones that know how to shoot?"

Paul looks at her like she's grown another head.

"If I don't ask these things, the network will!"

Paul hangs his head and laughs. "Victor would fire us for this shit."

"Victor would win Emmys for this shit."

"Fucking bastard."

"Yeah."

Paul flips a whiteboard marker between his fingers and regards the list of mostly-rejected ideas. Under *combat dolphins* is listed:

Demons?

Alaska - too many parkas

Barbershop dark comedy

Ski lodge but not horror ski lodge, next to which Olivia has scribbled *WTF?*

Paul's been at this point of development before with *Winsome* and the other pilot that was never shot, but he's never done it without Victor. Olivia is more than capable, and more and more Paul is coming to rely on her as his right hand, but there's always going to be the question of what could have been. Not just with *M.A.R.S.* — which is struggling regardless of the time Paul is still dedicating to it — but with all the other stories Victor had in him. Every unmade universe feels like a loss.

Paul's own work isn't going to be any different. He'll never be able to tell all of the stories he wants to. At best he, like Victor, will leave behind people with the talent and drive to keep going when he's no longer there.

◆

Alex does not go climbing.

Instead he goes to Victor's house. Why just read a script when you can visit the set?

Pulling into the driveway feels more natural than it once did, but he still needs to take a deep breath before he unlocks the door. Despite its magnetism, the house is still difficult for him. He'll stay away from the basement; he always does.

But for all of the time Alex has spent at Victor's house over the years — and in the last terrible weeks — he has never yet been upstairs. Once he's retrieved another stack of diaries, he tries several doors before he finally finds Victor's bedroom. Alex hovers in the entrance, staring. He knows, from reading so much of Victor's life in Victor's own handwriting, that Victor was actually human. But standing in his most intimate space still feels bizarre, as though Victor's been waiting all this time for him to show up.

In the bedroom, the stark modernism of the rest of the house is only slightly muted. An occasional accent of turquoise or cream interrupts the sea of gray and white. The bed is made neatly, and Alex is unable to avoid the image of Victor making it each morning, as if it that were something that mattered in his busy and expansive life.

There are built-in shelves bracketing the bed, that are less full than Alex might have expected given how crammed the bookcases are in the rest of the house. The things here are more lovely, however — small pieces of artwork, and books that aren't about the industry.

Alex is curious about the rest of the bedrooms, but the nape of his neck is prickling now and he wants to get out of the house while he's still ahead. He's careful to lock the door behind himself when he leaves, and then check the handle to make sure it's really locked.

◆

As unsettled as Alex is by the house, he can't stay away. The next time he's there is while Paul is at work thinking he went climbing again. It takes a few attempts before Alex can bring himself to open the bedroom door he can tell, just by looking through the crack, is Liam's. When he finally does, he has to lean against the wall to stay upright.

White walls, white bedding; it's all as described in the journals. There are human touches too, visible in a way they aren't in Victor's bedroom, that scream Liam: a battered paperback thriller on the nightstand, a t-shirt folded messily on a slat-backed chair in the corner, the door to the wardrobe cracked open in a manner Victor would never tolerate. What rocks Alex back the most, though, is that the bed is unmade.

He knows that bed hasn't been touched since Liam got out of it on the morning of the day Victor died. He also knows, as far as the diaries go, that Liam never spent a night in Victor's bed other than after the terrible day Liam filmed the material around the death of Alex's character, Zach, in *Fourth*.

Standing here, Alex can picture, with uncomfortable clarity, Victor sitting on the edge of this bed smoothing back Liam's hair. Liam nuzzles happily into a pillow until he decides he wants breakfast more than he wants to stay in his warm nest and be petted.

Alex remembers vividly his own last morning with Liam, in Liam's bedroom at his parents' house in New York. He wonders if it's a grace or an unkindness that they both knew it was a last morning, that they'd already said goodbye the night before to the possibility neither of them could fulfill, regardless of how much they wanted it. He wonders if Victor knew, when he bent to kiss Liam on the forehead before admonishing him about being late to the table.

♦

Paul, with Alex's blessing, talks to Sarah about their Very Tentative Plans for co-parenting their baby — assuming they have a baby — with Carly and Liam's kids.

Sarah, to Paul's devastation, is wary about the idea.

"I know this is not going to be my baby except genetically," Sarah says, "But I don't even know Carly and Liam."

"You know Carly," Paul points out.

"From *years* ago. I'm sure they're good people, but this is all really strange."

"Why? There was always a clan around when we were growing up."

"It's just different, Paul. Maybe it's not bad, but it's different. And then you, in the middle of this all — I don't know what you've told Alex and really I don't care, but I spent a summer visiting you after you landed yourself in the psych ward. I know the places you go when things get really bad for you. With everything that's happened the last six months, I don't know if you can handle a child. And I don't know if I can help you bring one into the world if I can't be sure what kind of life it's going to have."

♦

Darcy meets Alex at his shared trailer once he's wrapped for the day. She's bouncing up and down on the balls of her feet, and Alex greets her warily.

"Hi! Your blind is up," Darcy waves her phone at him. "Wanna see?"

Alex laughs. "Sure." Whatever crazy scandal Darcy has come up with for them, it's bound to be sexier and more entertaining than his and Paul's current drama.

Then he reads the headline.

"Darcy, what is this?" Alex's voice strains.

"Gossip! Not real gossip, obviously. But like it was super hard to top the whole public-sex thing, so I thought it would be a really nice spin on the 'look how awesome a couple Paul Marion Keane and J. Alex Cook are!'"

"This says we're having a baby."

He can't even be mad at her; Darcy has absolutely no reason to know what a hot mess of a topic kids are now. The universe really is too terrible sometimes.

"Yeah! Like, what says your relationship is awesome and solid more than that?"

Alex covers his face with his hands and moans.

25

Alex doesn't know what to think when he realizes Victor's diaries have become his comfort reading. As fraught as Victor's relationship with Liam was, it's not the kind of fraught Alex's own relationship is right now. He finds curling up on the couch when he's home alone and reading about all the weekends Victor and Liam spent together at an inn somewhere outside of town strangely lovely.

Alex knew they'd gone away from time to time, but he had no idea what those weekends consisted of and mostly tried not to think about them. There certainly was plenty of sex, at least what constituted sex for them, but Victor also recorded pages of conversation between them, about religion and philosophy and all sorts of topics their jobs and lives outside of each other didn't particularly touch.

When Carly is first pregnant with Ali, there are entries about children and family and a strange longing that stuns Alex for its abstract desperation. He realizes, for the first time, that his and Paul's own child, if they ever have one, will never know Victor. While Alex might once have made a grateful crack about that, now it leaves him feeling strangely sad.

About the really important things, at least as Alex considers them, the diaries are absolutely silent. Alex flips through pages over and over, sure he's missed something, but the entry for the day of Carly and Liam's wedding is another single sentence:

Liam got married today.

As much as Victor lies and omits and conceals, Alex can't believe that he hasn't left any more record of his feelings on the day than that. The next afternoon he can steal at the house, Alex digs into closets and cupboards he hasn't opened yet, looking for anything.

That's when he finds the flat files of sketches.

At first he thinks they're storyboards for old shows long finished or for concepts that never got made, and he starts to flip through them for anything conceivably useful for Paul.

It becomes evident, very quickly, that he has found no such thing.

Alex sits back on his heels and carefully lays the sketches out on the carpet. Some of them anyway. There are hundreds of them, and that's part of the peculiarity of them — to see so many studies, mostly of Liam, carefully preserved in the bottom drawer of a filing cabinet, never perhaps looked at after the process of making them.

For Victor, *this* is — was — sex, Alex understands. And not just because of their content.

Some are of Liam, asleep, which is an image Alex knows well enough himself that it's not shocking. In others, he's naked on top of the sheets, sometimes with his hand on himself, other times lying still on the bed with his hands up beside his head. Alex doesn't have to imagine what Victor was saying to keep him that way, because he has the diaries. Suddenly, everything makes so much more sense.

But then there are the others ones, also clearly Liam even if his face is never showing, because curly hair and Alex knows the slope of his back and his waist. They are of Liam tied up, but not in any simple hands-tied-to-bedpost way Alex has vaguely considered attempting with Paul.

Victor must have taken hours to get the lattices of rope and knots lacing Liam's arms together just right. There are multiple configurations, all of them beautiful and strange and erotic. Victor must have enjoyed the craft and care it demanded as much as Liam adored being touched and settled as he was turned into a work of art. It's visual evidence of the way they worked together that the diaries and all Victor's words alone haven't given Alex.

Alex is too staggered by the loss it represents for Liam to even worry about his own intrusiveness.

But now that he knows these sketches exist, he has no idea what to do. Eventually, like everything else in the house, they'll need to be dealt with, but he can't imagine how. Every option is a horror. They would, he knows, fetch a fortune at auction, which is high on the list of things Alex can't let happen. But he can't steal them, simply because he has no good way of getting them home without damaging them. Besides, there's weird, and then there's weird, and there are hundreds more in the lower drawers of the filing cabinet he hasn't even begun to go through.

Not all the sketches are of Liam. There's Carly, lounging by Victor's pool looking radiantly happy. There's even one of what Alex recognizes, after a shocked moment, as Paul, younger than Alex ever knew him, curled up asleep on a couch. That one, he sets aside, as a reminder to himself to demand the story from Paul at an opportune moment; there's no entry in Victor's diary that corresponds to it.

He's not surprised to find a sketch of himself, though it freaks him out. In many ways, it's less bad than it could be. Alex is not tied to a chair or naked in any physical way, just sitting on the *Fourth Estate* set, reading through a script. His head is down, and it could be any moment on any shoot in any of the hundreds of days Alex worked on that show, but Alex didn't know Victor ever watched him with an eye to draw him. It feels unsettling, and Alex feels like anyone could be watching him right now.

Packing the sketches up takes longer than he wants, considering how much he suddenly wants to get out of here. But he's careful, and sets the ones he wants to come back for on top of the pile. He slides the drawers safely shut again before he escapes back outside to his car, pulling in huge lungfuls of air now that he's safe from the land of the dead.

◆

Alex emails their assistant, Yancey, asking the best way to transport large volumes of unmounted artwork. He gets a useful if puzzled answer back and slips out of bed early one Saturday morning while Paul sleeps in, to drive to an art supply store and then to Victor's house.

He's never used anything in Victor's kitchen unsupervised before, but it's early and the coffee maker is tempting, so Alex puts on a pot to brew while he goes upstairs to deal with the sketches. He's gotten everything spread out on the floor to decide what he wants to take first — there's far too much to get home in one run — when the entire house starts to shake.

No matter how used he is to the little temblors that hit L.A. in waves that he now barely notices — many of them are indistinguishable from a truck passing by on a road it shouldn't — he knows what this one is right away because as the shake ramps up there's a brief sense of being on the water.

Rolling in these things is never good, and Alex scoots into a doorway as quickly as he can, although that's apparently bad advice everyone takes anyway. The movement is fading out by the time he gets there. Alex takes a moment to unclench all his muscles and stop willing the floor to become stationary once again. He hears car alarms up and down the block, snapped off in quick succession.

He shakily stands up to deal with his own. Nothing significant in the house seems damaged, although a few knick knacks shimmied off their shelves and onto the floor; there are no cracks in the wall, but all of Victor's pictures are now quite crooked. It's incredibly unsettling.

Alex hits the fob for his car from inside the house. All of Victor's neighbors are outside talking about the ground weather, and he has no idea what engaging that will look like. Something bad probably. He's not sure if he should straighten the house in response or not. Mostly, he wants to get the sketches and get out. The earthquake wasn't terrifying, but being in Victor's house now is.

He's just started getting them packed up when his phone rings. It's Paul, and given where Alex supposedly is this morning it's far better to answer.

"Are you okay?" Paul demands as soon as Alex picks up.

"I'm fine, I just got down," he lies.

"Oh God, thank God. I was scared you were free climbing."

"Nope, all good here," Alex says, tucking the phone between his chin and shoulder to keep packing. Paul thinking of all the ways Alex might have died is not making him feel better right now. The fact that he would have still been up a mountain, very possibly free climbing, if he weren't lying to Paul makes the whole thing orders of magnitude worse.

"Good. Are you coming home?"

"Yeah, just packing up now. Is the house okay?"

"Things got knocked over, and Todd freaked the fuck out. Olivia went home to check on her place, but we're fine."

"Okay. I'll be home soon," Alex promises, eager to end the call and get out of here. When he does manage to hang up, he's thrown by the sound of a car door slamming, too close to be one of the neighbors', and then the sound of the door opening downstairs.

Alex freezes. Once he recognizes the voices he doesn't know whether to laugh or cry.

"It smells like coffee. Why does it smell like coffee?" Darcy asks from somewhere downstairs. "Is it ghost coffee?"

Alex entirely cannot blame the note of near-hysteria in her voice as he hears Jackson soothing her. Then Jackson calls "Alex?" up the stairs.

He thinks mournfully that he really should have parked farther down the hill.

"Hi, I'll be right down," he shouts, trying not to sound sheepish or suspicious about it.

"What are you doing here?" Darcy demands when Alex thumps down the stairs.

"What are *you* doing here?" he counters.

"Why did you make coffee?" she asks.

"Because I needed coffee," Alex says.

Jackson finally has to interrupt their increasingly surreal conversation. "We came by to check on the house."

"Yeah," Alex says, wondering if he can get away with pretending to do the same. "Everything's fine. I mean, nothing's broken and nothing smells like gas."

"That's good."

"Yeah."

The silence is incredibly awkward. "I was sorting through some of the stuff in Victor's office," Alex finally blurts. "I'll just, um, grab that together and get out of here."

"Okay." Jackson shrugs, apparently deciding to roll with whatever is going on. "I'm going to check the basement, make sure the pipes are okay."

"Okay," Alex nods and escapes back upstairs before Darcy can pull him back into conversation.

It feels wrong to have other people in the house. This morning has gotten more fucked up than Alex could possibly have imagined, and he works as quickly as he can.

He gets out of the house without, thankfully, having to interact with Darcy or Jackson again. He spends the drive home debating whether Jackson will tell Paul, or anyone else who would tell Paul, and if it's worth confessing first to head off the awkward of that. He's got all the sketches in his trunk, in case he can actually get away with it all.

When he gets home, Paul hugs him tightly and Alex clings a little harder than necessary given that he wasn't actually ever in danger. But, *almost* is sometimes close enough.

"Have you seen Victor's keys?" Paul asks, pulling back and frowning a little. "I should go over and check out the house."

Apparently, this day has not yet reached its peak of fucked up. Alex takes a breath, digs the keys out of his pocket, and hands them to Paul. "The house is fine."

Paul looks baffled. "What?"

"I was at the house. I ran into Jackson and Darcy who had the same idea you did. Everything's fine."

"You said you were going climbing."

"Yeah, well, I lied."

Paul's apparently too stunned and confused to be angry. Yet. "Why the hell were you at Victor's?"

"I found some things I wanted to bring home."

"*When?*"

"The last time I was there."

"Which was?"

"I've been going, okay? Shit needs to be boxed up anyway, Nigel keeps nagging us."

"Yeah, but why do I feel like that's not what you've been doing."

"Does it matter?" Alex says petulantly.

"You're creepily hanging around the home of a dead guy you didn't even like, and I'm the one whose mental health we're worried about? Yeah, I'd say it matters," Paul says, just as petulantly.

"*My* mental health is fine."

"You're being a ghoul."

"It's not like I've been curling up in his bed or anything."

"You just said *that*. That is fucked up, Alex."

It's the weirdest argument they've ever had. Although, Alex has to concede it is justified. They go from their relative mental health to cheating, to the baby, back to the cheating — which is not useful to anyone now but it's a point Alex can plant his very pissy flag on — to Paul being incredibly angry about him lying about Victor's house.

Finally, Alex stalks out to his car to get the fucking sketches, so Paul at least can be furious at him in a specific direction. He drops the stack — carefully — on the kitchen island, glaring at Paul as he does so.

Paul stares. "That's a lot of sketches."

"Look at them," Alex says, in part because they are strange enough that he hopes they will get Paul on his side and in part because he's itching for Paul to get pissed off about naked Liam so they can scream at each other some more.

Paul gives him as sullen a look as Alex has ever seen on him and starts paging through them.

"Careful," Alex snaps when Paul accidentally almost creases one.

"Okay, curator of the odd and invasive."

"You're going to explain that one," Alex says when Paul flips past the one of himself on the couch.

"Maybe some other time," Paul says testily, and then falls silent. The sketch below is one of Liam tied up in the elaborate rope. "Oh my God," he says quietly, sitting down on one of the stools.

"Tell me it's not better for me to find that than someone random going through Victor's closets."

Paul doesn't answer right away, turning a few more sketches over. He wonders aloud, not kindly, how Alex could sort through all of them. "It feels so intrusive just to do this," he says.

Alex shrugs.

"I had no idea," Paul says, finally shutting the file.

"So maybe wait to be a dick about my choices before you see why I made them."

"And you have yet to offer a compelling and sane reason for why you were skulking around a dead man's house to begin with." Paul pushes the sketches toward him. "Now put these away."

26

Because Alex is out climbing — hopefully, actually, climbing — Paul should take advantage of having the house to himself, but so far all he can do is open Skype at his desk in his office and stare at Liam's icon. He needs to make this call, and he needs to make it now. But he also needs to not screw it up, and he's nohy t convinced of his ability to do that.

Finally, Paul makes himself click. He leans his chin on his fist as it rings through, hoping, foolishly, that Liam doesn't pick up.

He does, though, and Paul can see the walls of what he assumes is Liam's bedroom. The view on his screen shifts as Liam resituates his laptop.

"Hi," Liam says, once his face comes into view.

"Hi. Can you talk?"

Liam rolls his eyes. "Question on my abilities or polite social question?"

"Um." This is going to be exactly as hard as Paul has feared. "Social question."

Liam nods and settles himself more comfortably in his chair. "Yeah. Charles wants to take me out to a show later, but I'm here now."

"That sounds cool." Paul is aware of how pathetic he sounds. Liam, on the other hand, seems well.

"Have you ever seen a Broadway show?" Liam asks curiously.

"No," Paul admits.

"You should, it's awesome."

"Yeah," Paul says. "I'll try the next time I'm in New York and have more than an hour of downtime." He doesn't say it unkindly, but New York is a different place for all of them. It's home for Liam, hard for Alex, and for himself always too much work and too little sleep.

Liam smiles — which Paul doesn't know how to read — and then doesn't say anything for so long that Paul finally realizes he's not going to.

"Okay, so, well," Paul says. "I wanted to give you a call to talk about the co-parenting idea. Carly said you guys talked about it."

"We did," Liam allows.

"And?"

"And what? Like, if you want answers I need specific questions," Liam explains.

Paul chuckles nervously. "Okay. What do you think of the idea?"

"Carly didn't tell you that?"

"She did, a little, but if this is actually a thing the four of us are doing, you and I should probably be cool talking to each other about it."

"Okay," Liam says. "I have a few things to say."

"Yeah?"

"One, I think you're using the idea of this arrangement to manipulate Alex into having a baby, which is not cool and not something I want to be a part of. Two, you outed me to Alex, which is also not cool and you need to stop assuming stuff about how his and my relationship works. And three, stop trying to make decisions for everybody. You're not Victor. Yes, he was involved in all of our lives but he didn't do stuff like *this*."

Paul rocks back a little. Liam doesn't sound angry, but he's clearly not happy. Paul feels instantly guilty, and also worried about what this means for the viability of his, apparently shitty, plans. "I'm not trying to be Victor; I'm just trying to survive."

Liam tilts his head and stares at Paul for a long time. Of the four of them, they have always been the least close. That's been changing recently, although it's been awkward.

"That's okay, you know," Liam finally says softly. "If you need things, ask for them. Just don't come up with a scheme and pretend it's about what you think I need."

"It *is* about — "

Liam holds up a hand. "Look. Paul. This might be totally good for everyone. But you need to work out how to ask for the things you need and not make things harder for everyone else. 'Cause like, if we're all gonna raise each other's kids, you need to learn how to do that first and how to respect me — and Alex — as adults in front of them."

♦

Paul hits end on the call and takes a deep breath. That had been… more tense than he had expected. He can hear footsteps moving around upstairs; Alex is home, then. The footsteps approach the door at the top of the stairs, and the stairs creak as Alex comes down them.

Alex leans in the doorway to his office as Paul swivels his chair around to face him. He has new scrapes on his arms and his shorts have white streaks on them where he wiped his chalky hands; he really had gone climbing, then.

"How were the rocks?" Paul asks.

Alex ignores the question. "You had a fight with Liam?"

"No?" Paul says, though that's pretty much exactly what happened.

Alex looks unconvinced. "I heard your voices when I was coming in. You were arguing."

"You argue with him all the time," Paul protests weakly.

"I don't, actually, but that's not the point right now. What were you two talking about?"

"The same thing I talked to Carly about." Paul sighs. He doesn't want to rehash this right now, but he knows Alex isn't going to let him off the hook. Nor should he, really. "The same thing we've been talking about — family, and how it can work for all of us."

Alex sighs heavily and begins to pace.

"I know there are words that go with that." Paul tries to sound genial. He knows Alex's reaction, when it comes, will be something other than he wants, but he still needs to move the conversation forward without borrowing grief.

Alex stops walking and drags a hand through his hair before letting it drop. "We don't even know if Liam's coming home." He sounds more frustrated and confused than angry, but that's still not great. "We also don't know if Sarah's still willing to be bio mom. Even if we do have a baby anytime soon, you're going to be on a new project by the time it's born. I can maybe be single dad to one baby but, Paul, seriously, how am I going to be single dad to three?"

Paul blinks, waiting to see if there's more.

"I hope this is what Liam yelled at you about," Alex adds.

"Not exactly. But, it was in the neighborhood if that makes you feel better."

"Please don't patronize me."

"Look, you can't yell at me because you think everything is falling apart and we'll never have a baby at the same time you're yelling at me because you think you'll be stuck taking care of our baby," Paul tries to reason.

"Yes I can! There are so many fucking variables, Paul, we don't have the answers to *any* of them and every hypothetical decision you make keeps landing on me!"

"Is this you saying no?" Paul asks quietly.

"NO, THIS IS ME YELLING BECAUSE I HAVE NO INFORMATION WITH WHICH TO MAKE A DECISION AT ALL!"

27

The final *Winsome* readthrough has been on the calendar for weeks, but it still takes Paul by surprise when the day shows up in early September. So often he feels like the show has just gotten started. The fact that the show has been running for six years is hard to fathom. Harder still is the idea that his first show is almost over.

They have weeks of shooting left, but Darcy still shows up at *Winsome* office for the readthrough nearly in tears and sniffles her way through the first half of the script. Paul smiles behind his hand when he sees Alex rub her back during one of Ruth's last scenes.

For the rest of the read, though, there isn't much smiling. Paul and Olivia wrote most of this episode themselves, and Paul is as proud of it as anything else he's done. While he may not be as sadistic as Victor, he knows rural poverty and the shape of the violence it can create. The character Alex is playing may be the antagonist, but Paul wants to make his death punch the audience as hard as he can. Antagonists, after all, are the most compelling when they are vulnerable.

◆

The script for the *Winsome* finale is intense, and Alex needs a break when they're done with the read. Paul is going to be in meetings for hours more, and Alex doesn't particularly want to go home and be all by himself. So he treks up the stairs from the basement room where they do the reads, to Paul's office.

The lights are off, and Alex flicks them on before he tosses his bag on the couch. He stands there in the middle of the room. He's not often alone here, and it's a rare moment to take stock, not only of Paul's workplace but of their lives.

On Paul's desk is a paperweight Alex recognizes from Victor's office, years ago. Alex picks it up and turns it over in his hands. The thing is profoundly ugly, and Alex has no idea if Victor gave it to Paul, or why, or if Paul obtained it from Victor's now empty desk since he died.

He sets the paperweight down and settles himself in Paul's chair. From his bag he pulls one of Victor's diaries, the one that dates to his own final shoot for *The Fourth Estate*. Given the dead Jason material he's going to be playing, Alex is morbidly curious for Victor's take on that long-ago death scene.

He finds the exact date in the diary with trepidation. After all of the excruciatingly detailed accounts of Victor's intimate moments with Liam, Alex is afraid there are going to be pages of exacting description of his own agony.

But the entry, to his surprise, is only one sentence long.

J. Alex Cook doesn't have a single submissive bone in his body.

Alex laughs aloud in shock, then shuts the diary and puts it away. Victor had no idea, and it's hard to absorb the fact that Victor, who saw so much of him, never really knew him at all. It makes Alex sad, which in the midst of the terrible memory that day of shooting was, is confusing.

While Alex may have Victor's diaries and the deepest, darkest secrets he deigned to put on the page, they are a profoundly one-way line of communication. Paul is, thank god, alive and with Alex. The questions Alex wants to ask him he can, if he just takes the right approach. And while sex may have gotten them into their current mess, it — along with the things Alex has learned from Victor — may also offer them the road out of it.

♦

Paul walks into his office at the end of the day and finds Alex on the couch, reading something on his phone. Alex doesn't acknowledge him except for a vague hum.

"I thought you went home hours ago," Paul says, dropping a stack of notes on top of one of his cabinets and pulling a drawer open.

Alex turns a page, only half listening to Paul. "Are you done for the day?"

"Finally," Paul says, squinting at the labels on the folders.

"Cool, 'cause I really want to go home and fuck you," Alex says casually, still not looking up from his reading.

"Mm, good," Paul shuffles through his stack. Then Alex's words connect, and he looks up at his husband.

Alex slowly lifts his gaze to peer at him over the top of the script.

Paul drops his files back on his desk and barely remembers to grab his bag. Alex already has his slung over his shoulder by the time Paul gets to the door. They both race out of the office, Alex cackling as Paul pounds down the stairs behind him. Neither of them, apparently, wants to wait for the elevator.

They catch each other at Paul's car, and the reality of the situation hits them.

"Fuck," Alex says, still laughing. He grabs at Paul's shoulders when he tries to crowd him into the door; like he can't decide whether to push Paul away or pull him in.

"Why did we bring two cars?" Paul complains, but he's laughing too.

"Because we are terrible planners," Alex says. He sways in close enough that Paul thinks he's actually going to kiss him right here in the parking lot before he pushes back with a sly, challenging look. "See you at home!"

"No racing!" Paul shouts after him as he turns and jogs off toward his own car.

◆

Paul gets home first and waits in the open doorway until Alex pulls in with a flash of his headlights. He barely gets the car turned off before he's tearing up the walk and throwing himself into Paul's arms.

As soon as Paul kicks the door closed behind them, Alex shoves him up against it, biting and sucking at his neck until Paul digs his hand into Alex's hair and drags his head up for a kiss that's all tongue and teeth.

Alex moans into it before pushing Paul back far enough so he can look him in the eye. He holds Paul's gaze for a long moment, dark and even in the light filtering in from the street. Paul wants to film him, just like this, with all his power and intensity trained on him.

But then Alex leans in and murmurs in his ear. "Tell me what you need."

Paul lets his head tip back against the door.

Alex kisses along the line of his throat below his ear. "Paul," he says, scolding as he grinds his hips against him.

"Fuck my mouth?" Paul asks breathlessly.

"Is that what you need?" Alex asks.

Paul doesn't know whether Alex is making a highly effective attempt at dirty talk or is genuinely asking for information. Either way, it's impossible not to answer in glorious detail.

Alex buries his face in Paul's shoulder and eventually covers Paul's mouth with his hand.

"If you keep talking I'm going to come right here in the foyer. Not. The. Plan," he says breathlessly.

Paul kisses his fingers.

Alex's face goes very soft. He grabs Paul's hand to pull him upstairs.

◆

In their room, Alex strips out of his clothes before Paul can get his hands on him. When Paul tries to kiss him, Alex puts his hands on Paul's shoulders and shoves him down instead. He knows what he wants — and what Paul has asked for — and he is going to give it to him.

Paul gets the message and drops to his knees at Alex's feet. He runs his hands up the back of Alex's legs, and tips his head back to look up at Alex from under his lashes, asking for direction.

Before Alex can give him any, though, Paul pushes his hips back a little. "Hey," he says softly.

"Yeah?" Alex says, distracted and running his hands through Paul's hair.

"Condom."

Alex whines, but only because it's a delay while Paul reaches over and grabs one out of the bedside drawer and then helps Alex with it.

Paul settles back on his knees and gives Alex that same look.

Alex doesn't need to be asked twice. He grabs the back of Paul's head and feeds his cock into his mouth. They both groan with relief.

Paul keeps staring up at him as Alex starts to pump his hips. Alex couldn't look away if he wanted to.

Alex doesn't last long, and after he comes he collapses down almost into Paul's lap. There's fumbling with belt and jeans and underwear before Alex finally gets Paul's dick out. It would be funny if Alex didn't feel so victorious, and Paul weren't looking at him with that same too-much look.

Paul comes with his face buried in Alex's shoulder, Alex jerking him off, breathing encouragement in his ear.

♦

They drag themselves up onto the bed and lie side-by-side, staring at the ceiling and panting together. Alex rolls onto his side to deal with the sex trash and actually sways a little once he gets to his feet.

"Are you okay?" Paul asks. His voice is hoarse, and he rolls his head to the side to watch Alex.

"I waited for two hours in your office so I could jump you. I'm fantastic," Alex calls as he tosses out the condom, and pads into the bathroom to get a damp washcloth.

"Yeah, but why?" Paul asks when Alex crawls back onto the bed and hovers over him.

"Are you complaining about the fucking?"

Paul chuckles and pulls Alex down onto the mattress next to him. He doesn't give a damn about cleanup right now. "Most definitely not. I am questioning your motives, though."

Alex shrugs easily. "I'm into you. That hasn't changed. Even if everything else in our lives is one massive question mark." Alex tucks his head into Paul's shoulder, and Paul drapes an arm over his waist. The sweat is starting to cool on his skin, and Alex is warm.

Paul wonders whether he should mention that in their lives — and he suspects in all lives — nothing is ever resolved. It's the same struggles and misunderstandings over and over again. All you can do is learn from the last iteration and hope the knowledge makes the next one less painful.

"So in the interest of reducing future chaos," Alex says, "What should you tell me that you haven't told me yet?"

Paul practices the words in his head before he says them aloud. "You mean about the depression I've been dealing with really badly since Victor died and probably the entire time you've known me?"

"That would be it, yes."

Paul shrugs. "You've seen it in action,"

"Put it in words so we both know what the fuck is going on, before you decide everything is too crazy again and go fuck another random," Alex says. It's more gentle than it could be.

"I won't — "

Alex shushes him. "That's exactly what you would have said two months ago with just as much good intention. I do love you, and I do trust you. But I need you to do the work, not just make reassuring sounds about it."

"Apparently," Paul says. If Alex is going to initiate this conversation, he's willing to meet him halfway. "I'm not capable of being the sane adult all the time."

"Clearly." Alex grins.

Paul swats lazily at him. "We fell into a pattern," Paul says, "and it's a really good pattern, or at least, it's worked for eight years — "

" — Except for the time we almost broke up because you can't do work-life balance — "

" — I adore taking care of you. And I love the fuck out of my job. But sometimes, apparently, I need someone else to make decisions for me. In life or in bed."

"I'm not saying this defensively or with anger or to reject you, but I can take care of myself." Alex speaks slowly, listening for any signs of panic from Paul. "You focusing on yourself for a bit — your actual self not your coping mechanisms — can only benefit both of us."

"I know that. Intellectually. But…." Paul shrugs, jostling him.

Alex nods. Everything is always easier said than done. "And you want to bring a baby into this mess. And our friends."

"I thought we were doing help-Paul-figure-out-his-shit time, not lecture time."

"Shh. Related thought, not a lecture. You can't bring the self-destruction home if we have a kid. There are only so many choices I can make for you, and I can't make you be stable and okay all the time. So work out what you need to work out. Whatever that looks like, I will help, but the status quo of you wandering in and out of therapy and always saying no to the antidepressants is not working."

Paul frowns. It's an awful lot like the advice Liam gave him. "You've never asked me to do any of that."

"Actually, we fought about you doing therapy and then you passive-aggressived at me for years. I'm still not going to make these choices for you, because it's your life. But your choices do affect me and whatever offspring we have, so I am going to give you some pretty narrow parameters because everything I'm hearing from you is that it's necessary."

Alex's tone is softer than Paul expects, all things considered. He's also talking about a baby in a way that implies one actually might happen now, if Paul follows Alex's instructions for being a functional human.

This conversation is exactly what Paul needs, and so much of what he wants even if uncertainty, as always, lingers over everything. He runs his hand along Alex's side. "How did you get so capable?"

"I've always been capable. I just haven't always needed to be. At least, not since I got here."

"I'm glad you're here." Here, in L.A., in Paul's life, in his bed.

Alex smiles. "You have no idea."

Paul gets more stressed and more irritable the closer they get to the Emmys regardless of the fact that none of the work they're currently doing on *Winsome* or *M.A.R.S.* is up for the current awards cycle.

He's rambled at Alex about it so often Alex knows the spiel by heart. *M.A.R.S.* and *Winsome* are both up for Best Drama this year, much to Paul's dismay. Mark continues to be terrible and uncooperative. And either because of that or other reasons related to the showrunner dying, *M.A.R.S.'* ratings have been tanking. Which has not made Mark any more tractable to Paul's suggestions, much to Paul's infuriation.

Alex mostly leaves him to it; the focused anxiety is, as a rule, much better for Paul's psyche than the broad, scattered grief and insecurities he's been dealing with all summer. Still, the control and showmanship the event demands is exhausting. Paul is always charming on the carpet — more so than Alex ever would have expected years ago when he was first stepping into the public eye — but he's way more wound than usual.

Alex is worried but takes advantage of the setting — and their ongoing mission to be adorable in public — to stay closer to Paul's side than he usually does. Photographers and interviewers call out to them questions from benign to terrible. He loops his arm through Paul's as they get asked about who made their suits and how much they miss — and are grateful to — Victor.

Victor's absence is difficult, Alex feels the lack of Liam's presence too. Neither he nor Alex are up for anything this year, but Liam never misses a carpet if he can help it. Alex longs for his energy and enthusiasm. They've done this together, in one way or another, so many times.

At least Darcy is there, with Jackson as her date. She looks stunning and bounces between cameras and interviewers with a grace and energy that Alex respects even if it's exhausting to watch. Melissa is such a serious dramatic character that even after six years the audience hasn't entirely gotten used to the fact that the actress who plays her is so girlish and exuberant. Alex probably resents it more than Darcy herself does; it's one more way people choose to confuse their lives with their work to the depreciation of both.

Off the carpet, the social whirl is worse. They run into Mark in the lobby. Paul wants to hide, but Alex puts his hand on his back and smiles sharply. He dares Mark to actually say anything. Alex is perfectly willing to deck him once there aren't a ton of cameras around.

Paul hunts for something innocuous to say, but Mark greets them both as if he's done nothing untoward and then says, "You know, we're going to split the sympathy vote and both be fucked."

Alex cracks up.

Paul looks like he wants to kill both of them, but Mark doesn't give him the chance. With a crappy salute and a smirk, he wanders away.

"Alex!" he scolds, horrified, once Mark is gone.

"Paul," Alex mocks, still giggling. "Victor would think that was hilarious."

Victor lingers over much of the night. There is the obligatory *in memoriam* montage, and Alex wonders what Victor would think of it, his career boiled down to four seconds of sentimentality in a sea of other people he mostly didn't like. He suspects he'd love it, or at least love picking apart the pieces of the dying world someone else thought important enough to share.

Ellen wins Best Director for one of her *M.A.R.S.* episodes. When she gets to the microphone, she looks out at the audience, lifts her statue, and says "This one's for Victor" before exiting the stage. It's been a fuck of a year.

When the Best Drama category comes up, Alex leans over and whispers in Paul's ear about having his game face on in case *Winsome* doesn't win. Alex means it, but he's also being funny, grinning as he hisses a litany of "Smile, smile, smile."

Paul has to cover his own mouth so he won't laugh.

Winsome doesn't win. Neither does *M.A.R.S.*

"It would seem Mark was right about the sympathy vote," Paul says under his breath.

♦

The Emmys — and the consolation party Paul hosts for the *Winsome* people a week later — feels like a bigger milestone than Alex expected. Whatever is coming next, this phase of his and Paul's life is winding down. And if Alex is going to lay out parameters for Paul, he has to be as disciplined about his own life choices.

Soon he'll have to be on the road promoting *Icarus*, the movie he filmed in Australia before Victor died and the world changed. But aside from that, he doesn't actually have any other projects or obligations lined up. Alex is, for the foreseeable future, completely free.

Being able to do almost anything he wants is a strange kind of freedom. But instead of finding a new project or travelling for pleasure or climbing the ten hardest rocks in the state, Alex keeps coming back to the idea of going to school.

Paul can say he doesn't care Alex doesn't have a degree all he wants, but Alex does. With all the things Alex has in his strange and unlikely life, there are so many he lacks. Indiana lingers, and Alex has never been taught statistics or to do textual analysis or even to write a decent essay. He may have been able to learn some Farsi on his own, but self-study can only take him so far. If he and Paul do have a kid — the waiting game seems endless and, on some days, suffocating — Alex owes it to them to have enough of an education to at least be able to help them with homework.

And if they do end up in Paul's harebrained co-parenting arrangement, splitting his time between college and childcare would be a very good arrangement. Going to classes would certainly be easier than working on a project full-time while Paul is deep into a new show. And college would definitely be something new.

♦

Despite the offer of lunch, Alex has been avoiding calling Gemma since South Carolina. But if he's going to be starting something new, he also knows he has to make right with people that have come before.

He's grateful she's not too pissy when he finally does call, though she's completely entitled.

Lunch is awkward at first, which is weird. They always bicker, but they've never really been awkward. Alex hates this, and he doesn't know how to fix it.

He doesn't hate it any less when Gemma asks him again and again what's wrong. She's always been good at needling him, and today is no exception. In the face of her questioning, Alex demurs and struggles with words. He wonders if this was a terrible idea, and if she'll ever speak to him again. If this goes badly, Alex is totally blaming Victor.

Finally, he takes a deep breath and goes for it. "Look, I never was going to tell you this, okay? Not after it was obvious it wasn't ever going to happen."

"You're making me nervous. Are you okay? Do you have cancer?"

Alex tips back his head and roars with laughter.

"What?" Gemma demands, leaning across the table to swat at his arm and almost knocking over a water glass in the process. "What the fuck is so fucking funny? Alex!"

Alex presses his knuckles to his mouth and tries to control himself. Everything in his life is so fucked up. "I'm sorry, it's nothing, it's a really long story," he says.

Gemma crosses her arms over her chest. "Start talking."

"I just, no, I don't have cancer. Okay," he says, "So back when we were kids who told each other way too much about our shitty lives over the internet — "

"I remember." Gemma sounds wistful *and* annoyed. Alex wonders if she misses their terrible apartment too.

"We were going to run away and make it big in L.A. and live out all our dreams. You asked me once if I had a plan B because you had actually applied to colleges. You were worried what I was going to do if shit didn't pan out."

"I remember that too. You didn't. You're so fucking lucky shit panned out for you," Gemma says.

Alex gives her a tight smile. She really has no idea. "Well, I lied."

"Okay?" She has no idea what he's getting at.

"I did have a plan B."

"And?"

Alex shuffles his shoulders and makes himself keep looking at Gemma, not at the ceiling, because she deserves the truth from him, even if it was long ago and terrible. None of them will live forever, and now that Victor is dead, Gemma is the one he owes everything to. "You were my plan B."

Gemma narrows her eyes at him, confused. "Like, you were going to crash on my couch forever? Because that's kind of what happened anyway."

"No. No, not like that," Alex says. "Worse than that."

"Then maybe you should fucking say what you mean before I get completely freaked out." Gemma doesn't sound angry, merely puzzled.

"If L.A. hadn't worked out, and I had had to go back to Paragon it wouldn't have been safe for me to go alone."

"What do you mean?"

"Staying in the closet is one thing when you're a surly teenager no one wants to talk to anyway. But if I'd had to live my life there, without a wife or kids, people would've assumed things."

Finally, the penny drops. Gemma covers her mouth with her hand. "Oh my God."

"Yeah."

"*Alex.*"

"I'm sorry. Even if it never happened, I'm sorry."

"I don't know what to do with this! You're telling me if L.A. had been a washout we'd be living in a three-bedroom ranch right now with a dog and our 2.1 kids."

"That would have been the best possible outcome. For me at least. Yeah."

"I knew you were gay," Gemma points out.

"I fucked Carly. I could have gotten it up enough to have kids with you."

"You thought about that?" Gemma says, appalled.

"I thought about surviving."

"You couldn't have just, I don't know, moved to Ventura and worked shitty jobs to pay rent? Or like, Indianapolis? Why did you think you would have had to go back?"

"Because, sometimes, the worst thing happens. Usually, in my life. And then I got here."

"This entire fucking thing is surreal. And also screw you and your sense of entitlement. What if I had said no."

Alex stares back at her a little cruelly but says nothing.

"Yeah, fuck you too." Gemma laughs darkly. "Is that why you've been avoiding me forever? And why we went out to lunch today? So I wouldn't yell in front of people?"

"Do you want to yell at me? I mean, it's warranted. We can go back to my place, Paul's still at work." Saying Paul's name breaks the strange mood that's had him in its hold since he sat down; a reminder of the life he actually has, instead of the one he almost had.

Not for Gemma, though. "I want to know why the hell you were so fucking scared of Indiana you'd marry a woman just to stay in the closet."

"I would have married you, had kids with you, had a house — I would have been good to you. We would have had a good life."

"I'm ignoring most of that. But I do want to know why. Why this? Why this strategy?"

Alex shakes his head, relieved when she doesn't press. There's no more answer he can bear to give.

29

The shooting for *Winsome's* finale, at the end of September, takes them out to the desert. They're not going as far as Kelso; They need Arizona scrub, not Iran's rock-strewn desert. Still, Paul and Liam both spend the week before the shoot reminding him about staying hydrated, and heat stroke, and terribly timed media crises. Alex laughs and promises he'll take care of himself. Carly's due in a matter of days and joking about the way in which everything seems to happen at once among their group feels like tempting fate.

This desert shoot brings its own particular dangers. Alex can stay in the shade and drink as much water as he wants, but there are firearms in the episode and that introduces a level of risk beyond the weather. Their gun wrangler has drilled this into them, and every crew member seems to know some terrible story. People have died from being shot by blanks fired from prop guns. No one wants their set to be the next one an accident happens on.

Alex can't prep for Jason's death scene without thinking about Zach's. Alex has never told anyone the details of what went on in Victor's basement the day Zach died. At the time it was too private and awful. As much as Alex hated the process, and hated Victor, talking about it would only have made *everyone* talk about it.

Now, despite everything, Alex respects Victor — or at least his legacy — too much to have any of that known. Someone will eventually air their extended social family's dirty laundry, and Alex is determined it's not going to be him. He doesn't ever want anyone besides Paul to know Zach's tears when he was being tortured weren't pretend.

Alex grins at the effects guys and tells them he's fine after they test the exploding blood packets on his chest. It hurts less than getting hit in paintball, and he's grateful for procedure and safety and a shoot that's not in a fucking basement. Besides, having things actually impact his body makes the acting part of the job ridiculously easy. Alex asks them not to run through the whole sequence first; surprise is his friend.

♦

Paul does not, strictly speaking, have to be out on location for this. But someone has to keep a wary half-eye on an Alex who is, in his opinion, way too excited to try out the effects that will make it look like he's been shot. Ellen is directing, and while he trusts her and the rest of his team, he wants to be in the middle of everything now that it's all ending, not watching the rushes from his office a hundred miles away.

By the time they're ready to roll, Alex is jumping around and ridiculously ready to go. Paul gets it because Jason is a jangly, strung out, fuck-up of a guy. That Alex needs to keep his adrenaline up to make that work is reasonable. Even so, the degree to which Alex always seems so cheerful about death scenes — even in light of Victor being dead — freaks him out a little.

Paul's discomfort isn't helped by the fact that they're still occasionally snappish with each other since Alex's little revelation about his ongoing exploratory missions to Victor's house. On the list of shit they have to resolve in their lives — the cheating, Paul's health status, the baby, how to navigate Liam and Carly — Alex's adventures are fairly minor. But no matter how much they've agreed on that, and to table it, every conversation they have seems to come back around to it over and over. Sometimes they fight about which one of them is crazier. Sometimes they argue about Liam. And sometimes, they're blindsided by the ever-dawning realization that while Victor may have been a force of impish hostility and persistent destruction, they're all lost without him.

As the crew works, Paul tries stay out of everyone's way. He's there if they need him and for his own pleasure. But he will not unnecessarily interfere with a machine that has worked just fine without his excessive intervention since he stepped back enough to let *Winsome* find its stride at the end of its first season.

◆

Watching Alex as Jason beg for his life in front of Melissa's unsteady hand — in six seasons, Darcy's character has never actually fired her gun — is unsettling. It's also faintly hilarious, because only Jason could make begging sound like a *fuck you* that Paul hadn't known was in the script until the table read. Paul smiles as he leans his chin into his hand and watches them do the tight shots and the over-the-shoulders, knowing that their various forms of crazy serve all of them well.

During the wide shots things start to get fucked up. Without the camera right in his face, Alex is further away from himself. He is, Paul suspects, relying more on emotion and less on the uncanny physical control that initially attracted Victor to him as a performer.

Ellen doesn't let them get to the gunshots the first couple of times, which is a choice Paul agrees with. Alex will nail that. They don't need to burn time on resetting the effects part of the shot every time Ellen wants to bracket the lead-up.

Alex paces and rubs his hands over his face during their first couple of resets. Paul leans over to Ellen and suggests she give Alex and Darcy a moment, but Ellen shakes her head and Paul, not having been as quiet as he thought, gets snapped at by Alex for his trouble.

When Alex hastily pushes messy tears out of his eyes after the next take Ellen asks if he needs a minute. He growls that he's fucking fine. Because Alex is usually a sweetheart on set, no one really takes offense. A few crew members chuckle.

Paul is aware, however, that his own breathing is off watching this. Alex isn't entirely okay as far as he can tell, but Paul's not here to undermine his or, more importantly, Ellen's authority. He reminds himself that sometimes being not okay is part of the job.

Paul flinches when Darcy fires the gun and the first of the blood packets on Alex go off. The effect is startling, no matter how many times he's seen it executed in person. Alex, as Jason, is shocked that Melissa has the balls to actually pull the trigger.

Ellen eventually calls cut when the silence of Jason trying to process what has happened stretches out too long. A second and a half after that, everyone realizes the problem isn't Jason. Or acting. The problem is Alex, who still can't find his breath or his words and has gone an awful shade of shaking gray.

Paul doesn't understand how that's visible under the makeup, as the special effects technician, the first aid guy, and the gun wrangler run to him. Everything happens very quickly after that.

Darcy — despite all the training Alex and the crew have drilled into her — drops her gun and takes a step back. The look on her face is enough to make Paul realize that she thinks she's actually shot Alex.

Paul is out of his chair and trying to get to him so fast he actually knocks it over, tripping his way into where the crew guys are trying to get Alex on the ground and calm enough for them to see what's going on. That would be easier if Paul wasn't in the way, Alex wasn't fighting them off in a panic, and Ellen wasn't yelling at both of them to let the crew do their goddamn jobs. Darcy, who is progressively getting more freaked out, is louder than all of them.

"Alex!" Paul barks as he elbows one of the guys aside. "Words!"

That gets Alex's attention, but he freezes again for a moment before his eyes go wide and startled. Then he laughs, awkward and shocked and more than a little watery.

"I'm fine, I'm fine. Oh my God, I'm fine."

"Stop moving around and let them check," Paul says harshly because that seems to be what's working.

Alex acquiesces. Paul spares a second to exchange a look with Ellen. No, he has no idea what just happened.

When they finally get the all clear that Alex really is fine and Darcy didn't fucking shoot anyone, Alex staggers up and out of the frame.

"I just need five," he says, still breathless.

♦

Paul follows him back behind where the cameras are set up. "What the fuck was that?"

"Fucking terrifying," Alex answers, a hand half over his mouth. He feels like he's going to be sick.

"An answer I can understand, please."

Alex shakes his head and finally looks at Paul, who seems helpless and small. "Not now."

"WE THOUGHT DARCY SHOT YOU," Paul hollers, which sets Darcy off on another crying jag behind him. "TELL ME WHAT THE FUCK JUST HAPPENED."

"I thought she shot me too," Alex says in a small voice, still filled with that incredibly unsettling wonderment.

"Jesus Christ," Paul says in clear frustration. "I feel like I'm having a conversation with Liam."

Alex shakes his head and finally goes to Paul. He leans into him and tugs at Paul's arms to demand that he hold him in a way that has always been against the rules for them on a set — regardless of the power dynamic in play, crisis at hand, or public media image they're trying to project.

Paul, heedless of the fake blood Alex is getting all over him, squeezes him tightly around his waist. Alex props his chin on Paul's shoulder and looks out at the infrastructure of make-believe they've hauled into the desert. He is aware of it — and of what they must look like against it — in a purely cinematic way he doesn't generally consider. He blames Victor's diaries and cries.

30

When the van finally drops them off at the *Winsome* lot, Paul insists Alex ride home with him.

"Two cars," Alex says, apparently too tired to even be petulant about it.

Paul unlocks his car and opens the passenger side door for him. "We can get yours tomorrow. In."

"I'm *fine*," Alex says but slides in anyway, pulling the door shut behind him.

"You had a panic attack you still won't explain, and then you sobbed on my shoulder for ten minutes," Paul says, getting into his own seat. "I'm driving."

"It wasn't that long," Alex protests. "Right now I just want to crawl into bed and sleep forever."

Paul is happy to drive them home in silence. After Alex got himself back under control, his makeup was fixed, and the effects were reset — and Darcy had been calmed down — he went back out to the cameras and absolutely nailed the shot.

It was everything Paul could have possibly hoped for and he knows, from the look Alex gave him as they wrapped, that Alex is proud too. Jason died with a small, satisfied smile on his face. It was unwritten and completely disturbing, but only in a way that Paul appreciates as making fantastic TV.

All that remains is the question *why*. Paul waits until they're home — and Alex has dragged himself upstairs to face-plant on their bed — to ask again.

Alex rolls his face to the side so he can look at Paul and also actually breathe. "What do you want me to tell you?"

"I want you to tell me why today went to shit. What happened in your head?"

Alex shrugs.

"Why are you being so cagey about this?"

"Remember how you didn't tell me about your wrists for two years?"

"Can this not be a competition about who is fucking crazier for five minutes?" Paul snaps, exasperated.

Alex sighs and rolls over onto his back to give Paul a tired glare. "Victor's dead. We're still waiting for your test results. Sometimes when you're an actor weird shit happens. Can we just not talk about any more mortality right now?"

Paul holds his gaze for a long time. He knows Alex is lying, but he also isn't wrong. Everything today and in the last six months has been so strange and full of death and so many uncertainties. He sighs and lets it go.

"Okay," Paul says, crawling onto the bed and stretching out beside him.

Alex smiles faintly and lets his eyes close when Paul starts dragging a hand from Alex's chest to his stomach.

Paul thinks he's fallen asleep and startles when Alex says, "I kept thinking about Victor."

Paul makes an encouraging noise.

"After they got me down on the ground, I kept waiting for him to come and tell me I was okay and shove me back onto my feet."

"Alex," Paul says softly.

Paul softly strokes Alex's stomach while Alex blinks at the ceiling. He doesn't look like he's going to start crying again, but his eyes are still red and bruised-looking. "Apparently, I'm finally mourning Victor. That's uncomfortable. And overwhelming in a way I don't know how to handle. I have to live with that, and with knowing that no matter how much I hated Victor, he took care of me in a way nobody else — not even you — ever could."

♦

They wake up from their unplanned nap sometime in the small hours of the morning. Alex says he's starving. Paul tells him he can get his own damn snack, Paul has no ability to get out of bed again, and Alex teases him about being old until Paul throws a pillow at him.

Alex brings back leftovers and two forks, because he is awesome. He and Paul end up passing the container back and forth while talking aimlessly about what happens next. Paul scrolls idly through his phone, checking messages he missed while they were asleep.

"Oh," he says quietly.

"What is it?" Alex asks.

"Voicemail from the doctor's office."

"Oh," Alex repeats quietly.

Alex wraps his arms around a pillow and stares at Paul as he punches in his pin and listens to the message, and doesn't move until Paul hangs up, tossing the phone to the end of the bed and turning his head to stare back at Alex.

"Good news or bad news?" Alex asks, clearly freaked out.

"That was the doctor's office. Test results came back."

"*And?*" Alex demands, sitting up. He has exactly zero patience with Paul's sense of dramatic tension right now.

"Everything's negative. No HIV. Or anything else to worry about."

"Oh my God," Alex breathes, collapsing back onto the bed and staring at the ceiling.

"Mhmm," Paul says, crawling up the mattress to hover over him. There's no intent, but he wants to be in Alex's line of sight for whatever conversation happens now.

Alex gives a strange, gasping laugh. "It had to be today."

"What's wrong with today?"

"I thought I was dead!" Alex shouts, before giving a hysterical giggle and clapping his hand over his mouth.

"Well, you're not."

"I'm really happy about that," Alex admits. "But do we have to talk about babies right now?"

"We don't have to talk about anything," Paul says because he's learning how to time things with Alex better. Also, today has been hard enough already.

"I kind of feel like I owe you the conversation. I mean, two tests, three months, baby back on the table, this was the deal. And realistically speaking I was sort of exaggerating the HIV risk anyway. Which you never called me on, so thank you."

Paul nods, because Alex is staring intently at him and is clearly working up to something. When minutes go by without Alex saying anything, though, Paul touches his cheek gently and then sits back. "Words, Alex."

"The last six months have been *terrifying*." Alex begins to tick items off on his fingers. "Victor died, Liam left, you cheated, and I'm not even going to get started on the baby drama. You are still alive and we're still together and I'm afraid to say that out loud in case I jinx it, which is probably fucked up. But you still have mental health issues. I'm still overwhelmed, and what if you can't curb the self-destruction the next time disaster hits? I can't put a kid through losing you."

Paul stretches out on the bed and rests his head on Alex's shoulder. Alex automatically wraps his arms around him.

"I am working on my bad crazy. You're working on your bad crazy. But I've had some really fucked up experiences, and I'm ten years older than you. Victor may have been the first person you kissed who died, but he's not going to be the last. The chances of both me and Liam outliving you are really, really low."

"What about Nick?"

Paul takes a second to realize who Alex is talking about. He laughs. The memory of catching Alex making out with his old intern is absurd and also precious.

Alex gives him that look he gives the camera sometimes. That always freaks the fuck out of Paul — it's so quietly indicting.

"You're telling me we can only have a kid if I'm not going to die," Paul says. "I can't promise you that. But I am trying to have the best, longest life I can with you."

"I thought we were done with talking about mortality for today," Alex says.

"You alluded. I'm trying to reassure. Besides, we're talking about babies now, too."

"Okay," Alex says.

"Okay what?" Paul says cautiously.

"Okay, let's have a baby. If our fucked-up family hasn't completely scared away your sister. And if it has, we can talk other options."

"You don't have to make that decision right now. Or anytime soon," Paul says. The last thing he wants is for Alex to make a decision too quickly only to reverse it later.

"Me saying yes doesn't equal automatic baby. This is just exchanging one set of unknowns for another," Alex reminds Paul.

He nods. Alex isn't wrong, but he wants this so desperately. "What's your stance on the co-parenting thing?" he asks. If everything is back on the table, he wants to have all of these conversations while Alex is willing and verbal.

"If Carly — and Liam if he ever gets back — want in, I'm in."

"Yeah?"

"Yeah. If it makes our collective lives easier, that's awesome. Clearly, we're a family anyway whatever we choose to do. But whether our friends are involved or not I want to do this."

"You know, if I knew you were going to say yes so easily I would have been a lot less stressed the last three months."

"We should go away," Paul suggests fifteen minutes later, peeling Alex's fingers away after he claps a hand over Paul's mouth to stop him from trying to discuss baby names when Alex just wants to keep making out.

Alex raises his eyebrows. "How?"

"You, me, a car, some fucking B&B somewhere. Your birthday's coming up and we should do something for that. I want some time alone with you before the rest of the world starts demanding things from us. 'Cause it's only gonna start wanting more."

Alex snorts, because *understatement*. "Can you get the time away anytime soon?"

"We have a week left of shooting. I'll take a long weekend once that's done."

"I know a place," Alex offers, too quickly.

"Please tell me this isn't where Victor took Liam," Paul says warily. Alex has told him about those entries. With the whole thing with the house and the sketches, Paul has good reason to be suspicious.

Alex shrugs.

"Alex!"

"What? I checked it out on the internet. It's pretty."

"You are so fucked up."

"L.A. Victor. *Fourth.* Famous. You. Stop sounding so surprised."

31

As soon as they get onto the 101 and the promise of L.A. falls back behind them, Alex rolls the windows down, flips on the radio to the same sort of shitty country rock he still hasn't managed to outgrow, and smiles at the still too-dry landscape whizzing by. It's the first week of October and winter is coming, but it still hasn't rained.

Paul is eager to talk. So much has been strange lately, but Alex looks more unencumbered than Paul has seen him in what feels like years. His ease is a silent admonition for Paul to let go of some of the tension in his shoulders and worry in his heart. They have four days and more than words to remind themselves that they've always known each other's secrets. Paul decides to smile and let things go.

That they are on the way to Liam and Victor's secret getaway is, at this point, only humorously weird. Alex made a compelling point regarding pre-vetted discretion. Then he sucked up making the phone call to make sure they weren't going to wind up with the same room as Victor and Liam. As if all the beds in any accommodation don't see hundreds of guests per year. But Alex played grief and apologies — not insincere, just not his style — to delicately raise the issue. Either it worked or they'll at least hopefully never know if it didn't.

They talk quietly. Not to hash out any of their many lingering issues, which seems to have been all they've talked about recently, but simply for the pleasure of the conversation. They talk about filmmaking, not in terms of the thing that dictates their lives, but in the abstract, about art and story. Alex is a font of interesting trivia and curious questions about the process of filmmaking. Alex brings up the school thing, and talks seriously about going to college. And then they talk about their friends.

"I can't believe Liam and Carly don't know what sex the baby is," Paul blurts at one point when he's taken over driving.

"Dirty hippies," Alex laughs.

"I'd want to know. Wouldn't you?"

Alex nods. "Seems odd to be able to know and not know." Then he asks, "Which do you want?"

"Don't care," Paul says.

"Liar," Alex says with a completely smug smile.

Paul chuckles. "Why, what about you?"

"Girl," Alex says easily.

Paul's face goes soft. "I didn't know that."

"Mhmm. Just not with the fucking freckles. For her sake," he adds.

"Your freckles are sexy."

"They're weird."

"*You* are sexy."

"I am also weird."

Paul laughs with delight.

They stop at a little store on the way, because wine and cheese and bread are necessities. Alex leans against their car in the parking lot, of his sunglasses in his teeth as he checks their onward directions on his phone and utterly not giving a shit about anyone else in the vicinity who is not Paul.

When Paul kisses him, a peck at the corner of his mouth, Alex grins at him, his eyes crinkling up.

♦

Late afternoon sun pours in from a window looking out over a valley that is ridiculously bucolic and totally gorgeous. The floorboards and knotty pine walls glow in the light. The furniture, rugs, and bedding are all patterned in rich reds and browns, and the whole place feels about as far from the hideous modernism of L.A. as it is possible to get.

They make out on the bed forever, lazy and playful until Paul bites hard at Alex's shoulder and Alex whimpers, his head falling back against the pillows and his limbs going loose and pliant.

"Requests or protests?" Paul asks, starting to pull off Alex's clothes.

Alex shakes his head.

Paul crawls up his body so he can be eye to eye with Alex. "You cool with no condom?" he asks.

"Point of trip," Alex says, resentful of the intrusion upon his head-space. Although the trip is really about so much more than that. It's the culmination of their coming back together and getting everything back on track that Victor's death derailed.

Paul gives him a quick kiss on the lips before sliding down Alex's body, grabbing his ankles, and shoving his knees up to his chest.

"Efficient," Alex murmurs.

"I promise you're not going to mind," Paul says.

Alex huffs. Paul has ten seconds to get on with it, or he's going to whine.

Paul doesn't tease, not really, instead pressing his face between his cheeks and licking along his hole.

"Oh my God." Alex loves this. The sensation is the perfect mix of tease and actual action for him. It makes him desperate without being agonizing. This is also one of the first things they ever did together besides kiss, and after eight years together and everything that has happened in this one, it has a place in his heart. It's not something they do enough. With their work and their schedules, so much of everything in their lives is determined by what's fast and easy.

Their lives are going to get more chaotic with far less time for just the two of them soon, but there's a lesson here, in celebrating this choice and maybe mourning all the change that it brings. They have to be, no matter how exhausted and harried, more deliberate people. Not so that they'll remain together — that deal seems well and truly done and pretending otherwise at this point, even when things go grievously wrong, is absurd — but so that they can enjoy what they can't help but have.

Alex is certainly enjoying it now. Paul makes him delirious with want. He feels like he could ride this out for hours, like a drunk. Paul moans against him, the vibrations chasing up his body.

Eventually he says it's too much, meaning *fuck me now*, but Paul waits him out. He hovers close, petting at Alex's hip until he begs for more. Paul grins ferally, obviously pleased with himself.

"If you don't fuck me soon," Alex eventually manages, "I am going to kill you."

Paul shrugs. "I have a better idea."

Alex makes a noise that's somewhere between a laugh and a moan. This whole mess is the best sort of despair. He doesn't want to go back to their real life ever… not the old one or the new one.

"Two seconds." Paul dives over the side of the bed to fish something out of their suitcase.

"We said no condoms," Alex whines.

Paul comes back with a vibrator and lube, and raises an eyebrow at Alex.

"Not psychic," Alex snarks, letting his legs drop to the bed and palming his own dick.

"This fucks you while you fuck me," Paul explains.

It seems like so much effort. But worth it, and the whole point of this weekend is effort. "Less talk, more electronics," Alex says.

Paul smiles as he lubes up the toy and presses it slowly into Alex. Cold and mostly unyielding, the intrusion feels peculiar. He's not inherently opposed to peculiar, but it's perhaps not the intimacy he's been looking for.

At least that's what he thinks until Paul turns the damn thing on. He's expecting quick vibrations and a lot of buzz, instead what he gets is a sort of twisting, rolling motion that's deep and slow. If Paul taps the base of the thing one more time, it will probably be right up against his prostate.

"If you want me to fuck you," Alex says breathlessly, "turn it off."

◆

Paul laughs again and obliges, before helping Alex up onto his knees and getting down onto his own elbows and knees for the best angle.

Alex is having none of it. He pulls and pushes at him until he's on his back. "I want to see you."

Paul smiles at Alex's sweetness. He just hopes they're not too damn clumsy and desperate for this to even work at this point.

Alex insists on getting inside before Paul is allowed to touch the toy's remote again, which is probably wise. He can see the concentration on Alex's face from trying not to come too soon and the stretch and burn of having him inside him is still, always, surprising.

He lets Alex get a rhythm going, and it's so good it would be easy to forget the plan. But then he asks Alex if he wants more, with little more than an interrogative sound. Alex understands the unspoken question, and gives Paul a nod in return.

He pushes the slider up on the remote slowly and watches Alex freeze — mouth open, eyes closed — with the pleasure of it. He pushes the heel of his foot against Alex's ass, and urges him to move. Alex does then, and it's clearly all or nothing, because he slams into him with a joyous and deliberate outrage at being made to feel so much.

He doesn't last long, but Paul doesn't care, because it's extraordinary to watch and be both part and cause of.

♦

After he comes, when his hips still and his shoulders sag, Paul has the damn decency to turn the toy off. Alex is grateful and collapses, his forehead to Paul's chest, though he knows he's been spoiled and Paul hasn't come yet.

Eventually, when Alex feels like he can make words, he asks Paul what he wants. Paul tries to have a conversation with him about it.

"No," Alex says. "Tell me what to do."

Something in his voice clearly makes Paul understand that this is what will make him feel best. They're both grateful when Alex is on his knees again. He turns around so his ass is in Paul's face. Paul slowly works the toy out of him while Alex sucks his dick.

When the toy is removed and Alex feels aching and gaping and too emotional, Paul tosses it aside. He puts a hand on the back of Alex's head, holding him still while he fucks up into his mouth until he comes.

Alex sprawls the wrong way on the bed, both of them just breathing. Being here like this feels delightful and easy and not ominous at all. Paul hates that that's a thing to note but is so glad that they have arrived here

◆

Alex is jolted out of sleep by the sound of Paul's phone ringing. Apparently, they will never get through a month without that happening again.

"You have got to be fucking kidding," Paul says groggily, rolling over in bed and into Alex's feet; he's still lying the wrong way on the bed.

Alex pulls a pillow over his face until Paul picks the damn phone up.

"It's Carly," Paul says before he answers it. Alex takes his hands off his face to stare.

Paul doesn't say much, just, "Really? And "Okay," and "Do you need anything?" and "We'll be there." He hangs up, he stares at Alex.

"Do not tell me Carly went into labor three hours after we got away on vacation," Alex says flatly.

"She's on her way to the hospital now."

"Oh my God."

"Liam's flying out from New York."

"Oh my *God*," Alex repeats.

"And we really do have to put on clothes and drive back."

Alex covers his face with his hands and moans.

Paul flips on the windshield wipers as they roll out of the driveway and onto the road because it has chosen tonight — of all nights, after months of drought — to finally fucking rain. Alex laughs at the absurdity and sheer luck of their lives, and plugs in Paul's iPod for the drive back. All of the abstracts and hypotheticals they've been trying to make decisions around for the last six months have gotten way less hypothetical and abstract.

The closer they get to the city, the worse the traffic gets. Alex eventually reaches over and keeps his hand on Paul's thigh, because he is white-knuckling; entirely unnecessarily given that by her own account, Carly is fine and in good hands.

"Why aren't you freaking out?" Paul finally asks Alex as they get off at the exit for the hospital.

"You and Liam. Saving my strength."

◆

Ali runs chattering up to Alex as soon as they walk into the waiting room. She holds up a drawing done in purple crayon and waves it eagerly in his face... or as close to his face as she can reach.

Alex crouches down to see it better. "What's that?"

"Dragon! It's bringing the baby," she announces proudly.

Alex looks up at Paul to find him smiling down at them expectantly.

"Don't storks bring babies?" Alex asks her.

"No. It's a good dragon."

"That is totally awesome," Alex says, standing and swinging her up in his arms as he does. Of everything he expects he'll have to deal with in the next twelve or twenty-four or however many hours, the five-year-old is going to be the easiest.

"Hi, Alex." A woman he doesn't recognize greets him with a wave. As Alex walks Ali over to where her paper and coloring supplies are laid out on a table, two women sitting there say hi as well.

Alex looks between them, both thrown off and annoyed at the unfamiliar people. "I've never met you."

"TV. Carly. Why pretend?" the first woman says drily, waving her hand in disinterest.

Alex tries to ignore that it seems like she's had this moment planned for a while. "You're all here with Carly?" he asks instead, looking between them while Ali wiggles out of his arms again back to the floor. Carly said there would be people at the hospital with them, but she wasn't specific as to who or, for that matter, how many.

They nod.

Alex turns plaintively to Paul. "Nobody told me Carly has a coven."

The woman laughs. "You think you're joking."

♦

Alex spends the wait with his nose in one of Paul's film textbooks he'd brought for vacation reading. He also checks his phone at increasingly frequent intervals for any word from Liam. Both activities are better choices than berating Paul for apparently knowing these random women and, as is too often par for the course, never mentioning any of it to him.

At least Alex doesn't think Paul ever dated any of them, but his life is full of surprises and he expects an inevitable correction on the matter.

Several hours pass before another woman — another member of Carly's coven, Alex assumes — comes out and announces to the group that Carly's had the baby, it's a girl, and mother and baby are both healthy and doing fine.

Amid the whoops and hugs, Alex checks his phone again.

"It's a six hour flight," Paul says, when he sees him do it. There's no possible way for Liam to get here yet.

◆

They're sitting around deciding what to do next — no one's eaten dinner, and Ali is getting tired and cranky and insistent about seeing Mom and going home — when Liam finally arrives. He's dressed for October in New York, not L.A., and looks like he isn't completely sure how he's gotten there.

There's a raucous chorus of hellos from Carly's women, and Ali perks up and charges at him with full five-year-old speed, jumping up and down and chattering over everyone until Liam picks her up.

Alex stays put, because as much as he wants to tackle Liam himself, Ali comes first.

The hubbub finally settles down — Liam is verbally grateful to them all for being here, but is insistent that he really does need to get to Carly, and no one wants to delay him any further. He sets Ali down with a promise that he'll be back soon. Liam waves to Paul and then grabs Alex by the wrist. Liam smiles, his blue eyes sparkling, and presses a kiss to Alex's palm before vanishing through the double doors.

♦

Carly's awake and trying to ascertain if the fussy baby is hungry or still indignant about her arrival in a bright, loud world when there's a tap at the door.

Liam is hovering in the door. He smiles hesitantly. "Hi."

"You made it," Carly says cautiously. She's so glad to see him, but she's exhausted and isn't sure yet what happens from here.

"Yeah. Sorry I was late."

Carly laughs. Liam has, as far as she's ever been able to tell, never been on time for anything other than work in his life. That he's apologizing for being late because he's been in New York City for months is just one more reason their lives are strange, and wonderful, and fragile.

Liam's smile grows impossibly wider.

"Come in and see your daughter." Carly says when he doesn't move from the doorway.

He sits down gingerly on the edge of the bed and leans over to get a good look at the baby.

"She's beautiful," he says.

"Yes, well, we have good genes."

Liam runs a fingertip gently over the baby's downy head. "Hi, Victoria."

The baby squinches her face up. Liam laughs softly. He looks thoughtful, and his eyes are bright with tears Carly's not sure are happy or sad. Probably both.

"Can I stay?" he asks quietly.

"For good or for now?"

"Both."

"If you can, you may." Carly is thrilled and relieved to have Liam finally here, but she knows better than to take his presence or his functionality for granted.

"He should be here and he's not. It's always going to be hard. But I want to try."

Carly nods. "Do you want to hold her?"

◆

When Liam finally texts them to come in and say hi, Alex is unsurprised to find Liam not in one of the chairs but sitting at the head of the bed next to Carly, carefully cradling the baby. He shows absolutely no inclination to let anyone else have a turn holding Victoria.

"Sorry to interrupt your vacation," Carly tells them, more amused than apologetic.

"Wouldn't miss it," Paul tells her.

"You know this is only the beginning of the chaos," Carly says.

Paul looks across the room at Alex, who meets his eye and gives him the most private smile. "We can only hope."

"Do you want us to take Ali tonight?" Alex asks.

Carly shakes her head. "Nah. Risa's taking her back to our place, and Liam will be there. You should go back to your getaway. Rest up and all that. We'll need you when you get back."

Paul chuckles. "Yes ma'am."

♦

Finally, Liam lets everyone else have a chance to hold the baby. When it's Paul's turn, Alex steps back to dig out his phone and take a picture. Ali is curled up asleep on Carly's bed next to Liam, who's combing his fingers through her hair. Carly's smiling upon all of them.

Alex sends the picture to Sarah and then checks the time. It's already six in the morning here; on the East Coast, she'll definitely be awake.

He steps outside to make the call. The sun is just starting to come up, and there are puddles everywhere. For once, nothing smells like smoke.

When Sarah picks up, Alex says, "So if you say no at this point that is still completely fair; it's always been your decision, but I wanted to show you what our family looks like."

Sarah laughs. "The baby is adorable. Boy or girl?"

"Girl. They named her Victoria."

Sarah's quiet for a moment. "You all really are something."

"Good something or bad something?"

"*Something* something," she says fondly. "How's Paul doing?"

◆

Paul and Alex debate whether to drive back to the inn or crash at their own house. The sky is lightening with the coming day and they've not slept at all, but they're both too wired to sleep. Better to power through.

Sarah hasn't said yes or no, and in the current situation — new baby and Liam back, but who knows for how long — they're both a little wild with waiting. She asked for time to think, and Alex doesn't know if she's waiting to feel confident in her yes or doesn't want to mar everybody's new-baby happiness with a no.

Paul reaches across from the driver's seat to rub the back of Alex's neck, which at least drops the pitch of his nerves.

The room is exactly the same as when they'd left it fifteen hours before, and Paul crawls into bed while Alex is still taking his shoes and socks off.

"Please tell me your phone is off," Alex mutters, sliding under the covers and into Paul's arms.

He's asleep before Paul answers.

◆

It's early afternoon by the time they wake up again. Paul considers rolling over and going back to sleep, but lying in bed and stroking Alex's side as he slowly comes back to the world is pleasant too. They may never get enough sleep, but he also would like to be conscious and present for at least some of their holiday.

When he finally fumbles for his phone to check the time, he has a missed call and a voicemail, both from Sarah. He sets the phone on speaker and lets the message play so they can both hear it.

He's glad he does, because if Alex wasn't listening to it too, Paul would be afraid it wasn't real.

"So that's yes on baby," he breathes when the message finishes.

Alex nods mutely.

"What's that face?" Paul asks.

Alex's eyes crinkle up when he smiles. "This is the face I had on right before I said yes to Victor."

33

By the time they get back to Los Angeles proper three days later, Carly and Vic (Liam vetoed Vicky as a nickname almost immediately) are home from the hospital and Liam's parents have arrived in town. Alex is far less disturbed by them than Paul, who has clearly suddenly realized what he's gotten them into.

"All I could think about for that entire meal was the breakup pancakes," Paul says to Alex when they drive back from a particularly awkward brunch.

Alex tries not to look as victorious as he feels. This may be what they're doing, but Paul should still suffer a little.

That said, there's plenty of suffering to go around. No matter how much Alex whines, wheedles, and cajoles, neither Paul nor his mother are willing to make the call to Alex's high school to get his transcripts for his college application. To make matters worse, his mother suggests that it would be incredibly inappropriate for Alex to do anything but make the call himself.

"You're their most famous graduate," she says, when Alex informs her he'll just make their assistant do it.

"I'm their only famous graduate," Alex says sullenly.

"And you never visit or do anything to make these kids' lives better."

"I'll write a fucking check." Alex feels about as ugly as he ever has since fame has become a thing — and an increasingly normal thing — in his life.

"Those kids are not your enemy. Which you should probably get your head around, if you and Paul are going to have one."

"I'll like *our* kid."

"Sure," his mom says. "But how happy is anyone going to be if you're afraid of your kid's friends?"

◆

With *Winsome* days away from wrapping for good it falls to Alex to schedule all of the baby-related logistics. Their surrogate is over the moon that they're starting the process for certain this time, and Sarah is nervous but excited about flying to L.A. for a week for the procedure, a vacation, and to see Carly and Liam and meet their kids.

The schedule is a nightmare. Somehow, Alex doesn't realize that the day of the baby procedure is the same as the closing on Victor's house until he gets the email from Nigel reminding him of the date and stating that he's coming out to L.A. to finalize everything. That the *Icarus* premiere is forty-eight hours after all of this is just icing.

Alex isn't sure if he's horrified or relieved that Nigel has some common sense and suggests a final meeting of Team Victor at the house before the sale is finalized.

After he checks with Liam, Alex invites Sarah along. That will be a hell of a capstone on her whirlwind L.A. tour/medical trip, but also, if anyone deserves a glimpse into the house that made all of their lives possible, it's her.

♦

On the day, Alex is sorry Sarah doesn't get to see the house as it was when Victor was still alive. Most everything of any personal significance is long gone into storage or various people's homes. Much of what remains will simply be sold at auction. Modernist furniture may be ugly, but it's certainly valuable.

The emptiness and staging of the house doesn't make being there easier for any of them. The house is filled with ghosts, not of Victor, but of who each of them was in relation to him. Carly, with baby Vic in a sling, still seems happy in the sunlight of the kitchen. Liam is perturbed that the company that staged the house rearranged the living room, swapping the piano and the couch. Paul, his sister at his side, stares at the in-built shelves in Victor's office that used to hold his awards; those now live at the *Winsome* offices, at least until they get relocated to wherever Paul is next. Darcy and Jackson talk quietly by the dining room table. When Alex finds himself wanting to sit down on the floor by the now emptied filing cabinets, he forces himself to go down to the basement instead.

He's tempted to say *I was never afraid of you* to the echoing space, because that's what would happen in a movie. But it's not true, so he stands there, walking in a slow circle for the thirty seconds he can stand to, before he jogs back upstairs. At least he's sure it really happened now.

When he gets back upstairs, Carly's being impatient and sliding her copies of Victor's keys back and forth across the kitchen counter. The noise is intolerable to Alex, but when he looks around it's clear that no one else — not even Liam — cares. Possibly because Nigel is pouring out shots for all of them. On some level Alex is almost irritated. They've been doing this for months, and this doesn't seem like enough to have driven across town for. On the other hand, at least this is finally, *finally* going to be over.

Nigel makes a speech. His words are scaled appropriately — after all, there are only eight of them there — but it's still a speech. Everyone downs their shots with an enthusiasm that's a testament to how terrible the last six months have been. Liam still glowers briefly at Darcy when she slams her empty shot glass down on the piano.

Because Darcy is sometimes still a child, she makes an irritated face at him in response. He laughs at her before going back to fidgeting with the metronome on top of the piano.

With nothing left to do except be together, conversation turns to everything that's happened recently and is going to happen soon. Gemma should be here too, Alex thinks; she was the first member of his chosen family, and this moment feels like one for all of their clan.

After a few minutes, Liam makes a softly irritated noise.

"What are you doing?" Carly turns to ask him over her shoulder.

"The metronome's jammed," he says, frowning over the back panel of it.

"Why does Victor have a metronome? I didn't think he played," Darcy says.

"He didn't," Liam tells her. "The metronome was for writing."

Darcy is more interested in Alex complaining about Mark than in Victor's writing habits, and the conversation drifts away from Liam again.

Everyone is startled out of their grumbling about the social part of their very strange jobs by Liam fumbling the metronome as he finally manages to force the back cover off. Not only does it hit the top of the piano, causing Nigel to wince, the body of the metronome also skids out of his hands.

By the time everyone has turned toward the commotion, the dismantled timekeeper is not what any of them are staring at. A gold ring, which must have been what was jamming the device in the first place, spins like a coin on the top of the piano.

"Oh my God," Alex breathes. All he wants to do is turn and see the look on everyone else's faces, but he's afraid if he does, the ring will disappear. It doesn't seem fair to do that to Liam.

"You got anything on this?" Nigel asks Jackson, but Jackson just slowly shakes his head.

Even Darcy doesn't speak as they all wait for the ring to stop spinning. Once it does, no one moves.

"What the actual fuck?" Paul says quietly.

Sarah raises a questioning eyebrow at Alex. He shrugs at her.

"Liam?" Carly says quietly.

He shakes his head.

"Jesus Christ, it's not going to bite," she replies.

"Yeah," Alex says, "that's what you think."

Somehow that earns him a smile from Liam, who then, very politely, asks everyone if they could please stop staring. Then Liam snatches the ring up, opens the sliding glass door to the yard and pool area, and slips outside.

"So what are the chances that that was like his mom's wedding band or like something faintly sane?" Jackson finally asks.

Nigel gives him a withering look. "None," he and Alex say at the same time.

♦

"To be clear," Sarah asks, once she, Paul, and Alex are in the car, "We just witnessed a proposal from a dead man?" It's phrased as a question, but Paul knows it's not.

"Was there anything in the diaries about this?" he asks Alex. He assumes there was something, and that Alex didn't say anything at the house because Nigel and everyone else was there. Which Paul has to admit is somewhat fair, and even a touching bit of care and loyalty for Victor's privacy from a man who hated him so much when he was alive.

"Specifically, no." Alex says. "Generally, yes. Sort of. By omission."

Paul rolls his eyes over with a look that says *specify*.

Alex says, "Victor didn't write about the most important things."

"That doesn't clarify anything," Paul says.

"Then you haven't been paying attention." Alex sounds smug.

"I don't know what to think about it," Paul says. "Other than that Victor was a mysterious asshole."

"I've been telling you that for years. Why, what do you think I'm going to tell you?"

"I don't know, you were the one lying about skulking around a dead man's house for weeks," Paul shoots back.

From the backseat, Sarah makes a sound that Paul knows is her trying not to laugh. Clearly she and Alex are well suited to each other. Paul wonders how terrified he should be about their offspring.

"What?" Alex protests. "Victor never wrote 'I bought Liam a weird not-wedding ring today!' And it's not like I went through his bank statements or receipts or anything — "

"No, just his diaries and his drawings," Paul deadpans.

" — so fuck if I know anything about when or where he bought it." Paul gives him a skeptical look. "I swear!"

♦

Carly drives as Liam sits next to her in the passenger seat, staring at his hands. The rings don't match — hers with Liam is a wider band and platinum — but there's something to the symmetry that's probably pleasing to Liam beyond the obvious.

"Did you know anything about this?" Carly asks.

"No."

"Does it make any sense to you?" she asks.

"Not really," Liam says. "I keep thinking about what if we hadn't found it."

"It wouldn't have changed anything."

"Yes it would," Liam says. "It would have changed the story."

Carly smiles and shakes her head. While Liam's new ring maybe proves something, it also doesn't really prove anything at all. Love is faith. Whether you have jewelry to go with it or not.

34

The baby procedure goes routinely. They'll know if it worked or not in about a week; until then, all they can do is wait.

Liam, when Alex drops by their house to give him Victor's sketches, laughs way too hard at Alex's mortified account of his own role in the baby-making process. "In a *cup*, Lee," Alex whines.

Carly is completely unsympathetic, but Liam can't stop laughing.

Alex is afraid the sketches will ruin Liam's good mood. Liam does go quiet when he finally opens the box into which Alex has carefully packed all the ones he thinks his friend could possibly want. But then he smiles, carefully brushing his thumb over the corner of one of the sketches where a date is scribbled.

"That was the day Carly and I got married," he says so softly Alex can hardly hear him.

◆

Alex gets up early the morning of the *Icarus Experiment* premiere. Which is a questionable choice when he was up late driving Sarah to the airport and when their assistant and a stylist are coming over at two to get them ready for the premiere. But he lies to Paul one more time, and says he's going climbing, when he's really, really not.

He can no longer drive to Victor's house. Instead, he heads into Downtown, to a Los Angeles he essentially never sees, run by the people who pretend that the industry doesn't exist, and that they don't hate toiling not in its service, but its shadow. He parks in a garage a block from the Cathedral. He has no idea why he avoids its lot, but it's a creepy place, and he'd rather not be mistaken for being any part of it. He's here to visit the dead, and Victor had been sure to make it an ordeal.

He's as efficient as he can be, jogging across the street and through the courtyard with constellations etched into the concrete — a welcome to atheists or the city's stars, Alex isn't sure. He slips into the cathedral and walks along the somber hallway that wraps around the sanctuary. He tries to ignore the fact that, being Sunday, mass is on. He's grateful that Catholics seem to keep their heads bowed. The churches of his childhood were always filled with people turning their palms and faces up for blessings that, like rain, would never come.

He takes the stairs down to the mausoleum slowly, but only because he's pretty sure appearances demand it. He stifles a laugh at the thought of the gossip item — *J. Alex Cook seen running in church!* — and then wends his way to Victor's niche. It's in the back, past Gregory Peck and a maze of small chapels.

When he gets there, Alex frowns. While he doesn't necessarily expect to feel Victor's presence there, he wouldn't be surprised if he did. Victor was creepy like that, and if anyone could have the force to exist through ash it would be him.

"Well, this feels stupid," Alex says.

That he knows Victor would laugh helps.

"You know, you could have saved everyone so much grief if you'd ever told anyone the stuff you wrote down. Or the stuff you didn't."

Alex stares at the name carved into the marble. "Somehow it's even more annoying to get the silent treatment from you now." He sits down against the opposite wall, his back to a nun who died in the 1960s.

Alex has a lot to say, and most of it he doesn't say aloud, in part because he can hear other people moving around the space, which echoes spectacularly. He wonders how he'll know when he's done or that he's been heard. Even if he doesn't really believe in ghosts and spirits and souls, regardless of how essential Paul is to him or how many times he has probably known Liam.

Ultimately, he decides it's a choice, just like everything else. When he gets up to leave, he presses a palm against the stone too long for a man that had hated to be touched — which is exactly why Alex does it — and says thank you. Then he leaves, smiling smugly.

◆

That evening, Alex and Paul attend *The Icarus Experiment* premiere. After everything that's happened in the past six months, it's odd to see his castmates and director again. Australia seems like a lifetime ago.

Alex also has no idea when he'll next be attending an event like this for a project of his own; for the next couple of years, he'll be playing a supporting role to Paul's appearances. The reversal is odd to contemplate, but no odder than anything else that's changed in their lives recently.

Being happily on Paul's arm after so many weeks of performing intentional cuteness in public after the cheating scandal is a relief. With Victoria in the world, Liam back, Victor's house sold, and good news about their own future family hopefully being imminent, today is anything but a performance.

Alex always gets held up more on the carpet than Paul, simply because he's an actor and Paul's not. Today, Alex pulls at his husband's arm to keep him close and snarks back at a photographer that rudely hollers at him to get out of the shot.

"I love that," Paul whispers at him. It sounds dirty.

The photographers may be ruder, but they're easier to deal with than the video stuff. Alex struggles to focus on the questions in front of him amid the din all around him. He wonders how the hell Liam has ever managed to do this. That maybe Liam's brain is an asset in this strange, shitty business isn't a thought Alex has considered before, but it makes as much sense as anything. He wishes that he and Carly were here, but Liam's still adjusting and Victoria is so young. Alex knows he's being selfish.

He prattles something about the hilarious terrors of the plane ride into Darwin from Sydney when Paul's cell phone goes off. Paul awkwardly pats his pockets, apparently having forgotten how clothes or hands work.

Alex rolls his eyes and gives him an indulgent smile.

With a mouthed apology, Paul steps out of the frame.

"The horrors of the digital age," Alex quips.

When Paul slides back into the picture, he puts an arm around Alex's waist to whisper news from the doctor in his ear.

Alex's face splits into a grin.

"Something we should know?" the interviewer asks.

Alex shakes his head. "You shouldn't know anything," he says playfully. "But if you're very, very good, and we're very, very lucky, maybe we'll tell you next year."

More by These Authors

Visit www.Avian30.com to join Erin and Racheline's mailing list and get information about new releases!

The Love in Los Angeles Series

Starling, Book 1
Doves, Book 2
Phoenix, Book 3
Cardinal, Book 4, coming August 2018

Love in Los Angeles is a queer romance series, with elements of magical realism, set in and around the TV and movie industry.

When J. Alex Cook, a production assistant on *The Fourth Estate* (one of network TV's hottest shows), is accidentally catapulted to stardom, he finds himself struggling to navigate both fame and a relationship with Paul, one of Fourth's key writers. *Love in Los Angeles* is the story of Paul and Alex — and of their friends and family — as they navigate love, and life, both in and beyond Los Angeles.

A Queen from the North

A widowed prince in need of an heir, a not-so-united kingdom in need of healing, and an ancient prophecy that still lingers in the modern world are about to conspire to make Lady Amelia Brockett A Queen from the North.

The Art of Three

Two men. One woman. No love triangles.

The Love's Labours Series

Midsummer, Book 1
Twelfth Night, Book 2
More coming soon!

42-year-old John Lyonel has never been attracted to men before, but falling for 25-year-old Michael Hilliard is actually the least screwed up thing that's happened to him in years. Even if sometimes he thinks Michael's a changeling.

Short stories:

Sample and Hold
Off-Kilter
Lake Effect
Snare
The Omega's Reluctant Alpha
Alpha Bodyguard
The Hart and the Hound

www.ingramcontent.com/pod-product-compliance
Lightning Source LLC
Chambersburg PA
CBHW050546190726
48283CB00007B/2028